The Last Stop

The Last Stop

Michael H. Burnam

LODESTONE
BOOKS

Winchester, UK
Washington, USA

First published by Lodestone Books, 2016
Lodestone Books is an imprint of John Hunt Publishing Ltd., Laurel House, Station Approach,
Alresford, Hants, SO24 9JH, UK
office1@jhpbooks.net
www.johnhuntpublishing.com

For distributor details and how to order please visit the 'Ordering' section on our website.

ISBN: 978 1 78535 117 4
Library of Congress Control Number: 2015936388

A CIP catalogue record for this book is available from the British Library.

Design: Lee Nash

Printed and bound by CPI Group (UK) Ltd, Croydon, CR0 4YY, UK

The only constant in a biological system is change.

To Helena and Jonah: May you see every sunset as the promise of a glorious new day.

To Bradley and Joshua: Rejoice in life's uncertainty, for it is the wellspring of progress and opportunity.

To Jessica: my love for you continues to evolve. It grows stronger every day.

Michael Burnam, MD

3/13/15

Acknowledgements

My sincere thanks to my agent Susan Crawford for believing in a fledgling author at a time when the publishing market is increasingly difficult for amateur writers. The first thing Susan told me when I started this journey (after "I loved the story!") was that successful commercial writing is not an individual sport, it is truly a team effort. She was right, and I extend my thanks and admiration to my team:

Award winning sci-fi author John Nelson who helped edit the novel, and provided unflagging encouragement.

Jessica Burnam, my wife and in-house editor who added sparkle to my prose.

Suzanne Phillips, intellectual property lawyer and friend.

And last, but not least, to the real-life Ernie, who when asked how things are going always responds with the same signature phrase: "Excellent to superb, verging on magnificent." A few clones of him would make the world a better place.

Prologue

The disc pulled out of its orbit around the gas giant that sheltered its home and accelerated across space toward the third planet, a blue orb called by its inhabitants Earth. The database translated this as soil or dirt, which seemed an odd choice for its name as water covered the majority of the planet's surface. Then again, the hominids that had risen to dominance on Earth were now extremely unpredictable, which was precisely why the disc had been dispatched there to administer the Test. This wouldn't be the first time they had been tested; there had been other attempts over the millennia as the hominids continued to evolve, but all past generations had failed.

The creators of the Test would try again, but this might be the last time. As the hominids continued to despoil the biosphere at an alarming rate and use the pinnacle of their science for war, extinction seemed imminent. Yet, as their information age began to flourish, a generation arose that prized cooperation over militancy, openness over concealment. There was hope, even if this was…illogical.

The disc arrived in the Earth's atmosphere over a mountainous region and began to descend. To most observers gazing at the sky, it appeared as a shooting star against the black satin of the night sky, except it didn't wink out and disappear. Instead it slowed, leaving behind a glowing trail of vapor that twinkled for a few seconds, and then the disc settled into the waters of a marsh fed by the runoff of a waterfall.

The disc was ovoid, smooth, and about fifty feet wide and fifteen tall. At first it remained motionless, with the majority of its surface visible above the shallow water. Close inspection would have revealed its unusual silvery surface that felt wet to the touch; in fact, it could be dimpled with minimal pressure, and it was completely non-reflective.

As the first rays of the sun painted the sky with gold, a doe and its fawn warily approached the watering hole. While they noted the presence of the motionless silver disc, the two animals ambled to the water's edge. Reassured by the familiar sound of the wind through the trees and the buzzing of the cicadas, the fawn began to drink while its mother remained alert, standing guard. Suddenly the water rippled and struck their legs like a little wave and continued on a few feet to the bank. Startled, the two animals edged backward. When nothing else occurred and the water was still again, the doe tentatively stepped forward. It happened again. This time the wave was higher, flowing up and through their legs like surf on a beach. At the same time, the ground began shaking. The two animals scampered off and the cicadas were suddenly silent. Even the wind seemed to stop, as if the marsh itself was waiting.

Ever-stronger ripples emanated around the disc. As this phenomenon peaked, inexplicably the surface of the water turned into a whirlpool with the disc at its center. As the depth of the vortex's funnel grew, the speed of the water moving around it kept increasing until it was impossibly fast. The disc began to descend into an abyss created by the vortex. When it disappeared from view, the waters crashed down, and for a few seconds roiled like the surface of an angry sea, finally settling. Everything appeared normal as it had before the disc arrived.

The days of summer continued to pass. Each afternoon the wind creased the surface of the water and bowed the ranks of reeds that surrounded the marsh. In many ways it looked no different than when the Earth was young, when life here promised an endless pageant of possibilities. Yet, it could all come to an end.

The disc had returned when remote surveillance detected suitable subjects from Earth's younger generation. Beneath the water it awaited their approach, readying the test one last time.

The fate of two worlds hung in the balance.

Chapter One

The car shot up Highway 395 through the Owens Valley with Mount Whitney looming to the west.

"Damn!" David slumped back against the car seat. Even though he was sixteen, the same age as his best friend, he looked small for his age. His expression was perpetually brooding and nervous, the poster boy for "deer in the headlights." He handed the Game Boy to Mickey. "So close!"

Mickey was the larger of the two, slightly chubby (big boned, his mother said) and more outgoing, although not by much. "Which level did you die?" He started another game of Zombie Attack.

"Twelve. All I needed was eight more kills to upgrade to the mini-gun. With that bad boy, you can really mow them down!"

Mickey frowned. "I can't get past level Four."

"How many heads did you chop off? You need ten to upgrade to a…"

Mickey pushed the Game Boy back at him. "This game's disgusting!"

David smirked. "You're only saying that because you suck at it."

"F you."

Mickey's mother Jerry turned around and gave them both the evil eye. Her real name was Jeanette, but she preferred to be called Jerry. "Five more minutes to Independence," said Jerry. "You can get out and stretch your legs."

Mickey's mood instantly brightened. "And stand on the bridge," he said.

"And take a pee," chimed in David with a pained expression.

Five minutes later, they could see a stand of cottonwood trees up ahead and Mickey's father Max began slowing the car. It was a hot summer morning in the small California town of

Independence, a dot on the map at the end of the 110-mile stretch from Los Angeles through the Mojave Desert. For as long as Mickey could remember, his family had taken the same summer vacation, a camping trip to a resort called Twin Lakes in the High Sierra Mountains. Max always referred to it as a "camping" trip, but their destination was really a cabin with all the amenities. For several years Mickey's best friend David had come along.

Max pulled into the grounds at the edge of town and parked under a tree. Off to the side, an old wooden bridge with a rickety railing spanned a creek whose water originated as snow melt in the High Sierra Mountains that filled the horizon. As soon as the car stopped, Mickey jumped out, smiling at the bridge, and started running toward it.

David hung back and then ran toward one of the restrooms, the usual green-painted affair with a hovering swarm of flies around it.

Max caught up with his son in the middle of the bridge. He was a tall man with broad shoulders, and always had a loving smile. When caught off guard, his eyes sometimes looked wistful. Locking arms, they stared in silence at the swiftly flowing water. "Even though there's nothing here but this old bridge, my dad always loved this place," Max said. "It took me a while to understand why."

Mickey gazed up at his father. "I remember standing on the bridge with Papa."

Max brought his hand to the corner of his eye and turned away. "Last time the three of us were here together, you were five years old."

"Papa showed me how to dunk a line in the creek. Didn't catch anything." He stared at his father, could sense the emotion welling up in him, and it made him feel…safe.

Max's eyes glistened. He turned his back. "I remember."

Jerry stood beside the car looking fondly at her husband and son. After a few minutes, Mickey and Max walked back to the car.

Max still had his hand on his son's shoulder. David observed the two of them, and for a moment his face darkened.

Although the closest of friends, in some ways, the boys were opposites. Mickey was a fisherman, happy to sit for hours on the bank of the lake next to his father dunking a line waiting for "the big one." David had trouble sitting still for more than five minutes and preferred to hike. Both were well above average in intelligence and excelled in school, and both were considered nerds by their peers and socially shunned. This was one of the reasons why they hung out, that and the fact that they lived directly across the street from each other. But their friendship was more than proximity and a shared social stigma. They both had the same "moral compass"— Mickey's came from his parents, and David…well, it wasn't from his home environment, far from it. Maybe for him, trying to be a good person was just instinctual.

Chapter Two

Their final destination was a rustic cabin on the shores of a secluded lake ringed by snow-capped mountains. Actually there were two lakes connected by a small isthmus, not so creatively named "Twin Lakes." They drove to a resort on the larger of the two, the upper one not surprisingly named Upper Twin Lake. Mickey's family had been vacationing at the resort for three generations. From Independence it would take another couple of hours to get there. But after Bishop, the highway would ascend on the infamous Sherwin Grade that had caused more than a few cars to overheat. Only forty miles farther down the highway from Independence, Bishop was the logical place to stop, fill up the tank, and check the coolant level before making the ascent. Nevertheless, family tradition demanded a picture taken on the bridge over Independence creek, even though the creek was small and the bridge was ordinary. None of that mattered. Some things were more important.

Around five o'clock, they pulled into the resort and picked up the keys to the cabin from the general store. Mickey's pulse always quickened when he first saw the lake, a blue jewel set in a crown of snow-capped peaks. That scene was also one of his life's waypoints, like standing on the bridge in Independence. He sensed it was important to be in such a place from time to time, a place where the sky was bigger, and one could hear the sibilant rustle of the wind through the pines. His world too often became a small strip of time and place that spanned the distance between home and school, between adolescence and manhood. There's so much more to being alive, as his father often reminded him, and it's too easy to lose sight of it. His dad was right; it was important to be there, even for a little while. Mickey rolled down the window and inhaled the cold sweet air.

They drove through the campground to the cabin. After

arriving, everyone piled out of the car and Max and Jerry started unpacking. The boys made an attempt to look busy while standing around. His face just visible over the top of one of the boxes, Max smiled at his son. "Mom and I'll unpack. Why don't you two go stretch your legs? Take your rods and try off the main road just past the marina. Mickey knows the spot—there's a big red boulder next to a fallen tree. Usually good for a few fish in the late afternoon."

David shrugged. He didn't much care for fishing.

"I think we'll hike over to Horsetail Falls," said Mickey, after glancing at his friend and gauging his mood.

David nodded back at him.

"Do what you want," said Max. He continued unpacking the car. "But take your jackets and some insect repellant."

The two boys grabbed their lightweight jackets and started walking toward the trail leading up to the falls. After a few strides, Mickey stopped and turned around. Before he could say it, his father tossed him a can of insect repellant. Max shook his head, and then disappeared through the front door of the cabin.

The trail to Horsetail Falls swung around the lake, and then, where the creek emptied into the lake, veered steeply up the mountain. Most people stopped hiking at the bottom and gawked at the falls flowing down from high above. It was a thirty-minute hike to the creek without starting up the mountain. Since time was limited before dinner, the trailhead, not the falls, was the boys' destination. They walked along easily, enjoying stretching their muscles and seeing the familiar sights.

About thirty minutes later, the boys reached the far end of the lake within sight of the falls. They could taste the mist in the air and hear the sound of crashing water. It was an hour before dusk. That end of the lake flattened out into a small marshy area fed by runoff from the falls. It was thickly carpeted with tall reeds only cut by a single well-worn path. It wasn't possible to fish amongst the reeds, and a lot of bugs were always hovering around, so no one else was there.

Mickey and David were quiet for a while, soaking up the silence and listening to the wind. Mickey felt attuned again, like when he was fishing with his father. A short distance farther along the trail, something stirred below the ground. Unaware, they continued walking single file along the narrow trail between the reeds.

Mickey suddenly stopped. "Did you hear that?"

"Hear what?"

"I don't know…some kind of buzzing sound."

David looked panicked. "Maybe it's a rattle snake."

"Rattlers don't swim! It's probably a dragonfly on steroids." Mickey started walking.

David looked around warily, and then followed. "I don't see any dragonflies."

Mickey didn't see the hole in the ground that suddenly opened in front of him. He fell in with barely enough time for a cry of alarm.

David was still looking for something large flying around and didn't see Mickey fall, but heard the thud when he hit the bottom. He turned around, saw the hole, and knelt at the edge. "Jesus, are you all right?" he yelled down. "What happened?"

"I'm okay…I guess." David could hear Mickey's voice, but could barely see him in the dim light. "I was looking where I was going, but didn't see it. Must be some kind of sinkhole or something. Can you believe this?"

"Can you climb out?" David yelled.

"I don't know. I'm pretty far down, maybe fifteen feet. I landed on soft dirt, so I'm okay… It's kind of like a cave down here. Weird." Mickey's voice trailed off.

David didn't hear anything for a few seconds. "Mickey!" he shouted.

"I can't see any way to climb out! The walls are too smooth and they're slanted. I feel like I'm stuck in a flask. Damn! Better get my Dad. Tell him to bring a rope or something."

"I can't leave you down there." David stood and looked all around. He couldn't see anybody. What's more, it was starting to get dark.

"It's not like I'm going anywhere. Hurry, before it gets darker!"

"What if the walls collapse or the hole gets deeper?"

Mickey considered the possibilities but wasn't alarmed. He felt…safe, somehow. "No, I'm okay, just go!"

"Okay! I'll get back as fast as I can." He didn't look happy.

"Davie!" yelled Mickey.

"It's cold down here. Throw down your jacket."

Chapter Three

Mickey sat on the dirt with his back against the wall. It grew darker by the minute and colder by the second. He looked up at the sky and felt more irritated than scared. He knew it was only a matter of time before David returned with his father. All Mickey had to do was keep warm, not panic, and wait. As the temperature continued to drop, his breath started to steam. He wore his jacket zipped all the way up, but the cold penetrated his clothing anyway. He tried putting David's jacket on, but it didn't fit. So he threw it over his shoulders like a shawl and wrapped his arms around his chest. Total bummer.

The floor of the hole was unusually smooth. Mickey poked around with his foot and found it to be generally solid, like hard-packed earth. Trying to keep warm, he stood and walked around its perimeter. There was still enough light to see up the walls. He kept looking for any feature that might allow him to climb out, but couldn't find any. Then Mickey heard that strange buzzing sound again! It seemed to be coming from the floor and the walls, like some kind of surround sound. This whole thing was totally weird! He couldn't have missed a hole this big. And that strange buzzing sound—what was it? He leaned against the wall to collect his thoughts. He wasn't panicking, just uneasy.

After a few minutes, he began walking around the perimeter. He hadn't gone more than a few feet when his foot struck something soft and yielding. He bent down and felt as much as saw a piece of cloth. Mickey glanced up to see if somebody had thrown it down. For an instant in the darkening sky, he glimpsed a soaring shape passing over the aperture of the hole, but then it was gone. He began to wonder if he was the victim of a prank. He yelled, "Hey, I know you're up there!" He didn't hear an answer, or see a prankster's face leering down at him. Then again, if there was somebody up there connected to the strange appearance of the hole, maybe Mickey didn't want to meet him. A few minutes later the stealth drone circled back again, but it was now too dark for Mickey to see it.

He picked up the cloth and held it out for a better look. There was just enough light left to recognize some kind of a jumpsuit with a zipper down the front, like sweats for jogging. No, its material was too tough for a sweat suit. It was more like what a motocross guy would wear for protection. It seemed about the right size for him too. Wasn't that convenient! Maybe if he walked around again he'd bump into a cheeseburger and fries. Still, it was getting really cold. What harm was there in putting the jumpsuit on over his clothes?

Mickey pulled down the zipper and slipped into it. The cloth yielded easily and his legs slid right in. Although the outside of the suit was tough like leather, inside it felt downy soft. After putting his arms in, he zipped it up to just under his chin. It was exactly the right size. Suddenly he felt warm, even comfortable. What's more, for some reason he felt really energized. He started bouncing up and down as if he were on a trampoline, and was jumping at least a foot off the ground, maybe more. He'd never been able to do that in gym. Giddy with success, he kept bouncing higher with each try, but then that buzzing sound went off again and he stopped. Reality set in. This wasn't a moon-bounce at an amusement park—this was a weird hole in the ground. What if it closed up and buried him?

To shake off his fear, Mickey started walking again—about halfway around the perimeter, his foot struck something else, this time solid. Bumping into it stubbed his big toe right through his sneaker. In a little pain, he bent down and saw that it was a motorcycle helmet. By that point it was too dark to see it clearly, but his hands felt a visor and a cloth cowl attached to its base. He'd watched enough motorcycle races on TV to know what it was. The bigger question, of course, was what was it doing there? One minute he was hiking with his best friend, happy as a clam, and the next he was trapped in hole which appeared out of nowhere with a motorcycle suit that just happened to be his size. Come on, he thought! Way too much to be a coincidence!

It dawned on Mickey that this must be a test. What else could it be? And if so, the helmet was the next step. He examined it with his fingers. It seemed perfectly smooth and was made out of fiberglass or some similar material. He spread the cowl with his hands and slipped it on. It fit perfectly. Another surprise—yeah, right! Now his head felt warm too, not a bad thing. The only part of his body still cold was his nose. In fact, his nose was both stinging and running at the same time. So he pulled down the visor.

Strange things began to happen. First the cowl pulled taut and stuck itself to the top of the suit. After that, with a whoosh of air, the visor settled deeper into the face of the helmet and became completely flush with it. Mickey wondered how he could breathe, but then relaxed. He was breathing just fine. So far nothing encountered in the hole seemed harmful or threatening, far from it. Except for being stuck down there, he had to admit he'd never felt better. Mickey now tried to pull up the visor but he had nothing to grab onto. He put his hands under his chin, and tried to push the helmet off, but it wouldn't budge. Definitely exasperating—there had to be a way to get the thing off! That was when he noticed a blinking red light on his left forearm.

In the glow of the small red light, he could see a rectangular insert of some sort with a line of discs on the length of it. They were all dark except the first. It blinked steadily and looked like a button—perhaps an on/off switch. So Mickey touched it. Immediately the visor popped up and the bottom of the cowl separated from the suit. Startled and relieved, he took off the helmet and placed it on the ground. He stared at it and then noticed that the red light was still blinking on his arm. This had become a challenge, another test of some kind, and he was determined to master it.

He reached over, picked up the helmet and placed it back on, and he immediately felt better all over, except for his nose. Taking a deep breath, he pulled the visor down and once more felt instantly warm and comfortable with that almost euphoric feeling; his nose stopped stinging too. He kept his finger poised over the red button on his sleeve—just in case.

After sitting comfortably for a few minutes with the visor down, suddenly the hole appeared brightly lit, as though someone had switched on the lights. The visor must have a night-vision gizmo, like soldiers use. How cool! Maybe this was some kind of secret military installation. It had to be a test! They were watching him! He started spinning around, yelling, "I know you're there! Stop this and let me out! My dad's a newspaper guy!" No one answered, but after a moment the buzzing sounded once sharply. Now he got it—this was a signal of sorts, and something else was bound to happen.

With the visor down again, Mickey noticed a blinking light at the lower left corner of his vision on the *inside* surface of the visor. He was certain he hadn't seen that earlier; it was too annoying to miss. This whole suit thing was becoming weirder by the minute, but also exciting! Mickey felt a sense of adventure, which was cool—nerds seldom had adventures. This had to be leading to something and he would figure it out, even if a bunch of military goons were watching him. This nerd wasn't going to back down. "Okay, bring it on!" he shouted. "I can take it!" The blinking light inside the visor resembled the cursor on his computer screen at home. The light remained at the periphery of his vision and rhythmically blinked. Mickey kept expecting it to race across the visor and leave behind a message, like "This suit is the property of the US Army. You're under arrest."

With new purpose, he began walking around the hole again, this time the night-vision feature allowed him to get a better look at his surroundings. Halfway around, he noticed a rock protruding from the wall, and another one spaced a few feet above it. Both looked stout and broad enough to provide a handhold. Unfortunately the first rock was a good six feet up from the floor, and the second another four feet above that. He could never jump that high. The bitter memory of the rope climb in gym class suddenly came back to him. He could only climb three feet off the ground before falling and landing on his butt—not his greatest moment. Everybody laughed at him—except David. Mickey now glared at the rock with angry determination, plus something else—a newfound power. He would climb up this time! Besides, if he failed, nobody else was around to see—well, maybe.

As Mickey needed to see what he was doing, he left the visor down. Moving to the farthest point away from the potential handholds, he took a running start, all of four steps, and jumped as high as he could. Ordinarily this would have been about a foot. Somehow, he managed to jump completely out of the hole and hit the ground twenty feet away! Landing hard, he crumpled into a pile of legs and arms and lay there for a moment panting, unhurt but startled. It was just that kind of a day.

After Mickey raised himself on his elbows, he looked around. He was somewhere in the marsh. All it had taken was a leap like the astronauts had done on the Moon, except this wasn't the Moon. It had to be the suit, but it was more than that. He was the one who'd fallen into the hole, and found the suit and helmet that perfectly fit—a suit with super powers! He wondered if he'd been selected, but for what, and by whom? He shouted again, "Okay, now what? Do I get a certificate or something?" The wind through the pines and the distant echo of his voice were the only responses.

He touched the red button and the visor popped up. Once again, the lights went out. He couldn't see the hole twenty feet away slowly disappearing. Immediately his face started stinging from the cold, so he pulled the visor down turning on the lights.

At first he didn't notice the two small dancing lights moving toward him from the direction of the Lodge. The first flashlight was almost on him, and the other was at least a hundred feet behind. Using the visor's night vision and some magnification that had just conveniently appeared, he could see that the leader was Ernie Santos, a friendly ex-army guy who worked at the marina. He'd taken Mickey and David up to Horsetail Falls the first time. The second flashlight was held by his father Max followed closely by David. Being familiar with the terrain, Ernie walked well ahead to ensure that the path was safe.

Before they arrived, Mickey decided to make another jump. Until he figured it all out, he decided to keep the suit's super powers a secret—except for confiding in David, of course. He readied himself by bending his legs fully into a crouch like a sprinter in the starting blocks. This was great stuff for a teenager who couldn't climb up that damn gym rope! He felt bolder and more exuberant than ever.

Chapter Four

In the darkness, all Ernie could see was a blinking red light. He panicked and started running. If it was a flare or fireworks, it could start a forest fire! Running well ahead of Max and David, Ernie rounded a bend in the trail just as Mickey took off on his jump reaching a full twenty feet in the air. Ernie stopped and crouched behind a stand of reeds watching the whole display, too perplexed to move.

When Mickey landed, Ernie stared at the blinking red light. Because the suit was matte black, that's all he could see. As Mickey brought his hand near his face to straighten his hair—a teenage thing—the red button briefly illuminated his face. His head abruptly appeared in the darkness resembling the disembodied Cheshire cat in *Alice in Wonderland*. Ernie was transfixed, unable to move a muscle.

Mickey yelled out, "I'm over here, guys!"

Max and David heard him, stopped, but couldn't see anything.

"Mickey?" shouted Max.

"Dude, where are you?" hollered David, cupping his hands.

Still shocked by what he'd seen, Ernie tentatively stood up. He blinked his eyes, in case he was imagining things. In the dark he could just make out Mickey's silhouette. "He's over here! I see him," Ernie yelled. His eyes never left Mickey.

Max and David came running up. A few moments later, Mickey parted the reeds and stepped out.

"What happened?" asked his father sounding relieved.

"I fell in a hole." Mickey recognized Ernie. "Hey Ernie!" Mickey looked forward to seeing him. Ernie always had a ready smile and was happy to help Mickey or any other kid operate a boat, catch a fish, or just sit and tell a story. When Ernie was asked how things were going, his signature response was always the same: "Excellent to superb, verging on magnificent!"—but not this time.

Ernie looked suspiciously at him. "Where's that hole, Mickey?"

Mickey pointed off into the dark. "Over there."

Ernie shined his flashlight where Mickey was pointing. "Don't see anything…" Ernie said and looked back at him.

David stared quizzically at his friend. "How did you get out of the hole?"

Before Mickey could respond, Max stepped in front of him. "Are you all right?" A tinge of irritation crept into his voice.

"Yeah, Dad, I'm okay."

Max studied his son. "Where'd you get that suit?"

"It was in the hole. It was friggin' cold down there, so I put it on."

Max looked skeptically at his son. "Are you two trying to pull one over on me?"

"Dad, you've got to believe me—it happened just like I said!"

Ernie reached out and touched the smooth fabric. "Looks like that suit fits you real good, like it was made for you. I guess whoever left it must have been almost exactly your size." Ernie moved a few steps out from the others, his flashlight sweeping the area. "I still don't see any hole, but it's dark. I must be missing it." He stepped back. "I'll come back in the morning and try to find the darn thing." He frowned at Mickey. "Better put a warning flag next to it before anyone else disappears."

Max pulled his jacket's zipper up to his chin. "I'm freezing. Let's go back." He stamped his feet a few times. "We'll sort out your story in the morning. You kids be sure to follow Ernie. Only one accident allowed per night, got that?"

Ernie swept his flashlight beam around one final time, shrugged, and started walking back to the resort. The other three followed in single file with Max bringing up the rear. David tiptoed along as if afraid the hole would reappear at any moment.

They walked along the trail through the reeds toward the well-lit area around the general store. The nearby campground was filled to capacity in the summer. They could see numerous campfires and lights streaming from the windows of parked RVs. As they passed by the marina, Ernie said good night and headed for his cabin behind the boathouse. He kept glancing back at Mickey and almost tripped over a rock marking one of the campsites.

A few minutes later, Max and the two boys walked up to the cabin. Jerry was waiting for them on the porch with the front door open behind her. The warmth from the fireplace pouring out and the aroma of dinner were both comforting and inviting.

"Thank God!" Jerry anxiously called out. She glared at her son with her hands on her hips. "What happened?"

Mickey smiled at his mom. "We were hiking. I fell in a hole."

"A hole in the ground nobody can find," said Max, sounding more annoyed.

Smiling sheepishly at his father, Mickey climbed the steps to the cabin, followed closely by David.

Jerry followed the boys in and then turned to her husband. "Close the door before you let in a thousand mosquitoes." A swarm of flying critters buzzed about the light mounted outside the cabin door.

Inside the cabin, Jerry looked at her son. "What's that get-up you're wearing?"

"Says he found it in that hole nobody can find," her husband said, skeptically.

Jerry glared at the two of them with her lie-detector eyes.

Mickey blushed. "Jesus, Mom."

"I saw it, Mrs. B," blurted David. "I was there when he fell into it."

"Take that thing off right now!" insisted Jerry. "It's probably full of bugs or God knows what!" Mickey unzipped the suit, stepped out of it, and held it up. They gathered around him. In the light, the whole outfit, including the helmet, looked matte black, and reflected no light at all. It was also completely plain, without embellishments or a brand name, and it resembled a diver's wetsuit more than anything.

"Looks like it just came off the hanger," said Jerry, looking puzzled. "Never mind. Put it outside on the porch in case something still needs to crawl out of it. Then wash up and sit down before these burgers get cold, like that glass of root beer next to David's plate."

David smiled at her.

"Okay." Mickey went outside and placed the suit with the helmet on top of it on the wooden bench on the porch. He noticed that the red light on the sleeve was dark. Maybe the batteries died, he wondered. After staring at the suit for a moment, he went back inside, ready for one of his mother's famous High Sierra cheeseburgers.

Later that night, a figure sheathed in black removed the suit from the bench and took it into the woods behind the cabin. The figure laid out the suit on the ground, photographed it from multiple angles, and took readings inside and out using several electronic instruments. When this process was completed, the suit was returned to its original position on the bench, laid out exactly as it was before, and the figure in black once again dissolved into darkness.

Chapter Five

Mickey and David rested in their sleeping bags on top of the twin beds in one of the cabin's bedrooms. The lights were out, and the door was closed. The wind outside rustled through the pines, and a buzzing sound indicated at least one mosquito made it inside. After his experience, the buzzing sound made Mickey slightly nervous. Although the curtains were drawn closed, the colored neon lights from the Coors Beer sign in the general store's window seeped through the thin cloth and played across the teens' faces.

David turned on his side and propped his head on his elbow. His glasses lay on the nightstand, a polished tree stump. Everything in the room had a Wild West cachet.

"You goin' tell me what really happened?"

Mickey rested on his elbow too, his face painted with oranges and blues from the beer sign. "Okay, I'll tell you, but I'm warning you—it's totally weird. You can't tell my folks until we figure this whole thing out. Swear it!"

"Okay!"

Mickey explained how he found the suit, tried it on, and how it not only kept him warm but also made him feel better. He told about next finding the helmet and discovering its night-vision feature. "I could see everything inside the hole as bright as day. That's when I saw the handholds."

Still wrapped in his sleeping bag, David tried to sit up, but fell on the floor with a thud. "Jesus, Mickey!" he said from the floor. "Must be some kind of secret military shit!"

"That's what I'm thinking too. It was left there as a test."

David hopped back into the bed. "You used that night vision to find the handholds and climb out?"

Mickey shook his head. "Not exactly." He paused. "I just kind of jumped out."

David got up on his knees, and in the process almost fell off the bed again. "Wait a minute! You can't jump fifteen feet! In gym you can't even jump six inches!"

"Yeah, well I did, whether you believe me or not."

David thought for a moment. "What did you mean about a test?"

"I kept hearing a buzzing sound down there, and think it was some kind of signal."

"What does that mean?"

"Dude, things kept happening one after the other! First, I fell in the hole. Then, I found the suit, then the helmet, and after that, the handholds that weren't there before! The buzzer went off each time to keep me going." Mickey shook his head. "Totally weird."

"You're right. Gotta be military."

"Yeah, but that's not all." David looked back at him in eager anticipation. "The suit fits me perfectly, like it was made just for me."

"I see what you mean."

"Yeah, and putting on the suit made me feel different…not just strong, but confident…I don't know—powerful."

"Because you knew it gave you…super powers!"

"Except I still feel wired, and I'm not wearing it."

"Try jumping again."

"I did. Nothing happened, but I still feel…powerful."

"So it screwed with your brain."

"Maybe."

"Holy crap! We gotta tell your dad!"

"Not yet. First, I want to take another look at the suit in the light, try it on again, and see what happens."

"I'm thinking this wasn't just some random hole you fell into," David said excitedly. "Maybe it was dug by some secret military outfit and they're testing people!" His voice started to rise.

"Shhhhhh! We gotta keep this a secret until we figure it out!"

"Okay, but they gotta want their suit back," David added. "I mean, a teenager isn't supposed to have it."

"Yeah, we could be in a shitload of trouble if they think we stole it."

"What do you mean *we*?" David asked.

Chapter Six

The next morning, after a breakfast of pancakes soaked in maple syrup, fresh cooked bacon, and steaming hot chocolate, Max and Jerry prepared to leave for their favorite fishing spot. Max wore his fishing vest with its countless pockets, and as usual, he'd brought five rods and reels with him. Jerry, sporting a broad straw hat and sunglasses, carried a folding chair with a book in its sleeve and a small Igloo cooler with sodas and sandwiches. As far as she was concerned, vacationing meant always being well fed.

"Gonna catch that legendary three pounder this year, Dad?" asked Mickey smiling at his father. His father appeared determined. "Yup, I think this is the year." In reality, Mickey knew his father had a simple philosophy when it came to fishing. Max was a newsman. His career was often stressful and frequently involved long hours. A few summers before, Mickey had been fishing next to him at the same spot his dad was heading for now, when he saw him cast his line into the water without any bait. Shocked, Mickey demanded to know why his father would do such a thing. At that moment, Max was peacefully sitting on a fallen log at the water's edge. He stretched out his arms, looked up at his son, and smiled. "You're probably too young to get this," he said, "but some day you'll understand the fish can be a nuisance." That day hadn't arrived yet.

Max rubbed his hands together with anticipation. "You coming with us?"

"We're going with Ernie to look for that hole." He glanced at David.

Jerry appeared none too happy. "You think that's a good idea?"

"Ernie knows every square inch of this place," said Mickey, sounding a little anxious.

"Okay, but be careful," his mother urged.

After piling their breakfast dishes in the sink, Mickey and David went out on the porch. Mickey picked up the suit and helmet, tucked them under his arm, and they started for the marina. After they were out of sight of the cabin, Mickey stopped and held up the suit's sleeve with the buttons. All of them were dark. "I guess the batteries ran out," he said.

"Probably imagined the whole thing," David said. "No such thing as electric motorcycle suits."

"I'm not making this up. After we find the hole, we'll ditch Ernie and go somewhere private to examine it."

"Now I understand why ass and hole are used together."

"F you!"

It was a beautiful morning, bright with sunshine. The lake was flat calm, perfect for fishing. In the distance, Mickey heard the sounds of outboard motors sputtering to life. As he and David walked along the gravel road, they could see several boats leaving the marina headed out for a morning of fishing for rainbow trout and land-locked salmon, the latter a red-gold colored fish called Kokani. Mickey had never actually seen anybody catch one. He figured the Kokani were too smart to eat chartreuse Power Bait like a hatchery trout.

They reached the marina office near the launch ramp. Inside, several fishermen were standing at the counter buying tackle or renting boats. Ernie was waiting on them. He waved as Mickey and David entered and continued packing a bag full of hooks, sinkers, and other fishing paraphernalia. Since Ernie was occupied, the boys busied themselves looking around the shelves. At one point, Mickey glanced over and noticed Ernie frowning while he eyed the suit and helmet under Mickey's arm.

Ernie Santos was a fixture at the Lodge. Mickey's family had known him since before Mickey was born. Ernie loved to hang out with kids. Now a man in his late fifties, he looked younger than his age and was physically fit with well-muscled shoulders and arms. He liked to arm wrestle and boasted that he never lost—certainly never to any of the kids. In fact, arm-wrestling Ernie was a regular activity for kids at the resort. Ernie's strength probably resulted from all the hard work in the thin mountain air. When asked, Ernie said it was from clean living, and then he would wink as if he had some kind of secret.

Seemed like Ernie could never do enough to make sure kids of all ages had fun at the lake. If one of them hadn't caught a trout yet, Ernie had a secret spot he could take him to. Ernie didn't have a family and lived by himself year-round in one of the Lodge's cabins, the only one to stay the winter. Most people knew his wife had left him years ago, and his only son died in Iraq. The Lodge was his entire life now.

"Hey, guys, how's it going today?" Ernie asked, his eyes flicking down to the suit.

Mickey and David blurted out, "Excellent to superb, verging on magnificent!" They all laughed. Ernie loved being the butt of their jokes, one of the guys.

"I've been waiting for you two to finish your beauty sleep," said Ernie. "I pulled out a couple of flags from storage, the ones we use in the winter to mark the trails in the snow. Need to mark Mickey's hole before anybody else…falls in." He looked over at his assistant who stepped up to the counter, and then Ernie started for the door.

"Why are you still carrying that motorcycle suit around?"

Mickey blushed. "Maybe the guys who left it are still around." He hesitated for a moment. "Anybody looking for it?"

"Well, there were some…guys in black suits and shades nosing around." Mickey and David looked startled. "Gotcha!" said Ernie.

"Sure they weren't looking for you?" David asked sounding a little miffed.

"I'm not the one making claims about mysterious holes."

Mickey looked nervous. “I told you…I fell in a hole.”

“Okay, if you say so.” Ernie nodded his head. “Let’s head out.”

The three headed for the trail back to the marsh. Ernie carried two slender poles with yellow flags, something like the ones marking the cup at a golf course. A smaller surveillance drone shaped like a dragonfly followed them.

“Ever see any military guys around here?” Mickey asked Ernie as they walked along.

“So, you’re thinking that thing’s military, not motocross?”

Mickey shrugged his shoulders. “Maybe.”

Ernie pointed to the suit Mickey carried under his arm. “As I’ve told you guys, I was an Army Ranger, and the military plasters serial numbers all over their stuff. That suit’s somebody’s motorcycle outfit, that’s all. Somebody was doing some off-roading last season and thought he was going to get caught, so he stuffed it down that hole to bury the evidence.”

“Yeah, must be,” Mickey said.

When they arrived at the outskirts of the marsh, the teens starting looking around trying to remember where they were the night before. They walked for a few minutes as the trail twisted through the tall reeds, then Mickey suddenly stopped.

“I’m pretty sure this is where I was.”

“I think so too,” said David. He stood still with his feet tight together as if afraid he was on the precipice of the hole.

Ernie put down the flags and surveyed the area. There weren’t any holes in the ground he could see. He shrugged his shoulders. “Sure isn’t anything here now, nothing worth flagging. I’m heading back to the Lodge. You guys coming?”

“Nah,” said Mickey. “We’re going to hike around for a while. Probably go fishing in the afternoon.” The two boys stood there, waiting for Ernie to leave.

Ernie picked up the flags. “Okay, have fun, and don’t fall into any more holes, real or imaginary.” He shook his head, and then started back carrying the two flags.

When Ernie was out of sight, Mickey faced David. "We both know I fell into a hole, and it was right here." Mickey spun around 360 degrees. "Where's the friggin' thing?"

"Maybe it really is a secret military base and it's camouflaged," whispered David. "Maybe they're watching us now."

"Chill out, Dude. You heard Ernie." Mickey patted the helmet. "If there's no serial numbers on it, it's not military."

"Yeah, well according to you, it's no plain old motorcycle helmet either, unless you imagined all that other stuff you told me."

"I keep telling you—I didn't imagine anything!"

"Then put it on again and test it!" said David, pointing at the helmet.

"Fine, but let's go up to the falls where nobody can see us."

As they started down the trail to Horsetail Falls, Ernie waited until they were far enough ahead and began tracking them off-trail.

Chapter Seven

Mickey and David hiked to the far shore of the lake. Every few minutes, boats trolling lures would pass by offshore. Except for the boaters, nobody was in sight. They continued picking their way along the shore until they reached the creek fed by Horsetail Falls. They were now directly across the lake from the marina. A trail marker bore the legend: Horsetail Falls, 2 miles. Someone had scratched another message below it: "Not for the faint of heart." They started up the steep trail that hugged the side of the creek.

Halfway up, they stopped to drink from the creek's ice-cold water. It had a sweet taste of its own. There was nothing like it in a bottle. After another hour of hiking, they reached a clearing and stopped to rest. Not surprisingly, no one was around. They sat on a fallen log and watched the torrent of white water.

"Crap! We forgot to bring food," moaned David.

Mickey frowned. "Yeah. My stomach is rumbling." He grinned. "But we're not going to be thirsty!" He splashed some water at David who returned the gesture.

Mickey now put on the suit and helmet. When he pulled down the visor, the red light on the sleeve went on, just as it did the first time. With the visor down, he held up his arm so David could see it. Then, Mickey pushed the red button, the visor opened, and the light went off again. "See, I told you!" he yelled.

"Sweet!" David said.

Mickey pushed the button, and the visor closed again. "Can you hear me through the visor?"

David couldn't see Mickey's face. The visor had turned dark, like expensive sunglasses do. "Yeah, I can," said David, "but your voice sounds weird, like it's coming from a radio—it's freaky. I can't see your face either." He snickered. "Boy Scout becomes Darth Vader."

"Everything looks the same to me." Mickey sounded puzzled.

He tilted his head up toward the sky. "Dude, do you see an airplane up there?"

David looked up and saw the white line of a contrail. The airplane trailing it was much too high to see. "I can see the smoke trail. Why?"

"I can see the people in the windows and read the numbers on the plane's tail."

"Yeah, sure."

"I really can! This visor's like wearing binoculars!" He pushed the red button and the visor popped open. He squinted up at the contrail, but the airplane creating it was just a dot. "Jesus!"

"Got to be military!" said David. "We got to give the thing back!"

"Give it back to who? You want to go back and drop it in that hole again, like returning a video? Well, guess what? Nobody can find the friggin' thing, not even us!"

David looked thoughtful.

"Besides," continued Mickey. "I want to try something else."

"What?"

"Jumping like I did last night when I got out of the hole." He moved a few yards away from David.

"You mean the hole that isn't there anymore?"

Mickey extended his middle finger and closed the visor. Facing the creek, he flexed his legs and jumped, leaping at least twenty feet into the air. At the apex of his jump, he started waving his arms and shouting in that strange voice that came out of the helmet. "Holy shit!" When he came down, he landed halfway up a tree on the other side of the creek. Hugging the tree, Mickey looked back at David. "Holy stinking shit!" he yelled again. His amplified voice echoed up the mountain.

David stared, dumbfounded. "Jesus, I see what you mean!"

Mickey scrambled down the tree with relative ease and jumped back across the creek, this time pushing off less vigorously. He landed close to David, and after steadying himself like a gymnast sticking a landing, pushed the red button. As the visor popped up, he was beaming.

David smiled. "Hey, I have an idea. Lower the visor and try picking up that log." He pointed at the fallen tree they'd been sitting on. It was at least three feet in diameter. No human being would be able to budge it without a crane.

"You got to be kidding me! That thing's gotta weigh a ton!"

"Normal people can't jump twenty feet in the air either, asshole! Just put the visor down and give it a shot."

"Okay." Mickey sounded hesitant. He closed the visor and faced the log, focusing on a large branch sticking out from the side. "Here goes." As though it didn't weigh anything at all, Mickey picked up the log and tossed it to the opposite side of the creek. It landed with a loud crash and rolled down the hill, smashing into a boulder and breaking in half.

Both boys stared at the remains, speechless. Mickey pushed the red button and the visor popped open. "Did you see that?"

David pumped his fist in the air. "Sweet!"

Mickey's face was flushed with excitement, but then he stared at the broken tree.

"What's wrong?" asked David.

"Might have hurt somebody."

"There's nobody here," countered David.

"Squirrels count too."

David snickered. "What about spiders, Spider-Man?"

"Or bats. I think I prefer Batman."

"Then I'm Robin!"

"Exactly!" Mickey reached up his hand to high-five, but David held back. Mickey looked quizzically at his friend. "What?"

"I still need my fingers," said David.

"You're right. I don't know what this thing can really do. Better take this slow."

"Like what?"

Mickey lowered the visor and pointed at a fair-sized rock as big as a pumpkin and at least one hundred pounds. He picked it up as if it weighed nothing at all and tossed it into the air with one hand like a tennis ball. After catching it with his other hand, he pitched it like a monstrous-sized fastball at a much larger boulder higher up the hill. When the smaller rock impacted the larger one, it disintegrated, in the process cracking the larger rock down the middle. The sound of the impact was almost deafening. David covered his ears and cringed. Mickey stood looking at the carnage with his arms at his sides.

After the dust settled, still with the visor down, Mickey turned slowly back around. David stared at him and stepped backward. Mickey picked up another large rock and crushed it in his hand like it was an egg. He stared at his gloved hand covered in dust and then opened the visor. This time he wasn't smiling. Mickey removed the helmet and tucked it under his arm. "Not sure about this," he said.

David kept staring at Mickey's hand. He blinked and seemed to refocus. "Kind of scary."

"Yeah."

David looked pale. "We've got to give it back."

"Great. Have the phone number for the Pentagon handy?"

"We'll tell your dad. He's a news guy. He knows people in Washington."

"How about we tell your dad. He's a cop."

David's face blanched. "Not him, okay?" After four years of being David's best friend, Mickey knew the rest of the story.

Mickey put his hand on David's shoulder. "I think it's military all right—part of some test."

"A test just for you, a dude on summer vacation who just happened to be out for a hike? Gimme a break!"

Mickey had a faraway look in his eyes. "I say we go back to the cabin, put it in a box, and take it back home. It could come in handy on the mean streets of L.A."

David smiled. "Awesome idea, Dude." They high-fived.

"Jesus, I'm hungry."

"Let's go." Mickey took off the suit and they started back.

Ernie was watching everything from behind a boulder farther up the trail. When the boys started back down toward the resort, he stood up, wiped the mist from his face, and headed for the rock Mickey had smashed as easily as popping a paper bag. He kept up on hi-tech military gizmos by reading books at night, and he never missed the Military Channel. Ernie had an absolute passion for that sort of thing. He always wanted to be an engineer. When he joined the Army, he was hoping to start down the hi-tech road, but it never happened. He couldn't handle the book stuff, but as an Army Ranger he saw plenty of action and learned how to handle himself "in-country."

Ernie picked up one of the broken shards of rock and remembered a TV show on exoskeletons, special suits that enhanced a soldier's powers like a suit of armor with motors inside. Looked like Mickey had stumbled on one of them. The story about the hole didn't make any sense, and Ernie couldn't figure out why a hi-tech super-secret gadget would be lying about at the lake. Had to be military! *Maybe* it did belong to one of the soldiers training in winter survival. *Maybe* Mickey was right. *Maybe* it was a test of some sort. The fact that the outfit fit Mickey like a glove was probably just a coincidence. Ernie would have to figure this out of course, maybe contact the Army. If he helped them recover it, maybe he could work on the project as a way of keeping his mouth shut. That seemed fair. But for now, while he tried to decide what to do, he'd keep his mouth shut anyway.

A technician inside a curtained Winnebago parked in the resort's campground asked his associate. "What do you think he's going to do?"

"He's an Ex-Army Ranger guy. He'll phone it in to somebody wearing a uniform."

"Do we want him to?"

"It'll be the best cover in the world."

Chapter Eight

On a tree-lined street not much different from where Mickey and David lived, two teenage girls, classmates of the boys, sat on Pam's front porch whiling away the last days of their summer vacation. Pam's leg braces were off, propped up against her lawn chair.

"Looking forward to next week?" Pam asked.

"You think some cute guy's moving into the neighborhood?"

"I was referring to school—learning things, reading great books, *that* kind of thing?"

"Getting all sweaty in PE, learning all about the birds and the bees in Health from Mrs. Briscoe who's probably still a virgin..."

"What's wrong with being a virgin?" asked Pam.

Vickie rolled her eyes.

"We could have been in Honors Biology this year, you know?"

"With all the geeks? Like, maybe you want to be a social pariah—not me," Vickie said, tossing her head of curly blond locks.

"A couple of the smart guys are damn cute."

Vickie took a close look at her friend and shook her head in feigned despair. "You don't mean that guy David, do you? He's a head shorter than you."

"So what? He's got gorgeous eyes behind those rims, and the cutest dimples. And, you know, his friend Mickey isn't that bad either."

Vickie looked shocked. "Don't even go there. If I can't do better than *that,* I'm jumping off the nearest bridge.

Pam looked away. "Don't you want to get married some day and have kids?"

"Married? What's the point? Kids...why would I want to bring another brat into this messed up world?"

"Stop being so bitter!" She pointed at her leg braces. "Try wearing one of those for a few days."

Vickie looked down. "Sorry."

"I do…"

"Do what?" asked Vickie.

"Want to get married, and have kids. One of each, a boy and a girl…maybe twins."

"All the screaming and crying, changing diapers. Who wants to deal with that shit?"

Pam bit her lip. "I can't imagine anything better. The chance to do everything right for someone." Her voice trailed off.

"If David's your sperm donor, your kids are going to be shrimps."

Pam's face reddened. "At least they'll be smart, unlike the dufus you hang out with."

"Ever hear of *the Pill*?" asked Vickie with air quotes.

"You mean aspirin, I assume," Pam said with a smirk, then opened her laptop. "Get a load of what I found on Facebook?"

"You've got Wi-Fi?" Vickie asked.

"Yeah, my…*adopted dad* is addicted to the Internet. He's got the whole house wired."

"Why do you still call him that?"

Pam gave her a penetrating look, and then started scrolling across the page. "Looks like you've got competition for Prom Queen." She showed Vickie the Facebook page.

"Lacey. She only wishes." Vickie studied the computer screen. After a moment, her jaw dropped.

"I know! I think her new boobs are a bit much," said Pam.

"Like, everything about Lacey is too much—her clothes, her car…like, her mother must've paid for them, like she does everything else."

"You're having a *like* attack again," Pam said with a grin.

Vickie knitted her brow. "Like, what's that supposed to mean?"

"It means every time you talk about Lacey and her crowd, you slip into their 'like' lingo, *like* too damn much!'"

"Pisses me off! She's got everything, and I've got nothing—a mom who doesn't give a crap about me, and then there's Brandon, her new boyfriend. Now there's a real deadbeat."

Pam reached out and took her hand. "Sorry, Vic. Didn't mean to...*like,* bring you down." They both laughed.

They watched an old Ford truck sputter around the corner and stop in front of Pam's house. "Speak of the devil," said Vickie, frowning.

As the fiftyish guy with graying temples scooted across the passenger seat to roll down the window, Pam noticed Vickie tugging down her skirt, which struck her as odd.

"Hey, Vickie, get your stuff and let's go," called out Brandon.

"I'm sleeping at Pam's," shouted Vickie.

"Your mother said to pick you up. She'll be home in an hour. I'm cooking dinner."

"If you really want to impress her, why don't you get a job?"

"Watch your mouth!" Brandon opened the door and slid out of his truck. "Get in the car, you little bitch!"

Pam's mother Phyllis stepped out onto the porch. She was a tall statuesque woman in her mid-forties who had worked in corporate America for twenty years. "Is there a problem, girls?"

"Psycho Brandon says I have to go home with him," whispered Vickie behind her hand.

Phyllis gave the man on the sidewalk a closer look. "Good afternoon, Brandon," she said. "Please forgive me...I meant to call Judy earlier. I've asked Vickie to stay for dinner and spend the night. Pam has an appointment in the morning with her surgeon and wants Vickie to come along for moral support. I'm sure you understand." She took out her iPhone and began texting.

"You should've cleared that with Judy," snapped Brandon.

"I just texted her and she said it's okay. Sorry for the inconvenience. I'll bring Vickie home tomorrow afternoon."

"Yeah." Brandon glared at Vickie as he drove off.

Phyllis winked at Vickie. "Dinner's in an hour, young ladies. Turkey burgers. You two can make the salad." She went back into the house and closed the front door.

"You can uncross your legs now," Pam said to Vickie.

Vickie pulled out a pack of cigarettes and lit one.

Pam leaned away from her. "Jesus, Vic, why do you do that?"

"You try living with Brandon."

"You're sure that's all that's going on?" Pam asked.

Vickie looked suddenly uncomfortable. "He stares at me, okay," she added. "He tries to get me alone with him." She let Pam digest this tidbit. "Like my mother called him and said to cook dinner." Vickie smirked. "Their idea of fine dining are TV dinners."

"Has he messed with you or anything?"

"I don't give that pervert a chance. I make it a point to not be home very much."

"That's why you're always here?" Pam asked.

"I checked your fridge—no TV dinners."

"You should talk to my, um, mother. She's done sexual harassment trainings at work."

"Stop choking on the word *mother*! Don't you have any idea how lucky you are?"

Pam started to protest.

"These two people adopted *you*! They wanted *you*! You're *their* daughter! My mom used to cringe every time she checked 'Have Children' on an Internet dating site."

"They're still not my *real* parents!"

"Do you remember anything about your *real* DNA donors?"

"I was three years old when they died." She pointed at her braces. "When I got these."

"Any aunts or uncles, maybe a grandma in a nursing home somewhere?"

Pam lowered her gaze. "No."

"How about a cousin in Chicago who drinks and doesn't have a job?"

"There's nobody." Pam looked uncomfortable.

"Any pictures?"

"No!"

"Don't they keep records at the...place you came from?" persisted Vickie.

"You mean the orphanage?"

"Yeah."

"I never went back."

Vickie looked surprised. "Why not?"

Pam began strapping on her braces. "Time to pick the salad dressing and set the table."

"There has to be something somewhere!" persisted Vickie.

"Why is this so important to you?" Pam asked angrily.

"Don't you want to understand your roots, know who your people were?"

"So I can drive by my first house and put flowers on my mother's grave?"

Vickie felt terrible. "I'm really sorry."

"I don't want to discuss it anymore." Pam levered herself into a standing position.

Vickie looked at her friend with tears in her eyes. "I'd trade with you if I could, braces and all."

"What?"

Tears began rolling down Vickie's cheeks. She pointed at the front door. "There's real food cooking in there, and people who don't see you as an inconvenience. You may have more of them out there somewhere. Don't you want to find them? I'd settle for one."

Pam didn't respond, but looked at her braces.

"What's up with your appointment anyway, and why didn't you tell me?" asked Vickie

"It's no big deal. I'm hoping they can do something so I can get around better." Pam laughed. "Maybe a sports version of these braces." She slapped one of her leg braces.

Vickie stood up and smiled. "So you can chase 'Little Dude Davie' down the hallway after school?"

Pam reached out to swat Vickie, but she dodged her. "Or give somebody I know a swift kick in the A double S."

Chapter Nine

The new school year was in session. One evening, while watching TV, Mickey heard a knock on the front door. He opened it and saw David standing there looking miserable. Mickey had seen that expression before and stepped aside to let him in.

Mickey stuck out his closed fist, which David tapped with his. It was like a high-five, but more simple. To adults, no communication between teenagers is simple anymore. In days past, kids just waved and said "hi" or shook hands, like adults. Nowadays, there are endless permutations of a simple salutation: high-fives, low-fives, chest-thumps, backslaps, and more. Yet by far, nothing confuses adults more than the word "Dude." To teenagers, the word "Dude" can substitute for any word in the dictionary at any time, but despite that, no kid ever seems to get confused. Parents are clueless with how "Dude" works, which is undoubtedly the point.

The boys headed for Mickey's bedroom. On the way, they passed his parents sitting at the dining room table. Max was reading the evening newspaper while Jerry studied her latest Mahjong card. Recognizing David's haunted expression, they exchanged knowing looks.

"Hey, Davie," said Jerry, starting to get up.

"Hey, Mrs. B," replied David, casting his eyes downward. He kept walking toward Mickey's bedroom. After exchanging a knowing glance with his parents, Mickey followed.

After the door was closed, the boys hopped on the bed, lying on their backs facing the ceiling.

"What happened?" asked Mickey.

"Same as last night, except worse. Think your mom would mind if I slept over?"

"She never minds. What happened?"

"Jake got home. He and my mom got into it like they always

do, and then my dad started screaming at her, telling her to leave Jake alone. When the doors started slamming, I bugged out." He closed his eyes.

Jake was David's older brother. He'd graduated from high school two years before (but barely), and he still didn't have a full-time job. David said he was working at a motorcycle shop part-time, or at least that's what Jake was telling everybody. Whatever the truth, Jake seemed to have ample spending money these days, and he had to be getting it somewhere. He spent a lot of time and money customizing his bike, buying fancy equipment, doing a custom paint job and souping it up. Obviously, fixing motorcycles part-time paid well. When Jake came home at all hours of the night, he made a point of roaring up and down the street on his chopper, making as much noise as possible and waking everybody.

One evening last week, Mickey happened to be looking out his window when Jake came roaring down the street. Just as he passed the neighbor's house, Jake leaned over with a big silver wrench in his hand and knocked down their mailbox. Mickey knew there was no point in complaining to the police. David's dad was a cop, and for some reason, his father thought everything Jake did was cool.

Nobody in the neighborhood liked Jake except for his father Dick. It was also clear that, for whatever reason, Dick had little use for his younger son David. Mickey wondered if this was because Dick and Jake were so much alike. Both were over six feet tall, liked loud music, beer, and motorcycles—the noisier the better. David was short and slight like his mother, introverted, and wore thick glasses. He once confided to Mickey that his father was ashamed of him, but David wasn't sure why.

The year before, David and Mickey were riding home from school on their bikes when Jake and his biker buddy Rob, a fat dirtbag who always wore leather, came roaring up on their motorcycles and cornered the boys in an alley. After taunting them, Jake and Rob knocked both boys off their bikes and sped away howling with laughter. David's lip was split and bloodied, but Mickey was uninjured. Immediately after, they rode straight to David's house and told his mother. She was furious. But when his father arrived home that night and Linda told him, it was David who was punished, not Jake. In fact, Mickey remembered hearing Jake and his father in the garage laughing about the incident. Mickey then watched Linda walk into the kitchen and pour herself a small glass of liquor from a bottle in the cupboard.

There was a knock at the door to Mickey's bedroom. "Can I come in?" asked Jerry. Without waiting for an answer, she opened the door and stepped inside. She was carrying a plate of cookies and a quart of milk, and placed it on Mickey's night-stand.

"Thanks, Mom." He glanced toward the door.

Jerry got the signal. "Let me know if you guys want more," she offered and then left.

David took one of the cookies. "Have you tried out the suit again?"

"Too busy with school."

"Where do you keep it?"

"Under the bed."

After hesitating, David took a sip from the carton and handed it back. His mood seemed to brighten. "My mom bought me my own motocross suit and a helmet. Let's ride to the park tomorrow and do some serious dirt biking."

"Sure."

Smiling, David stuck out his fist and they did that hand thing again. After knocking off the rest of the cookies and milk, they fell asleep.

Chapter Ten

The next day was a Pupil Free Day, so students were off while teachers went into work. After breakfast, David ran home to get his bike and put on his new motocross suit. When he went into his house, he didn't see his mom. She was probably still in the bedroom with the door closed. He hurriedly put on his new red and silver jumpsuit, donned the matching helmet, then extended his arms and smiled as he admired the shiny material. The whole get-up totally rocked! When he went into the garage, he was relieved to see that Jake's motorcycle was gone.

David got on his dirt bike and pedaled over to Mickey's house where he skidded into the open garage.

"That's so cool!" shouted Mickey.

David's visor was up and he had a sideways grin on his face. "It's a lot fancier than yours, except I can't smash boulders or see in the dark."

Mickey quickly spun around to check that they were alone. "Shut up! I don't want my folks to know!"

"Nobody's going to believe that shit we did up at the lake, anyway."

Mickey put on the black helmet and hopped on his bike. "Sometimes I don't believe it either." He glanced at his sleeve. The small red light was off. He dropped the visor and the light came on again. "Must've recharged itself somehow."

"With that gizmo, anything's possible," said David.

Reassured the suit still worked, he lifted the visor and nodded to David, and they took off on their bikes.

They headed toward Verdugo Park paralleling the train tracks along Chandler Street. It was a sunny weekday with a fair amount of traffic. They kept to the side of the road.

Mickey and David were two cool dirt bikers having a carefree adventure. They rode for ten minutes with the wind in their faces. A few blocks from the park, they could hear the unmistakable growl of motorcycles. They glanced over their shoulders and saw Jake and his buddy Rob roaring up behind them. Jake was pointing his finger at them and leering.

The boys veered into an alley just past Catalina Street, but Jake and Rob had no trouble catching up. Instead of pedaling faster to escape them, Mickey stopped his bike and turned around.

David stopped next to him with a look of panic etched on his face. "What are you doing? We gotta get outta here! They're going to beat us up!"

Mickey looked at his friend with steel in his eyes. "Not this time." He lowered his visor and looked at his left forearm. The red light was blinking, but now a second button lit up beside it. This one was yellow, and it blinked insistently. Mickey noticed it and looked up. "Get behind me," he urged.

"What are you going to do?" David sounded frantic.

"Nothing."

"What do you mean nothing?" David shouted.

Mickey stared at his sleeve again and didn't answer.

Jake and Rob pulled into the alley and flanked the two boys blocking their way. They both wore motorcycle jackets with a club emblem on the back, something with a skull and a dagger through it. Cigarettes were dangling out of the corner of their mouths. Jake wasn't wearing a helmet. Before getting off his chopper, Jake gunned his motor. The sound was deafening in the confined alley space. He slowly got off his motorcycle and, with a wry grin, approached the boys. His buddy Rob, who had gained a few more pounds, remained on his motorcycle staring menacingly. His black tee shirt kept riding up on his belly.

"Well, well, what do we have here?" Jake walked around the two boys, giving them the once-over. He touched his brother's jumpsuit. David flinched. "Did *Mommy* buy that Halloween costume for you, little bro?" He sneered, took a drag on his cigarette, and deliberately exhaled smoke rings in David's face. He coughed. Jake chuckled, and then looked at Mickey's suit that was matte black and featureless. With his visor down and the faceplate once again opaque, Jake couldn't see his face.

"Now these threads, Mickey—that is you under there, right?" Jake pounded on Mickey's helmet, but Mickey didn't react. "This get-up isn't looking too swift. Probably got it out of some dumpster." He and Rob laughed.

"Leave us alone!" yelled David.

Jake faced his brother with a glare. "Or what, little bro? Gonna tell Mommy on me again? Think I give a shit?" Jake threw his cigarette on the ground and stomped on it. "Don't get all bent out of shape. Rob and me, we're here to do you little men a real favor today. Ain't that right, Rob?" Rob spat out some chewing tobacco and remained seated on his motorcycle. "Seeing as how you boys are real serious bikers now, we're going to let you join our biker club, that is, if you can pass the initiation." Jake poked David hard in the shoulder. "You do want to join our club, don't you little brother?" Between each of his words, Jake poked David progressively harder, until he finally fell off his bike. Jake loomed over David, sneering down at him, and raised his leg as if he was going to stomp on him.

"Stop it, Jake." It was Mickey's voice, but it sounded artificial, like it was coming from a radio.

Jake wheeled around. A head taller than Mickey and twice as broad, he took a step forward and pounded on Mickey's helmet again with his fist, this time harder. Still Mickey didn't flinch. "Is that some cool GI Joe thing with a walkie-talkie in it? Take it off! I want to see it."

"No," replied Mickey without moving a muscle.

"Whoa!" Jake stood up straighter and stared at him. "Hey, Rob, did you hear that shit? This little dude doesn't know the first rule of our biker club." Jake peered at Mickey's visor but couldn't see his face. "When I tell you to do something, you do it, cause

I'm the president of the club. Get it? Now take that damn thing off before I rip it off!"

"No," said Mickey in the radio voice.

"We'll see about that!" Jake started to reach toward him, but before making contact, Mickey effortlessly pushed him away. Jake fell backwards and skidded on his back, ripping his leather jacket.

Jake stood up with murder in his eyes and dusted himself off. David looked frightened. Mickey didn't budge. Jake looked at his torn jacket and glared at Mickey. "You're going to pay for this, asshole, big time!" He walked back to Mickey and lashed out with his right palm, striking Mickey in the middle of his chest. Mickey didn't move an inch. Jake felt like he'd hit a brick wall. He yanked back his hand grimacing in pain.

Jake rubbed his hand and scowled at Mickey who remained standing like a statue. "What the fuck!" exclaimed Jake. His face turned beet red with rage. "You got body armor under that thing?" He went to his motorcycle and pulled a large silver wrench out of the saddlebag. He leered back at Mickey, brandishing the wrench. "We'll see about that."

Mickey turned to David. "Get on your bike and go."

David scrambled to his feet. "Where?"

"Doesn't matter, just go! I'm right behind you."

David ran to his bike and tore down the alley. Mickey followed after him.

"You got to be kidding me!" yelled Jake, laughing. He turned to Rob. "Let's teach these losers a serious lesson." He mounted his motorcycle, gunned the motor, and raced after them. Rob followed.

A block away, David kept looking over his shoulder. He was pedaling as fast as he could, but he heard the rumbling of motorcycles drawing closer.

Mickey followed right behind him. Because of the power of the suit, he was pedaling effortlessly. "David, turn right at the end of the block," he directed in the amplified radio voice.

"What are you going to do?" David shouted while gasping for breath.

"I'm going left, taking those two assholes with me."

"Are you nuts?"

Mickey looked at the buttons on his sleeve. "Just do it. I'll be fine."

Now, at the end of the block, they could see the two motorcycles closing the gap. David saw his brother brandishing the large silver wrench. David broke right as Mickey instructed. Mickey slowed until Jake was twenty yards away from him, then turned, lifted his arm with his middle finger extended and took off to the left.

Enraged by Mickey's gesture, Jake yelled back to Rob. "I'll deal with my brother later. Let's get that asshole in the black pajamas!" He took off after Mickey with Rob close behind.

When Mickey was sure both bikers were following him, he started pedaling faster. Because of the suit's power, he sped up suddenly like he'd been shot from a cannon.

"What the hell?" roared Jake. He poured on the throttle and peeled rubber after Mickey. Rob tried to keep up with him.

Mickey turned and saw he was too far ahead. He slowed his pace, and when he was sure Jake was still on his tail, began taking a course that would lead them back to his house.

Chapter Eleven

Mickey stopped his bike in the middle of the street between his and David's house. Stepping off his bike, he crossed his arms and waited for Jake and Rob to catch up. Mickey noticed the yellow button blinking brighter and faster, demanding his attention. He touched it, but nothing obvious happened.

Jake and Rob stopped their bikes on either side of Mickey, bracketing him. Still holding the wrench, Jake dismounted and faced Mickey. He slapped the wrench against his gloved hand. "Say your prayers, asshole," Jake said. When Mickey didn't flinch, Jake started towards him. Still Mickey wouldn't retreat. Jake raised the wrench high over his head. "Let's see how solid that armor of yours is!" He brought the wrench down hard on Mickey's helmet. Just as the wrench contacted the top of Mickey's helmet, there was a brief flare of light and an electric sound, like a short circuit. The wrench vibrated violently and flew out of Jake's hand fifty feet up into the air hitting Mickey's roof, making a series of banging sounds as it tumbled down and landed on the porch. Jake fell backward onto the street with shocked disbelief plastered on his face.

Hearing the commotion, Max ran out the front door, followed by Jerry. Mickey was standing next to his bike. He'd taken off the helmet.

Jake slowly got up off the pavement. He looked scared. He pointed at Mickey and started bellowing, "You ain't heard the last of this! You hear me?"

Max ran to his son. "You okay?"

Completely unperturbed, Mickey replied, "No biggie, Dad."

Max took a step toward Jake. "I've had enough of your B.S.!"

At that moment, still pedaling as fast as he could, David careened down the street just as his father Dick stepped out onto their porch. David pulled up on his bike. Dick approached Max.

"What's going on?" he asked, sounding official like a policeman.

"Just having a little fun," Jake said.

Dick turned to Mickey. "What happened?"

"Nothing," Mickey replied with a neutral expression.

Jerry walked over to David. "Tell me what happened."

David looked first at Jake, then at his father. He seemed to withdraw into a shell. "Nothing, Mrs. B," he said under his breath. Jerry spun around and looked at Max.

His face flushed with anger, Max glared at Dick. "When are you going to control your juvenile-delinquent son?"

"Your kid said nothing happened! You heard him." Dick turned around and pointed at David. "Get in the house!" he ordered.

David walked away with a backwards glance at Jerry and went into his house. Dick followed him, leaving Max, Jerry, Mickey, and Jake standing in the center of the street.

Jake glared at Mickey. "This ain't over, Dude."

Max stepped up to him. "Yes it is! Touch my son, and I'll put you behind bars!"

"Yeah, right," said Jake smirking. Leering, he raised his middle finger and followed his father into the house, slamming the door.

Max turned to his son, put his hands on his shoulders, and said, "You're sixteen years old. Jake is a man hanging out with a bunch of outlaw biker types. You can't handle it, but I can." Max glared at Jake's house across the street.

With her arm around his shoulder, Jerry began steering her son back toward their house. As they walked, she grabbed hold of some of the suit's black cloth. "Isn't this the thing you found at the lake? I thought you tossed it."

"I've been goofing around with it. No big deal." Suddenly self-conscious, Mickey reached to cover up the buttons but noticed they were both dark. He dropped his arm and followed his mother inside their house.

That night, like most nights lately, David showed up at Mickey's house. On the way to Mickey's bedroom, Jerry pulled him aside. "Hey, mister," she said, sounding concerned. David looked unusually withdrawn, even for him. Jerry teared up.

"Hello Mrs. B," David replied, avoiding eye contact.

"Everything okay, honey?"

"Yeah. See ya." David started toward Mickey's room. When he closed the door, Jerry wiped her eyes dry.

David flopped onto Mickey's bed next to him. Mickey was lying with his head hanging over the edge staring at the suit and helmet on the floor. Both were silent, staring at the suit.

"When Jake caught us, another button lit up, a yellow one next to the red one," said Mickey. "If they hassle us again, they're both in deep shit."

"Did you see what happened to that wrench? The suit's got a force field."

Mickey rolled over onto his back. "Maybe."

David frowned. "Why did you take Jake's shit and not pulverize him?"

"What do you mean?"

"You could've tossed him and his bike down the alley like a friggin' tennis ball."

Mickey shook his head. "Remember that Kung Fu movie? The monk would defend himself, but he wouldn't hurt anybody."

"Yeah, I remember," said David. He didn't sound happy about it.

"I won't use the suit to hurt anybody either, not even your asshole brother."

"I guess so," David added.

"Anyway, maybe he'll leave us alone now."

"Find where the batteries go, just in case," David said.

Chapter Twelve

Ernie stood at his cabin window gazing out at the mountains. Winter was approaching—the leaves on the trees had all turned yellow and orange. In another month or so, the first snow would arrive and he'd be confined to his cabin for days on end—his only entertainment a big screen TV; his only decisions, which frozen dinner to thaw out and what to read from a pile of military books and magazines. One of them was open on the table in front of the TV. He was reading an article about exoskeletons and super-powered soldiers of the future.

Ernie couldn't stop thinking about the suit that Mickey had supposedly found in a hole by the marsh. Ernie had gone back several times and never found anything larger than a gopher hole, let alone any high-tech military gear lying around. If he hadn't seen Mickey tossing trees and smashing boulders while wearing the suit, he'd have accepted the discarded motocross suit explanation. Part of him still didn't believe what he'd witnessed, even though he'd hiked up to the falls and touched the scarred face of the boulder that Mickey had pitched a rock at like a missile. It was true, all right. Now the question was, what should he do?

After considering it for several days, the decision became obvious. Ernie was a patriot, a former Army Ranger. It was his duty to report it. The problem was, to whom? The Army is a huge organization. It wasn't like he could call Lost and Found. Besides, he wasn't even sure the suit was theirs. Air Force, maybe? Could be. The CIA seemed wrong. The suit was currently in the possession of a teenage kid, not some spy. The FBI made the most sense. He sat on the couch, stared at the magazine picture of an exoskeleton one more time, and picked up the phone.

"FBI, Washington DC. How may I direct your call?"

"This is Army Sergeant Ernest Santos...retired. I want to

report some missing top secret military hardware, Ma'am."

"The FBI doesn't usually handle this kind of thing. What is it, if I may ask?"

"An exoskeleton."

"A what?"

"A suit that gives the wearer super powers. A kid has it, about sixteen years old. Used the thing to toss a whole tree across a creek like it was a twig…and he crushed a rock in his hand like it was an egg! His name's Mickey. Nice kid. Lives in L.A. He didn't steal it," Ernie hastened to add. "Says he found it in a hole up at the lake."

There was long silence. "I see. And this alleged incident occurred where exactly?"

"At Twin Lakes in the High Sierra Mountains. That's where I work. Great place."

"Mr. Santos, can I ask you a question…not related to the military equipment?"

"Sure, anything."

"Do you take any medication?"

Ernie looked quizzically at the phone. "A Tylenol once in a while. Are you going to take my report now?"

"I've been doing it while we've been talking. Got your phone number. Even pulled up your service record."

"That's because you're the FBI!"

"Right! So don't worry, we know how to find you. I'm sure the army will look into this…um…*incident,* and they'll be in touch."

"Not sure the suit belongs to the Army, Ma'am."

"Don't worry! I'll make sure everybody knows about it."

"Great!"

"Bye now." The operator sat back in her chair and muttered "Jeez!"

The operator next to her noticed. "Hey, girl, you look like you just got a wild one."

"They must be showin' *X Files* re-runs on cable. Every time that damn show airs, the kooks come out of the woodwork and start phoning in all kinds of weird shit."

"At least it wasn't another UFO."

Meanwhile, in the sub-basement of the Defense Intelligence Agency (DIA), the super computer that monitored every phone call and email in the country made a recording of the conversation, cross-referenced it against key words, and filed it away. A duplicate of the file was transmitted to another location without the DIA's knowledge.

Days later, it was lunchtime on the day of the After School Dance. At this point in the school year, many of the sophomores already had official girlfriends. Mickey and David weren't among them. Social pariahs, they ate their lunch in solitude sitting on the cement steps behind the Science Building. Misery loves company.

"Want to go to the dance tonight?" asked David, holding half a tuna sandwich. Mickey's usual answer would be no. Although both were introverts, David was usually the more socially intrepid of the two, until Mickey discovered the suit.

"You got that right, Dude," replied Mickey.

David stared quizzically at his friend. "What gives? You never want to go."

"I'm going and thinking of wearing the suit," said Mickey, taking a bite of his PB and J.

"You can't wear that thing to the dance. You'll look worse than a geek!"

Mickey frowned. "Maybe you're right."

"Why would you want to, anyway?"

Mickey looked embarrassed. "When I wear it, I feel different."

"You mean stronger?"

"It's more than that. Confident, like I could ask Vickie out."

David laughed. "If I were you, I'd stick to crushing rocks!" Mickey looked annoyed. "You just can't wear that thing to the dance!"

"I know…but I'm going to stash it in my locker, just in case."

David nodded. "If the dance is a downer, we can go to the dump and toss around old cars, or something."

"Yeah, cool," said Mickey.

They high-fived.

That day Pam and Vickie violated the boy's refuge behind the Science building. The four had a Biology class together next period, but of course sat on opposite sides of the classroom. Today the girls were behind the Science Building thirty minutes before class, and to Vickie's dismay, within a social radius of Mickey and David.

The girls were arguing as they approached. Vickie, always a bundle of nervous energy, danced around Pam to compensate for the slowness of Pam's lumbering gait. "I don't see why it's such a big deal," Vickie said. "So what if we hand it in late?"

"I've never handed in an assignment late in my life, until I got stuck with you as a lab partner," replied Pam sounding irritated.

"You're not the only one with an A in the class," sneered Vickie. With a look of disgust, she eyed the two boys. They stared back like deer in the headlights. "But I'd rather get an F than suck up to those two losers," Vickie said. "Somebody might see us!"

"Suit yourself," said Pam. "But I'm not turning in anything late!" she said it out of the side of her mouth, and then smiled at the boys as she hobbled over.

"Hey, guys," said Pam.

"Hi, Pam," said David, answering for both of them. David liked Pam, but he never had the guts to speak to her outside of class. While this brief interchange occurred, Vickie held back a few steps.

"Guys," Pam went on. "Vic and I have a *little* problem, and we're kind of hoping you'll help us out."

Mickey looked up at the mention of Vickie. "What's that?"

"You know the questions on the Science lab we're supposed to turn in today?"

"Yeah."

"Well my lab partner," Pam said pointing at Vickie, who gave her a somewhat pained smile in return, "left ours at home."

"Why don't you copy ours?" said David, too eagerly.

"That would be *so* nice of you," Pam replied brightly. She turned to Vickie and poked her in the ribs. "Wouldn't it?"

"Yeah, sure," mumbled Vickie, afraid someone in her social clique might hear her. Pam glared at her friend.

David pulled the assignment out of his notebook and handed it to Pam, while Mickey looked on. In days past, Mickey would have climbed under the nearest rock. But he felt different now, like he could talk to Vickie, even ask her to dance—well, almost.

The two girls sat on the steps and started furiously copying. When they finished, Pam planted her feet and then pushed herself up. "Thanks." She looked at Mickey. "Maybe I'll see you at the dance?"

"Sure," said Mickey, smiling. He was looking at Vickie. "You going?"

Vickie stared at Pam in dismay. "I don't know."

Looking embarrassed, Pam said, "Thanks, guys. We'll *both* see you later." Pam hobbled off with Vickie in tow.

"Yeah," mumbled David half-heartedly.

When the girls were out of sight, David stared at his best friend. "Jesus!"

"What's the big deal? We said we were going."

"Dude, you talked to Vickie…sort of."

Mickey got a dreamy look. "Her eyes are hypnotic."

"So are a boa constrictor's."

Chapter Thirteen

That night, after storing the suit in Mickey's locker, the boys entered the Men's Gym. David wore a fresh pair of tan slacks and a blue long-sleeve shirt not tucked in to look cool. Mickey was similarly dressed in a dark shirt with the lines running down. His mother called vertical lines "slimming." Various clubs had decorated the gym with posters, nothing very catchy, and a DJ blasted music from the corner. As far as the boys were concerned, this dance looked like the other social disasters they'd attended—and never hung around for more than five minutes. All the boys stood on one side staring at the girls, while some of the good-looking girls danced together in the center of the gym—the rest of the girls lined up on the opposite wall pretending they weren't staring back at the boys. Several teachers were lurking in the shadows making sure everything remained genteel, but mainly they were shooting the breeze with each other. One teacher plugged her ears with cotton. David and Mickey's usual strategy was to walk in, mill around for a few minutes, and then make their escape.

Pam and Vickie had already arrived. Pam waved to them from across the gym. Vickie frowned and turned away, not wanting to create any illusion of a social connection. Most of the girls looked alike—the same blonde hair, usually dyed, same red lipstick, and same style of dress. Nevertheless, as far as Mickey was concerned, Vickie stood out. Her hair seemed blonder, her lips redder, and her dress...he sighed. And, she was smart too. Vickie tried to hide it, but Mickey had seen some of her class assignments—all As. The perfect woman.

"What do you want to do?" David asked, eyeing Pam and Vickie across the gym.

"Talk to some girls. That's why we came here, isn't it?"

David looked nervous, but stiffened his back. "Yeah, let's do it, Dude." They walked across the gym toward Pam and Vickie. The closer they got, the farther Vickie edged away.

David smiled at Pam. He hoped she couldn't see his knees shaking. "Was the lab assignment okay?"

Pam glanced at Mickey. "We had the same answers as you guys, except dingbat Vic left them at home." Pam forced a laugh.

Mickey looked over at Vickie. She had already put a good twenty feet between them. With her back turned, she was engaged in animated conversation with several of the other in-crowd girls. When Vickie didn't turn around, Mickey turned back to Pam. "Looks like we separated you from your friend."

Pam glanced toward Vickie and looked uncomfortable. "Vic's okay. You just have to get to know her."

"That would be kind of difficult since she won't let us get within a mile of her." Mickey sighed. David laughed until he realized the joke was on him too. They talked with Pam for a while. She couldn't dance, so they stood around.

After that, their prospects decidedly worsened. Jake strolled in with two buddies. All three had graduated two years earlier and weren't allowed on campus. From across the room, Jake glared straight at Mickey and the message was clear. Seeing Jake and smelling trouble, one of the teachers, Coach Dunivant, immediately angled over.

Jake smiled and patted the coach on the back. "Hey Coach," shouted Jake over the din of the music. "You're lookin' good, man. How much weight did you lose?"

Coach Dunivant frowned. "Cut the crap, Jake. You know you shouldn't be here."

Jake held up his hands in mock surrender. "Just want to check on my little bro, Coach." He beckoned to David in a voice loud enough to catch everyone's attention. "Ain't that right, Davie?" David looked back but didn't answer.

Coach Dunivant's expression hardened. "You know the rules. You and those other two juvenile delinquents can wait off the school grounds. Got that Jake?"

"Sure thing, Coach." Again he spoke loud enough so David and Mickey would be sure to hear. "Hey, little bro, me and my posse'll wait for you outside. Mommy ain't home now, so she can't come get you." Jake and his buddies grinned at each other.

Mickey maintained a neutral expression. David didn't look happy.

Jake and his two friends left the gym.

David turned to Mickey. "Now what do we do?"

"We go to my locker and get the suit. Jake won't come near us if he sees it."

Pam looked concerned. "My mom is picking up Vic and me in a few minutes. Do you want a ride?"

"No thanks," said Mickey. "We brought our bikes."

"But what about…?" Pam started to ask.

Mickey ignored her and turned to David. "Come on."

"Yeah, let's go." David turned to Pam and forced a smile. "Nice talking to you."

The boys' lockers were side by side outside of one of the bungalows across the campus. As soon as they arrived, Mickey opened his locker and slipped on his suit.

"Show me your sleeve," replied David.

Mickey held up his arm so David could see the blinking red and yellow lights.

"Good to go," he said. He put on his own motocross suit. "Let's make tracks!"

They stepped onto the field and headed for the parking lot. Halfway there, Mickey stopped and grabbed David's arm. "Hold up."

"Why?"

"Got company," Mickey replied, pointing into the dark. With the visor's night vision, he could see Jake and his two buddies hiding behind the bushes.

"I don't see anything," said David, peering into the dark.

Jake and his buddies now stepped out into plain sight. David tensed for a few seconds, but then forced a smile and slapped Mickey on the shoulder. "Okay, it's time for some payback!" David tried to sound mean but wasn't very convincing.

Jake stopped in the middle of the field, and his two buddies circled around him barring any escape. "Hey, guys," Jake said back over his shoulder, "look who we ran into, GI Joe and Little Bro. Ain't that a coincidence!"

"Leave us alone," Mickey commanded in the radio voice.

"Can't do that," Jake replied with a snicker. "I gotta teach you a lesson. That's why you go to school, right?" His two buddies chuckled.

"You're the one who's getting a lesson!" David shouted.

Jake stood up straight and glared at his brother. "When I'm done with your friend in the Halloween suit, *asshole*, we're having a nice brotherly chat."

"Leave us alone," Mickey repeated.

Jake took a step closer. "And if I don't?"

"I'll defend myself," Mickey replied without gloating, crossing his arms over his chest.

Jake laughed, and then lunged forward grabbing Mickey by the shoulder. Faster than anyone could see, Mickey flicked his arm away with such force that Jake stumbled backwards and fell. Mickey turned to David. "Let's go," he said.

David stared back at his friend. "Is that all?"

"Yeah," replied Mickey. "We're leaving." He turned and started walking toward the bike racks.

"You're kidding me!" exclaimed David. He glanced back at Jake. His brother raised himself off the ground with murder in his eyes.

Mickey spotted Pam and Vickie in the back seat of a car across the parking lot. He stopped, raised his visor, and locked eyes with Vickie.

"What are you doing?" David asked. He turned and saw Jake

advancing on them.

"You two scumbags are gonna get it...big time!" Jake yelled. He motioned to his biker buddies to follow him.

"Mickey!" David yelled in alarm.

Without turning around, Mickey stuck out his arm.

Jake and his buddies stopped for a second, but when Mickey didn't move, continued on.

"That's enough!" shouted Coach Dunivant. "You and your two Juvie Hall buddies get off my campus now or I'll call the real cops, not your father. Got that?"

Jake straightened up and grinned wryly. "Don't worry, Coach." He laughed. "Me and my boys have had enough fun, *for now.*" As he uttered the last two words, he leered at Mickey. Jake and his friends started walking away. "See you later, guys," he called over his shoulder.

"You two okay?" asked the coach.

Mickey broke eye contact with Vickie and turned around. "Yeah, Coach."

"Want me to call your parents?"

"It's okay. We have our bikes," Mickey replied.

"What about those motorcycle goons?" the coach asked. He pointed toward the retreating forms of Jake and his friends.

Mickey looked toward Jake and frowned. "They were just mouthing off."

"Have it your way, but I'm staying with you two until you're on your bikes and on your way home."

"Thanks Coach," said David. He looked at Mickey and nodded his head. David flashed on the Kung Fu movie Mickey had talked about, and the peace-loving monk who could kill people with his pinkie, but never did. He kind of understood now—maybe.

Coach Dunivant walked the boys to the bike racks. "Last chance, guys. Sure you don't want me to call your parents?"

"Nope," said Mickey as he mounted his bike.

The coach looked around once more. "Then beat it out of here so I can go back and keep an eye on the other juvenile delinquents." He shook his head and walked back to the gym.

The boys hopped on their bikes and started down the driveway. Mickey made a point of veering toward Pam's car and stopping when they pulled even.

Pam and Vickie were in the backseat, but there was no sign of Pam's stepmom.

Pam leaned out the back window. "We saw the whole thing! Mickey, are you all right?"

Mickey smiled. "I'm fine."

David frowned. "Me too."

"You want a ride home?"

"No thanks," Mickey replied. "We're cool."

"You sure?"

Mickey nodded and then glanced at Vickie, but this time she averted her eyes. He dropped his visor and started pedaling away. After picking up speed, he jumped the divider soaring several feet into the air, and after a perfect landing sped off down the street. David pushed his bike over the divider, hopped on, and followed after Mickey.

"See you at school," shouted Pam at their retreating forms. "I can't believe how Mickey stood up to David's brother!" she exclaimed, settling back in the seat.

"Yeah," Vickie softly replied, still watching Mickey pedal away.

Chapter Fourteen

Four hundred miles away at Twin Lakes in the High Sierras, the snow-covered ground in the marsh began to shake. A patch of reeds trembled. Moments later, this same area began to move with a circular motion throwing snow into the air until a white vortex rose above the marsh. No one was there to witness the strange sight since the Lodge was closed for the winter. As the speed of the vortex increased, the ground beneath it started dropping until the reeds were no longer visible. This left a large hole, and then the ground stopped shaking. At that point, a silvery saucer rose from the hole, hovered for a few seconds over the marsh, and shot straight up at an impossible speed leaving only a faint popping sound in its wake. The saucer arched across the sky like a shooting star and began descending over Griffith Park, traveling four hundred miles in just a few seconds.

Six thousand miles away, a tall, distinguished-looking elderly gentleman wearing a business suit stood behind a technician. Both were viewing the satellite imagery of the saucer. The man picked up a phone. The orange jewel in his ring glinted in the artificial lighting. "Are you watching?"

"Yes, and we've also spotted the Aurora Spy Plane in the sector. Its bound to spot the craft," answered the voice on the phone.

"Yes, one wonders about the timing."

"The military will muck it up and we'll lose everything."

"They won't if we're patient."

"What do you propose?"

"Continue the current business arrangement—sell them the drones and the satellites with linkage, and then steal the images and keep them under our thumb. A solution will present itself."

"We should snatch the suit and help those kids go missing!"

"Too soon. We don't know what the game is yet."

"Game?"

"After all this time, our alien friends return and land in a swamp in the middle of nowhere. Why now? They leave a suit with unusual powers in a hole so a teenager can find it. Why? No my friend, the only reasonable course is to allow our military to continue doing the work for us until we know how to act decisively."

After a few blocks of riding, Mickey and David saw that Jake and his buddies were nowhere to be seen. Feeling safe and needing to burn off their adrenaline rush, they decided to take the longer route home and started riding toward Verdugo Park. It seemed like a sensible precaution to try and evade Jake by avoiding the usual streets. Mickey held up his arm for David to see the flashing lights. At least the suit's batteries still worked. David pumped his fist in the air in acknowledgement.

After pedaling in the chilly evening air for a few minutes, Mickey glanced at his sleeve and noticed another change. A third light appeared, and it was pulsing green. Startled, he quickly stopped at the curb. Not expecting this maneuver, David almost ran into him and sailed past another twenty feet before slamming on his brakes and skidding to a stop. David walked his bike backwards until he pulled even with Mickey. "What's up?"

"There's a green one now."

David peered at Mickey's arm. "What does that one do?"

Mickey left his visor down and spoke to David with the radio voice. "No idea, but let's find out." He touched the green button and sat back on his seat. "Wooo!" he exclaimed. He stared straight ahead as if looking at something.

"What's happening?" asked David.

Mickey ignored him. He seemed to be concentrating on something in the distance.

David looked off in the same direction. He saw nothing unusual.

"You know that blinking light I always see on the inside of the visor?"

"Yeah."

"It just streaked across the visor, zigzagging all over the place, and left a map right in front of my eyes."

"A map to where?"

"Not a clue, but let's follow it." Mickey pushed off and pedaled down the street.

"We don't know where it goes to. What if it's Death Valley?" David called after him. When Mickey didn't answer, David pushed off and followed.

They started pedaling down Buena Vista Street again. Continuing south on Buena Vista, they passed the NBC Studios and crossed Riverside Drive. At that juncture, the cursor careened right, so they did too. They were now paralleling the freeway heading toward Griffith Park. Mickey signaled for a halt again and David pulled up alongside him.

"It looks like the cursor thing wants us to head into Griffith Park," said Mickey in the radio voice. "It'll be dark soon. What do you think?"

"I say we check it out," said David sounding unusually resolute. "We both got lights on our bikes. And you've got night-vision gear."

Mickey was surprised by his friend's bravado. Not wanting to be outdone, he hopped on his bike and sped away. David tailgated right behind him.

They rode down Riverside Drive and, following the map, turned right into Griffith Park. As the sky darkened, they turned on their lights. The map on Mickey's visor indicated that they should ride up the road that led to the Observatory. They'd both been there before. The astronomy shows were cool.

It was a steep climb. Halfway there, Mickey pulled off onto a dirt road and stopped. He opened his visor and waited for David to catch up.

A few seconds later, David came chugging up the hill.

"Where are we?" asked David.

"Below the Observatory."

"What's that GPS map thing saying now?"

"To go down this road." Mickey pointed into the dark.

David squinted. "You mean that trail?"

"Yep."

David picked up his bike. "Okay. We've come this far."

Mickey held up his gloved hand for a high-five.

"Dude," said David, holding back. "Don't break my wrist, okay?"

Chapter Fifteen

The dirt road led steeply down through the trees. Both boys needed to ride their brakes. At one point David's wheels skidded, but he recovered before falling. After fifty yards, the trail leveled off and ended in a small clearing…a plateau on the edge of the mountain that had the Observatory on its summit. It appeared to be a picnic ground with wooden tables and a fire pit marked by blackened stones. They were pretty high up, at least for Los Angeles. The boys could see the city lights twinkling through the trees.

Mickey raised the visor, looked down at his arm, and saw another blinking light. This one was purple. Brighter than the others, it pulsed frantically. He inclined his arm toward David.

David glanced at it. "Thing's lit up like a Christmas tree. Friggin' unbelievable!"

Mickey stared at his sleeve. "What do you suppose it means?"

"Each time another one of those things lights up, you end up with another super power! Push it and see what happens."

"Think I should?"

David pulled his arms across his chest. "Dude, it's cold up here. Just do it. We both know you're going to anyway."

"I'm not cold," said Mickey, matter-of-factly.

David stamped his feet. "Push the damn button!"

Mickey touched the purple button and the visor closed on its own. At first he stood there casually, as if nothing happened, but then Mickey sat down on the ground and began stabbing the red button. As soon as the visor popped up, he yanked off the helmet and set it down on the grass. He had difficulty catching his breath.

David hunched down next to him. "Jesus! What happened?"

Mickey panted, "All of a sudden I could see the sky and the clouds— like I was looking out an airplane window—but everything was coming at me, fast, like I was in the cockpit of a jet! It was making me dizzy."

"What d'ya think it means?"

"Not a clue." Mickey stood and grabbed his head.

"What's wrong?"

"Still feel sick. Better wait before I put the helmet back on. Otherwise, I'm going to toss my cookies and drown in my own barf." They both laughed.

David tensed. "Mickey, what's that?"

"What's what?" Mickey sat on the ground holding his head with his eyes closed.

"The ground is shaking."

"It's California," replied Mickey.

David looked up. "Mickey?"

"What!"

"Look up!"

"Can't. I'm still sick."

"Mickey!" David insisted. "Look up!"

Mickey looked into the starlit night. "Holy shit!"

A large silver saucer as big as a house was descending over the clearing. Too startled to move, they watched it settle to the ground at the edge of the clearing.

David grabbed for his bike, as if he to make a run for it, but stopped. "This is all part of the same thing, isn't it—the test with the buzzing and all that? I mean, first you're picking up trees like they're toothpicks, and now a flying saucer lands next to us. All this shit has got to be connected!"

"I think the suit has a tracking device!" said Mickey. "I bet it called that flying saucer!" He stared at the saucer. "The suit probably belongs to whoever's inside that thing! It's gotta be part of the test!"

"Well I think we just reached level ten," David said, his voice strained, "but this is no video game!"

Mickey nodded his head and pointed at the saucer. Beginning like a vague blemish on its silver side, a darker rectangular area began to appear, twice the size of a normal door. When the margins of the rectangle appeared distinct, it began flowing to the ground like a liquid, and then re-solidified in the shape of a ramp. A bright light streamed from the opening. The boys held onto their bikes too frightened to move.

After a few seconds, during which nothing further happened, a red light appeared beside the doorway and started blinking.

Mickey elbowed David. "See that red light on the side of the thing? It's just like the one on the suit! I think it's a signal—we're supposed to go in."

David whipped his head around. "You're not going up there."

"Yeah, I am. You coming?"

David's eyes were riveted on the saucer. His emotions were at war. On the one hand, he knew any sane person would get the hell out of there. On the other hand, the prospect of exploring the saucer felt strangely exhilarating. "Maybe."

Mickey laid his bike on the ground. "I'm going to take a look."

"You're serious?"

"This whole thing fits together somehow. Dude, the suit always protects us. Right? I've gotta trust it and climb up that ramp. I'll holler if it's safe."

David gaped at him.

Mickey stared back. "Dude, like you said, it's all part of the test. We've come this far, and everything's been fine."

"Yeah *fine*, except now there's a friggin' flying saucer!"

"I'm going. Are you coming with me?" Mickey pulled down the visor, and with a confident stride, walked up the ramp and disappeared inside the saucer. David took a step forward, stopped, and stared up at the doorway.

Mickey noticed that as he ascended the ramp, its surface briefly yielded as if he were stepping through shallow water, not solid ground. David could hear Mickey's radio voice coming through the doorway. "Davie! You're not going to believe this..." he heard Mickey gasp.

Chapter Sixteen

"Come up here!" Mickey beckoned.

David warily approached the ramp. He touched it with his foot, saw it dimple, and quickly backed off.

Mickey stood at the door looking down at him. "Dude, get over it!" He disappeared inside.

"Easy for you to say. You're wearing the Superman suit," muttered David. Slowly, he ascended the ramp, its surface briefly liquefying under each step. He tiptoed like a cat running along a fence. When he reached the top, David stopped and peered into the brightly lit interior. It was completely plain inside, an empty room. Mickey was standing in the center, his matte black suit in sharp contrast to the interior made of the same silvery material as the saucer itself. The only things visible inside were a pair of four-foot protuberances of the silver material bulging from the floor. They were smooth and angled upwards away from the wall farthest from the doorway. The protuberances looked like the final dollop of yogurt that drops out of a dispenser, and the two were spaced roughly six feet apart.

Mickey stood beside one of them with his visor raised. David joined him and asked, "Do you think this is some kind of stealth plane or NASA gizmo that got lost?"

"Dude, it's a flying saucer."

David looked around slowly, afraid he might discover something. "See any aliens?"

"I have a feeling there aren't any," said Mickey. He reached out and touched one of the protuberances. It shuddered at his touch, like the way Jell-O quivers when poked at with a spoon. He poked it again, harder. This time, in addition to quivering, there was a subtle change in its overall shape, which continued quivering until it transformed into something that resembled a chair. Mickey tentatively sat on it.

David gaped at his friend. "What are you doing?"

With Mickey sitting on it, the chair-like shape continued to morph, finally assuming the familiar shape of a contoured easy chair. In fact, it fit Mickey's body perfectly in every dimension. Reclining, Mickey's hands now rested on two armrests made of silver material. Under his left arm were the familiar buttons, all lit, except now there were five of them—red, yellow, green, purple and white.

"Davie, sit down."

David didn't budge. "No way!"

"Don't you get it? It's part of the test."

"Yeah, but it's your test, not mine. You're the one with the friggin' buttons!"

"Like it or not, you've been part of this from the beginning."

"Then where's my Superman suit?"

"Maybe that's not what you're supposed to do."

"Great. Then what am I here for?"

Mickey stared at his friend and suddenly got goose bumps. "Something…for sure." He smiled. "See that white button?"

David leaned over a little. "Yeah."

"I'm going to push it, and I've got a feeling you better be sitting down when I do."

"Why?"

"Dude, sit down!"

Mickey stared at David with his finger poised over the white button. It was now blinking faster. "You know I'm going to do it."

"Okay!" yelled David. He sat down on the other protuberance, and within seconds found himself reclining in a silver chair perfectly conformed to his body. On David's left armrest were two lit buttons, not five like Mickey's—only a red and a white. He started to relax. "Looks like I have buttons to play with too. Should I push one?"

"The red one."

David paused for a few seconds with his finger poised over his pulsing red button. He had a devilish look on his face. "Okay, it's my turn!" He stabbed it and three things happened: First, the ramp retracted into the doorway, and the doorway then disappeared leaving a featureless silver wall. This took less than five seconds. Second, a large rectangular portion of the wall directly in front of them changed to a pewter color, and then seemingly disappeared. Through it, the features of the Griffith Park clearing were plainly visible. Moreover, everything outside appeared perfectly lit as if it were midday, though the boys knew it was night. Third, David was feeling different—not just relaxed, but comfortable. He settled back with a content smile, as if he had popcorn and the movie was about to begin—ignoring that he was inside a flying saucer.

Mickey stood and approached the window. He reached out and touched what he presumed to be an open space, but his hand was held back by something solid. It was a window made out of a perfectly transparent material. He rapped on it with his fist. The surface under his hand seemed to liquefy briefly, just like the material of the ramp. He turned to David still sitting in his silver chair. "Now touch your white button."

"You know, I get what you mean about the suit making you feel different," said David. "This chair is making me feel...*good*." He drew out the word good. "Totally weird."

"Dude, push the white button."

"Can't I just sit here for a while?"

"Push the white button!"

Even though David had no idea what the white button did, for some reason this didn't bother him at the moment. So he pushed it, and his chair began to morph. First it further reclined to a 45-degree angle. Then it molded around his body, encasing him like a cocoon.

"Whoa!" David yelled. It happened too quickly for him to panic, not that he was going to. In less than five seconds, the portion of the chair behind his head changed to pewter and then became perfectly clear, like the window in front of them. As David was about to say something, the chair flowed over his head forming a bubble. With his head completely encased, David began to panic…a little. He stabbed at the red button. Immediately the entire cocoon withdrew from around him, and once again, he was sitting in the reclining chair. He leaped out of it, spun around, and stared back. "Jesus!" he yelled. "What was that?"

Mickey looked thoughtful. "I think I'm starting to get it." He sat down in his chair, pushed his white button, and was soon encased in a cocoon including a bubble over his head. But instead of hitting the red button to remove it, he turned to David. As he did, the bubble turned with him. His voice had that same familiar radio timbre. Mickey smiled at his friend. "Dude, sit down and push your white button again."

"I'm not sure about this."

"It's some kind of a spacesuit! The temperature inside is perfect, and the air is fresh, like up at the lake."

David didn't move. "Halloween's over. Maybe we should go home."

"You just said it felt 'good'! Try it again."

David stared at the silver chair. He seemed to be wavering. "It did feel good."

"If you don't, I'm going without you."

"Going where?"

"Wherever this flying saucer wants to take me."

"You can't be serious!"

"There's no way I'm quitting now. Like I said, I trust…whoever's behind this. It's not just me. You're supposed to go too!"

David looked around the interior of the saucer. "You think so?" He sat down again, eyed the white button, closed his eyes, and pushed it. He was immediately encased with a clear bubble over his head. After his breathing slowed, he turned toward Mickey. "What does your purple one do?"

"One way to find out."

Mickey smiled mischievously, hit the purple button, and the view through the window started to change. Either the city's lighted buildings were sinking, or the saucer was rising—slowly at first, then faster.

Although there wasn't any sense of motion, the view shifted sharply to the side.

"I hate rollercoasters," Mickey mumbled. He closed his eyes.

Both cocoons further reclined and the silver material flowed around their bodies until they were covered up to their necks. Only their heads were visible inside the bubbles. They couldn't move.

The disc began to accelerate. Moments later, they were in the clouds and couldn't see anything, except for the clouds speeding by. Before either of them could comment, the clouds cleared away and they could see blinking lights with a familiar shape.

"Where do you think we are?" asked Mickey.

"You got an A in Geography, don't you recognize it?"

"I'm a little queasy! Just tell me."

"It looks like the outline of California…at least it did. Jesus, now it's the whole United States! No, North America! Oh my God! This thing's hauling ass!"

Mickey's response was a moan. He couldn't handle roller-coaster maneuvers; in fact, he got seasick in the bathtub.

Within moments the view changed to the blackness of space, and the face of the Moon raced to the center of the window. Unfortunately, at precisely that instant, Mickey opened his eyes. "Fuck. I'm going to puke," he groaned through clenched teeth.

All David could say was, "Oh my God, oh my God," over and over.

Chapter Seventeen

With each passing minute, the Moon grew bigger and brighter. Then suddenly, the sensation of motion ceased. Fortunately Mickey hadn't actually tossed. Now, besides the ever-growing disc of the Moon, uncountable stars crowded the window.

"I think we're in space!" exclaimed David.

"No shit, Sherlock."

"What do we do now?"

"Enjoy the ride, unless you can steer this thing."

"Do you think it's taking us to Mars?"

"Look!" The Moon filled the window with its pockmarked face. It seemed like they were skimming its surface.

"Where are we heading?" asked David.

"I think we're going around it, to the dark side."

The motion stopped.

"Why did we stop?" David blurted out.

Mickey squinted at the window. "Jesus, look at that!"

The unmistakable shape of a satellite slowly drifted into view. A rectangular section of the window changed, forming a frame around it. Within the frame, the satellite's image appeared magnified. They could make out the detail of the satellite's structural features. The writing on its solar panel said ESA Lunar Orbiter. Once the satellite flew by, the saucer began accelerating again.

"I'll bet our ride was waiting for the satellite to go by," said Mickey.

"Why?"

"ESA stands for European Space Agency. I've read about it. They're scouting for landing sites."

"So?"

"Thing doesn't want us to get our picture taken."

"Hey, we're in a UFO! We could have been in the National Enquirer."

The saucer continued its course to the dark side of the Moon. One of the craters there appeared to be illuminated by artificial lights along its rim. As the crater with the ring of lights moved to the center of the window, the saucer began to decelerate towards it. When the boys could see individual boulders on the crater's floor and it seemed like they were about to crash, the view suddenly rotated and a white horizon replaced the face of the crater against the black backdrop of space. Mickey closed his eyes and counted to ten.

"I think we landed," said David.

Mickey belched. "I hope so."

"Are we on the Moon?"

"Yep, we sure are."

"What happens now?"

"Must be some reason the saucer brought us here."

"We can't just hang out here. I've got a book report to do. I haven't even read the book!" David said with alarm. "Dude, your buttons are dark. We can't control the saucer, even if we knew how."

"This sucks! What do we do?" David began to sound like his old self again.

"Let it happen, just like we've been doing since the day I found the suit."

David started to relax.

The saucer began to shudder. As it did, clouds of dust roiled in front of the window, then blasted across it as if they were trapped inside a tornado.

"Now I know how Dorothy felt," said David.

His eyes clenched shut again, Mickey muttered, "You're right."

"About what?"

"This sucks."

The saucer began descending, plunging them into total darkness. Before they could panic, the walls started to glow with soft ambient light. The motion stopped in less than a minute and they could see light outside again—the same soft shade present in the disc, yet they were under a roof of rock.

"I'm guessing we're in a cave," said Mickey.

"A cave with lights on the Moon. No one's going to believe this," David whispered.

"Which part?" Mickey replied. A blinking white light caught his eye. He glanced down and saw that the substance of the chair had partially withdrawn exposing his arms. When he touched the white button, his chair began to change. More of the material withdrew from around him, darkening as it did. It continued flowing away until all that remained was a form-fitting silver garment with a clear plastic bubble covering his head. With this transformation completed, the material returned to its original silver hue. The excess material dropped to the floor in a puddle and was quickly absorbed. This process left Mickey standing.

When Mickey lifted his right arm, the material briefly darkened and liquefied, but re-solidified and brightened as he held his arm still. The red button was now lit as well. He turned to David. "Is your white button on again?"

David gaped at him. "You're wearing a spacesuit!"

"Push the white button and get yours!"

Seconds later, David was wearing an identical silver suit.

"You get the honor of pushing the red button this time," said Mickey.

"What'll it do?"

"I've got a hunch," said Mickey.

"What?"

"Push it and find out."

David hesitated. "Are you sure that's a smart idea?"

"Nope." Mickey touched his, and then turned toward the opposite wall. The area where the door had darkened now flowed to the ground leaving a doorway that formed a ramp to the Moon's surface. "C'mon, let's take a look!" With a bounce to his step provided by the low lunar gravity, Mickey ambled down the ramp.

David didn't move.

"One small step for Mickey!" he hollered, standing on the surface of the Moon.

David stood at the top of the ramp. Mickey coaxed him, "Dude, you're on the Moon! This is a once in a lifetime gig! You gotta join me!"

They stood side by side at the base of the ramp. The saucer had taken them to a vast, well-lit subterranean chamber with rows of identical silver saucers, all with their ramps extending downwards.

"All those saucers look the same as ours," exclaimed David.

"Looks like nobody's home," said Mickey.

"What do you suppose it means?"

Mickey shrugged. "One way to find out."

"Every time you say that, something weird happens."

"We're in an alien base on the Moon. We have to at least look around."

David shook his head. "No way this is happening."

"Try jumping."

David pushed off and landed ten feet from the ramp. "Hey, I have super powers too!"

"No you don't! You weigh one-ninth as much because of the weak lunar gravity."

David laughed. "Coach Dunivant said not to lose any more weight."

Mickey frowned. "Can we go now?"

Chapter Eighteen

They set off for the nearest saucer. When they arrived, Mickey touched the ramp with his foot. "It's different than ours, solid like metal." He moved up the ramp and disappeared inside.

David heard Mickey's voice inside his bubble excitedly say, "Come up!"

David peered up the ramp. "What do you see?"

"Look for yourself! Believe me, it's worth the trip."

David ambled up the ramp and stopped at the doorway. He looked inside. Mickey's bubble projected a beam of light at what he presumed were two seats, except they looked strange. They were half the expected size, triangular, and had a peak in the middle reminiscent of a saddle. The wall where the window should have been was completely opaque.

David approached the opaque window. Within a few feet of it, his bubble projected a beam of light like a movie projector. The boys stood transfixed and watched a sequence of images beginning with a star chart. The star in the center of the chart was orbited by several planets of various sizes, twelve in all, three with rings like Saturn. The camera, or whatever it was, focused down on the sixth planet—a medium-sized one without rings. The sixth planet kept growing in size until they could see that it was mostly brown dappled with puddles of blue.

"Think those are oceans?" asked Mickey.

"Oceans of what?" replied David. "No way to know how cold it is down there. Could be lakes of methane, or who knows what?"

A halo of lighter blue-green surrounded the planet, its atmosphere. As the camera panned closer, clouds appeared, and finally below them…

"Jesus!" explained David. "Is that what I think it is?"

"A city, but it's not on Earth, that's for sure!"

The view continued expanding, until they could see broad thoroughfares connecting buildings with various geometric shapes and colors. Suddenly a flash of light engulfed one of the buildings, and then it was gone. This happened several more times. More flashes of light obliterated a large swathe of structures.

"What do you think that means?" asked David. His voice sounded strained.

"Nothing good!" Mickey shouted. "Look!"

Zooming in closer, the camera focused on the area around one of the buildings that no longer existed. For a fleeting moment, the boys thought they recognized shapes on the ground reminiscent of people, well not exactly. They could make out four limbs and something like a head…but before they could get a really good look, the camera panned upwards, so quickly that both boys nearly lost their balance. The maneuver didn't do wonders for Mickey's stomach either. Within seconds, the only image on the screen was the star chart, and then David's helmet projector winked out.

"Okay, what was that?" exclaimed David.

"I think it was a war on some alien planet," Mickey replied. "I'm not feeling good about this."

"Maybe we can change channels," said David.

Mickey returned to the two chairs. "These buttons are dead. This whole saucer's dead." He headed for the ramp.

David caught up with him. "We should check out more saucers."

"You're right. You go one direction and I'll go another. When you're inside one, call me on your radio."

"Roger that."

They went in opposite directions. David entered a disc one row down. It was dark inside, just like the first saucer. When he crossed the threshold, a light projected from the top of his helmet illuminating two silver shapes that looked like doughnuts. The customary buttons were there, but all dark, the same as in the other saucer. The window was opaque too. When David drew nearer, his helmet projected another movie, this one of a different star chart—a binary system with twenty planets. With growing dread, David watched as the view moved closer to one of the planets.

"Mickey?" David said into his bubble helmet.

"What did you find?"

"Another movie. Different place, different actors—what's left of them. Same ending." David sounded uneasy. "You?"

"Same," Mickey replied. "Any live buttons on the seats?"

"Everything's dark, just like the first one. Yours?"

"Dead. I have a theory. Meet me back at our saucer."

"See any aliens walking around?"

"If I'm right, we're the only ones here."

Mickey waited for David at the top of the ramp to their saucer. David bounded up jumping ten feet into the air with each stride. "Jesus, that's fun!" he shouted when he landed beside Mickey.

Mickey walked through the saucer's doorway. "We gotta talk."

"Okay." David looked out at the rows of dead saucers one more time, and then followed him.

Once inside, Mickey stabbed his red button. In response, the ramp retracted and the door re-solidified.

Mickey moved next to his chair. "Push your white button."

David moved next to his. "Why?"

"We're leaving, unless you want to stay around and watch more war movies."

"Not really."

"Me neither." Mickey poked his white button several times. The floor darkened and bubbled beneath their feet, and a pedicle of silver shot up from the bubbling fluid and connected itself to the back of their suits like a hose. This connection swelled as silver material flowed up from the floor reforming their chairs. Soon they were reclining in front of the window.

"Time for the purple one," said Mickey.

"Let's hope it works," replied David, feeling calm again.

"It will."

"How do you know?"

"It's all part of the test…the saucer, you and me being here, the whole deal. Has to be!"

David thought for a second. "All the saucer movies were about war. Maybe our planet's next, like *War of the Worlds*!"

"No way!"

"Then what happened to the alien guys who sat in all those weird-looking seats?"

"I don't think anybody sat in those seats."

"Why?"

"If you buy the test idea, maybe when the saucer saw all the shooting going on, it turned around and left without picking anybody up," Mickey said, thinking about his theory.

"One of them picked us up."

Mickey looked stunned, like a light bulb had just gone off in his brain. "Because we're still being tested!"

"In case you haven't noticed because you've been living in a cave, our planet's got a few bombs going off too, like every day! What if we already flunked the test?"

"But we're here. Maybe this is a warning. Maybe there's still time for us to evolve!" Mickey's voice rose as he finished his sentence.

"I guess that makes sense." David looked out the window again at all the dead saucers. "I'm sure about one thing…it's time to bug out of here!"

Mickey punched the purple button, but nothing happened. He did it again, repeatedly. Still nothing happened. "Not good!" he yelled. Not even the chair was keeping him calm.

"What's wrong with it?" shouted David. He also felt anxious.

"Nothing's happening!" Mickey continued stabbing at the purple button.

"Why not?"

"I don't know! Do you think flying saucers have an owner's manual?"

Finally, the saucer shuddered and started to rise. Mickey pumped his fist in the air and yelled, "Yes!" David closed his eyes with relief.

In less than a minute, the window showed only the blackness of space. Then the craft did a quick gyration. This time it was too much for Mickey. Fortunately, the substance of his bubble absorbed it all, a well-designed feature.

With the course correction completed, the window offered a welcome sight, a familiar blue orb rapidly growing larger. The saucer settled onto the clearing in Griffith Park. After the sensation of motion stopped, Mickey hit his white button and his chair withdrew. David did the same. Soon the boys stood on the floor wearing their own clothes. Mickey poked the red button on the suit. The door reappeared, admitting the sounds and aromas of life from the clearing. Smiling at each other, they raced down the ramp.

When their feet touched solid ground, the ramp flowed upwards, and within seconds the side of the saucer turned completely smooth. The boys darted away from the saucer, stopping at the base of the dirt road. The ground shook making it difficult to stand. They steadied themselves and watched as the saucer lifted off and ascended straight up, picking up speed until it was gone from sight. The clearing was empty, except for two astonished teenage boys and their bicycles.

Chapter Nineteen

The triangular airplane painted black shot across the sky over Idaho moving at 4000 miles an hour, more than Mach 5. No one on the ground could see or hear it, as it flew at the edge of space.

"Dark Cloud, this is Raven…over."

"Raven, this is Dark Cloud. You are not authorized to break radio silence… Repeat… You are not authorized to break radio silence. Over."

"Roger that, Dark Cloud. Raven is declaring an emergency."

"Say again, Raven."

"Dark Cloud, I repeat, Raven is declaring an emergency."

"Raven, this is Dark Cloud. State the nature of your emergency. Over."

"Dark Cloud, this is Raven. Raven is flying straight and level, fuel reserve is nominal. Do you copy?"

There was a pause on the radio. "Raven, this is Dark Cloud. We do not copy. Again, please state the nature of your emergency. Over."

"Dark Cloud, this is Raven." There was a pause. "That might be a little difficult to explain. You boys down there might want to make sure this here is a private phone call." When the pilot, call sign Raven, became nervous, his Texas drawl grew thicker.

"Raven, this is Dark Cloud. I copy. You are authorized to enter Corridor 51 for line of sight-only communication using your 55W laser. Do you copy?"

"Raven copies, Dark Cloud. ETA seven minutes. Will contact with 55W when in corridor. Raven out."

The pilot would be communicating with the ground via a laser. Unlike a radio signal, communicating with a light beam had to be line of sight. Even encrypted radio messages bounced off satellites could be intercepted and eventually decrypted with a powerful enough supercomputer. Thus far, nobody had figured out how to pirate a light beam.

America's newest stealth reconnaissance plane, the super-secret scramjet called Aurora, banked toward Area 51 in the Nevada desert. The pilot activated his intercom and spoke to his back-seater, or radio and radar officer. "Randy, do you still have that object on the radar?"

"No way, mon capitan. The fucker went straight up at Mach 9 plus!"

"Was it a missile?"

"That's a negative. According to the reverse track plot, it took off from downtown Los Angeles with no IR signature."

"Yeah, right. Your high-tech toys must be acting up. Try hitting it with a hammer. That's what I do when my TV goes out."

"You break it, you pay for it. Got an extra billion bucks lying around?"

"No heat signature? How do you fly a machine without a tail pipe?"

"Maybe it was a UFO."

"We're a UFO, remember?"

The Aurora dropped down to ten thousand feet and slowed to Mach two, about as slow as it could fly without gliding in for a landing.

"Dark Cloud, this is Raven. W55 is activated. Do you copy?"

"Raven, this is Dark Cloud. We are receiving your W55, five by five. You are authorized to download all data and return to base. Dark Cloud out."

"Okay, Jer, dump the data over that fancy laser gizmo of yours and let's grab a couple of cool ones back at the shed."

"You mean after a whole friggin' night of debrief?"

"Why?"

"Because we're not the only guys with a radar unit around here. You can bet somebody else saw whatever the hell it was. Those numbnuts in Intelligence will concoct some cockamamie story to cover it up."

"Why?"

"Its point of origin was a park."

"A *what*?"

"Griffith Park, near the Planetarium. Saw some great shows there as a kid."

"Could get messy. I'll bet half the city of L.A. saw it, at least the ones who weren't at the Lakers game."

"That's right! It's Ring Night. Kobe gets number five. We always miss the big ones."

"Somebody has to defend the US of A from terrorists launching rockets from friggin' parks."

"The usual UFO shtick probably won't work this time."

"Bet they blame it on the Planetarium laser show. Beats the old swamp gas or weather balloon stories."

Preparing to land, the Aurora cut it engines and dropped its wheels.

NORAD, Cheyenne Mountain, Wyoming

A junior officer wearing a black uniform and beret hunched over his radar screen. An older man dressed in the uniform of a general weighed down by rows of military decorations glanced over his shoulder.

"There it is again, Sir," said the junior officer.

"Lieutenant Latham, how do you know it's the same bogey?"

"Well at first, Sir, the computer classified it as a meteor. It came straight down from space, so it can't be a missile, unless they're shooting 'em off from the Moon, Sir."

"We don't have any missile bases on the Moon, Latham. If we did, you can be sure I'd know about it."

"Yes, Sir."

"What happened after that?"

"It slowed down and...hit the ground in Los Angeles, in a park near the Planetarium."

The man with all the medals scratched his chin and started spouting off questions in rapid-fire. "Meteors don't slow down, Latham."

"Whatever it was, Sir, it must be real small. I called the Planetarium, on the sly of course, to see if anyone saw anything unusual."

"Good thinking, soldier. What did they say?"

"They said tonight's laser show's sold out and put me on hold."

"How do you know it's the same bogey?"

"Because it took off straight up at Mach nine. It was exactly the same velocity vector, and no IR trace, same as the previous bogey at the same location."

The general with the medals stood up straight, drawing back his shoulders. "What is it, Latham?"

"Not a clue, Sir."

"Speculate, soldier!"

"Does Area Fifty-One have any, I mean, do we have any…antigravity-driven experimental planes, Sir?"

"We'll see about that!" The general was angry, feeling cut out of the loop again, and grabbed a red phone. "This is Westlock. Get me Spec Ops at Edwards!"

"Spec Ops, this is Marin," replied the voice on the phone.

"This is Brigadier General Moreland Westlock at Cheyenne. I am declaring a Code Blue at the following coordinates. Stand by to accept data."

"Standing by, General!"

"Latham, send him the coordinates where that thing took off."

"You mean the park in Los Angeles?"

"Just do it!"

"Done, General. He's got it now."

"Spec Ops, did you copy?"

"Yes, General, but…"

"Send a unit there right away! Damn it, send two units! I want to know what's down there, and I want to know now!"

"Yes Sir, General Sir! Two birds will lift off in thirty minutes, call signs Rapier One, and Rapier Two. Should arrive at Griffith Park in Los Angeles in ninety minutes."

"Thank you, soldier. Cheyenne Mountain out!"

"Err, General, Sir…before you hang up, what are we looking for…in that park?"

"Somebody's doing something…off-books from that park, soldier! And I want to know what it is!"

"Yes, Sir!"

An officer wearing Air Force blue got up from his chair and left the room. He walked to the men's room, pretended to comb his hair while he waited for a particular stall to become vacant, then went inside and closed the door. When he knew he was alone, he slid the toilet paper holder to the side exposing a hidden compartment. Inside was a phone connected to a micro fiber optic cable. He quickly texted the coordinates for Griffith Park in Los Angeles, slid the compartment closed, flushed the toilet, and left.

The special operations officer at Edwards Air Force Base hung up his phone and turned to another soldier sitting next to him in front of a similar screen.

"We're launching after some unknown activity or unidentified…objects launching from Los Angeles."

"Jesus! What are they?"

"Haven't figured that out yet. According to the radar plots, the thing went straight up and vanished."

"From a park?"

"In Los Angeles."

"You're shitting me, right?"

"No."

"We're sending two Black Hawks full of commandos to look

for…whatever?"

"Yep. Rev up two birds."

"How the hell are the choppers supposed to land in the middle of L.A. without somebody seeing them?"

"That's why they call us Special Ops! Tell 'em to improvise! If anybody asks, it was a navigational error, or they were running out of gas."

"Come on! This is gotta be some stupid-ass drill. I bet as soon as those birds are airborne, they call 'em back."

"Stop worrying. Nobody's going to be in that park tonight. Everybody in L.A. with a pulse is watching the Laker's game."

Chapter Twenty

After the saucer ascended from the clearing, it accelerated north touching down in the marsh around 10:00 P.M. The snow fell lighter now, dusting the area with powdered flakes. A clear halo of air surrounded the disc—an invisible barrier. Suddenly, a beam of light shot out from it, illuminating a window in a cabin two miles away. The Lodge was vacated for the winter, but this solitary cabin remained occupied. Smoke curled up from its chimney.

Ernie was startled when the level of light in his cabin intensified. He rose from his chair by the fireplace and went to the window to investigate. As he pushed aside the curtain, the light projected by the disc was so blinding that he had to shield his eyes and turn away. Before he could ponder this strange occurrence, the light winked out. Sensing this change through closed eyelids, he opened his eyes and gazed out the window again. It might have been his imagination, but Ernie thought he saw the marsh illuminated. Maybe soldiers were practicing winter survival, he reasoned, but the reflected light shouldn't have been that brilliant. Could somebody be out there with a searchlight? Not likely, especially with a frozen lake and the temperature just above ten degrees. What was the source of that light? Ernie earned his living being the Lodge's winter caretaker. If somebody, even soldiers, was doing something unusual around the lake, he needed to check it out. The owners of the Lodge were going to get their money's worth, even during the fourth quarter of the Lakers game. He glanced at the television. Thank goodness for DVRs.

Ernie donned his thick winter coat, a muffler, and pulled a woolen cap over his head. He added leather gloves and heavy boots, and grabbed a large flashlight. Swaddled in layers of clothing, walking would be more like a penguin's waddle, he thought, but at least he'd be warm.

Two Black Hawk helicopters lifted off from Edwards Air Force Base and headed for Griffith Park in Los Angeles. On board were two full teams, including twelve men in combat gear with night vision goggles and heavy weapons. Several technicians with top-secret sensing equipment were also on board. The plan called for the combat team to secure the area, and then the science team would figure out what was happening. It made sense, except no one had any experience attacking a public park.

"Rapier One, this is Dark Cloud, do you read?"

"Dark Cloud, this is Rapier One, I read you loud and clear, over."

"Rapier One, new orders are being transmitted via satellite uplink. Authenticate and respond when received. Dark Cloud out."

"Acknowledged, Dark Cloud. Rapier One out."

Rapier One's pilot turned to his copilot. "Bet they'll call this off. Fucker has to be a drill. Dumbest one yet."

The copilot began reading a printout spilling from a unit on the instrument panel. "Actually, it just got worse."

"Now what?"

The copilot activated his helmet microphone. "Dark Cloud, this is Rapier One. Message received and authenticated. Rapier One, out." He turned to the pilot. "Contact Rapier Two. They're still going to Griffith Park. We're heading somewhere else."

"Home?"

The copilot began programming his navigational computer. "Nope. Did you bring fishing gear?"

"Why?"

"We're supposed to fly to a lake half way between Mammoth, California, and Reno, Nevada."

"To do what?"

"They didn't say."

"Shit."

The helicopter, call sign Rapier One, began veering away.

Ernie opened the cabin door and was immediately assaulted by an icy wind. It pushed him back inside. Refusing to be deterred, he pulled his goggles over his eyes, hunkered down, and pointed his flashlight into the dark. The snow had picked up, further diffusing the light from the marsh. At best, he could see the trail for just ten feet in front of him. He closed the door and stepped into the darkness.

Poles topped with flags spaced fifty feet apart marked the trail to the marsh. The flags whipped around so violently in the wind it was amazing they weren't ripped away. Ernie trudged slowly between them, trying to follow the trail. Ahead he could make out something glinting in the marsh, but at that distance and through the sheets of snow, he couldn't identify it.

After thirty minutes of slogging along the frozen trail, navigating from one pole to the next, he spotted something ahead that appeared to be a glowing metallic shape. It had to be a vehicle, maybe a crashed airplane? People could be injured! Fearing the worst, he moved as fast as he could.

As he rounded a bend in the forest of reeds, Ernie froze in his tracks. He'd come upon a glowing, smooth silver shape whose dimensions were hard to make out in the diffused light. It was circular and kind of looked like a flying saucer from an old science fiction movie, which of course didn't make any sense. Ernie blinked his eyes to clear them, but the strange image remained.

Orbiting over the frozen lake, the pilot of Rapier One turned to his copilot. "Do you see that thing down there?"

"Yeah, except it's not there. Doesn't register on any of our sensors—no radar return, no IR, nothing."

"Has to be a stealth plane. Must have crashed. Call it in."

"Wait. There's one IR signature, and it's moving." The copilot pushed his head against the eyepiece of the scope. "It's a man with a flashlight. He's walking toward whatever it is."

"Rapier One to Dark Cloud, come in please."

"This is Dark Cloud, over."

"Dark Cloud, we have a visual, something on the ground—maybe a crash site—no IR or radar signatures. There's a man heading toward it. Any stealth planes reported in this area?"

"That's a negative, Rapier One."

"Black Cloud... What are our orders?"

"Stand by Rapier One...Rapier One, orbit but do not approach. Repeat, orbit but do not approach at this time. Use your light and send some imagery. Do you copy?"

"Roger, Dark Cloud. Rapier One will stand off and orbit. We'll light it up, but it's already glowing."

"Roger that, Rapier One. Standing by for image uplink. Dark Cloud out."

The helicopter descended and began orbiting. It activated its searchlight and the 50,000 candlepower beam illuminated the disc, along with Ernie. Blinded by the light, Ernie squinted his eyes and reflexively looked up, allowing the helicopter's sensors to capture an image of his face. The advanced military-grade optics showed every pixel of his face, even a mole next to his nose.

Within seconds, the marsh around the disc began to shiver, and then to spin.

"Dark Cloud, are you getting this?"

"Stand by, Rapier One."

"Jesus!" exclaimed the pilot. "What's going on down there?" The copilot was too stunned to reply.

A vortex of mud and ice swirled around the disc. In the searchlight's glare, it looked like the funnel of a tornado. The disc began to sink in the middle of it, until nothing was visible but a twisting column of snow. Hovering overhead, the helicopter buffeted wildly in the turbulence. The crew struggled to hold on. The chaos continued for ten seconds longer, and then the vortex collapsed leaving no sign of the disc.

When the turbulence cleared, the helicopter pilot regained

control. "Holy shit! What was that?"

"Rapier One, this is Dark Cloud. Is your image uplink stable?"

"Ah…sure, Dark Cloud." The helicopter's searchlight beam panned over the terrain illuminating the marsh, but the disc had vanished.

"Rapier One, this is Dark Cloud. Return to base. I repeat, return to base."

"Dark Cloud, this is Rapier One. I copy. What about the guy on the ground? Over."

"Is he still there?"

"Affirmative. Should we pick him up?"

"Why?"

"What if he talks, or goes on the Jerry Springer show?"

"Who cares? If he saw the same thing we did, nobody will believe him."

"Roger that, Dark Cloud. Rapier One is to ignore the civilian on the ground. Rapier One is now RTB, ETA ninety minutes. Rapier One, out."

Ernie shone his flashlight beam over the marsh where the disc had been. Although he hadn't been able to see it through the snow, he'd heard the distinctive sound of a helicopter orbiting overhead and saw its searchlight roaming the marsh. It must have been the searchlight that hit his cabin. The silver disc had probably been a mirage from the searchlight's reflection off the snow tornado, or whatever it was. He'd been at the lake for years and had never seen anything like it.

The searchlight winked out, and the sound of the helicopter retreated in the distance. Ernie trudged back to the warmth of his cabin and his DVR.

Inside Cheyenne Mountain, Brigadier General Westlock stood back as a team of experts poured over the images captured by Rapier One. For the past few minutes, all any of them could say was "Holy shit!"

General Westlock was growing impatient, not his most attractive frame of mind. "I need answers, gentlemen! What is that thing?"

One of the photo-analysts looked up. "Never seen anything like it, Sir."

"Except in an old sci-fi movie," muttered another one of them.

"Speak up, son!" commanded the general.

"I said it looks like a flying saucer, Sir… You know, like in that sci-fi movie *Forbidden Planet*?"

"The one with Robby the Robot?" said one of the others.

"Yeah, and the blonde—what was her name?"

The general cleared his throat. "I don't waste time with that kind of drivel."

The photo-analyst stared at him.

"Where is it now?" asked the general.

"We lost it after that snow-tornado-vortex-thing."

"Not good, son. You got the best technology there is. For all that money, you don't lose things."

The man looked down. "Yes, Sir."

The first photo-analyst looked up. "We were able to ID the guy on the ground. Military. Sergeant Ernest Santos, Army Rangers, Retired. Silver Star and two Purple Hearts in 'Nam."

"Go talk to him, soldier."

"Yes, Sir." He picked up a telephone. "Dispatch?"

There was a yawn at the other end of the line. "Yeah?"

"Where's Rapier One?"

"Just got back. In debrief."

"They're going back."

"It's two in the morning!"

The photo-analyst turned away and lowered his voice. "Westlock's standing next to me! You want to talk with him?"

"Hell, no."

Chapter Twenty-One

Winter always proved difficult for Ernie. When the snow fell hard, he'd be stuck in his cabin for endless days, watching television or reading. Limited physical activity and an amply stocked larder didn't help his weight either. He had a phone but nobody to call. His wife left him years before, right after he volunteered to serve his second tour in 'Nam. Back then, they had a three-year-old son. His wife was an only child and both her parents were dead. She told him in a letter that she feared losing him and being left all alone. A few days later, he phoned her from Saigon and exchanged some regrettably harsh words. He still wished he had the chance to take them back. After that, she refused to answer his calls or letters. When he returned from Vietnam, she had moved out of their apartment and he couldn't locate her. After years of searching, he finally found his son. He was killed in Iraq—a sergeant, just like his dad.

Both Ernie's parents were dead, and he was an only child. He felt alone in the world. Summers were easier to bear because he kept busy, the resort's Jack-of-all-trades. The owners were his family now. The best part of his job was greeting all the summer folk, some of whom revisited every year. Their kids became his kids. Seeing them smile when they reeled in that first fish, or laughing while they watched a bear stealing trash from one of the trashcans…those things became the spice of his life. He felt most comfortable in the company of young people, innocent minds more interested in experiencing the world than judging it. That was what Ernie lived for now. He was like a hibernating bear in the winter, holed up in the cabin waiting for the thaw.

On the rare day in winter when the weather turned mild, Ernie would bundle up and try to deal with his cabin fever. He'd make his rounds of the lodge area, ensuring that the roofs were holding up under the weight of blankets of snow, and that the doors were locked. Then he'd check on the marina. Of course the boats were pulled out of the water. The lake was frozen, at least the surface of it. The outboard motors were stored in the outbuilding with their fuel drained...always a messy job. The tackle store was locked and empty. Next season's inventory wouldn't arrive until March when the roads became more passable.

Ernie hadn't been able to sleep. He kept thinking about the strange lights in the marsh. At dawn, he hiked back to the area to investigate. By then the snow had stopped falling, but the temperature hovered just above freezing. Afraid he'd fall through the ice, he stayed on the trail and scanned the area with binoculars. He couldn't detect anything unusual, just piles of snow and frozen marshland.

The poles marking the trail still stuck out of the snow, in some places just the top two feet. Some still had their bright yellow flags attached. The footing wasn't bad, but Ernie walked carefully, testing the ground with his boot every few steps. The overcast grey sky added to his dismal demeanor. Even without wind, the cold still pierced him through four layers of clothing and a thick winter coat.

Spotted around the lake were a number of private cabins. Nobody lived there year-round, nobody but Erie, a few bears, and a ranger to the south. This time of year all the private cabins were dark, most with storm shutters closed tight and the electricity turned off. He sighed and resumed walking. Solitude and loneliness—how different yet how alike, he thought. Did any man, if given the choice, truly seek only his own company? It was at times like these, gazing over the frozen lake and the vacant cabins, that he wondered what life was about. How many more winters would he endure? How many more did he want?

After thirty minutes of walking, Ernie reached the marsh where he saw the lights and heard the helicopter. It was also near the spot where Mickey fell into the hole last summer—the hole nobody could find. He smiled at the memory. If there was trouble at the resort, a hole to fall in, or a raccoon with a bad temper, some kid would always manage to find it. In his earlier days, Ernie would have been that kid.

He stopped and looked around—again, nothing. Using his binoculars, he scanned the peaks to the west, half-expecting to find a sign of the soldiers, but he didn't see anybody or anything walking around, not even a wolf out scavenging. He headed back.

Below the frozen marsh, a red light started blinking on the buried saucer. Just as Ernie stepped down with his left foot, a silver tendril projected through the surface of the frozen ground. When it pierced his boot, Ernie felt a brief stabbing pain. He stumbled and grabbed his foot. The silver tendril had already withdrawn below the surface, so he saw nothing.

Ernie realized he had stepped on something, a discarded fishhook maybe? Those could be nasty. Although it was eleven degrees outside, he removed his boot and sock to examine the underside of his foot. He expected there'd be blood or an old fishing hook sticking out of his sole. He saw only a small silver dot, like a decal or a label, right in the middle of his sole. Probably had come off his sock. He scratched at it with his fingernail, but it wouldn't come off. Satisfied that he wasn't injured, Ernie put his sock and boot back on and started down the trail. His foot didn't bother him; in fact, he felt fine, maybe better than fine. The hike back to his cabin was unusually easy.

Back at his cabin, Ernie sat in the overstuffed chair in front of the TV and took off his left boot and sock to reexamine his foot. He rubbed at the silver dot with his thumb, but it still wouldn't come off. Wasn't worth fussing about. He'd scrub it off in the shower in the morning. He used the remote to switch on the TV, and then put his sock back on and headed for the refrigerator.

Just as he opened the refrigerator door, he heard a strange popping sound from the TV. He ran back expecting to see smoke coming out of it, or something worse. It seemed fine, except for a bunch of static on the screen. He just purchased the TV two years ago, and couldn't remember what he did with the warranty. Not good. Being stuck in the cabin for two more months without a TV would be disastrous! Slumping in his chair, Ernie started fiddling with the remote. He wasn't aware of it, but the silver disc on the bottom of his foot was flashing with a bright white light.

He pushed several buttons and the screen started to clear up. That was better! The picture continued to resolve and then became perfectly clear. Whichever station he'd randomly selected was showing an old sci-fi flick. It reminded him of that old TV show *The Jetsons*, except it wasn't a cartoon. He hated sci-fi, so he immediately changed channels, but the next channel had the exact same flick. In fact, it was playing on all the channels—something about a big bubble with a city inside. The whole thing appeared to be under water. Must be a problem with the satellite, he thought. Sometimes clouds blocked the signal. Or maybe it was the remote? He banged the remote on the chair's armrest a few times, but nothing changed.

Suddenly, Ernie felt really tired, as if his body weighed a ton. He turned off the TV, tossed the remote on the carpet, leaned his head back, and closed his eyes. Before long, he fell asleep. As his breathing became deep and rhythmic, the TV turned itself back on and the picture on the screen began to change.

Two hours later, Rapier One arrived over the marsh.

The copilot yawned. "Got any more coffee?"

"Blew through the last of it an hour ago," replied the pilot.

"What about the guys in the back?"

"You want to wake up a guy with a machine gun who hasn't had any sleep, you go ahead."

The copilot grunted. "What are we supposed to do?"

"Talk to the guy we saw last night."

"Why?"

"To ask him what he saw."

"If he's smart, he already forgot the whole thing."

"I'm turning right thirty degrees. That must be his cabin over there. We can land behind it."

A loud knock on his door awakened Ernie. In front of him, the television showed only static again, so he shut it off. He wondered how long he'd slept. Felt like it had been all night. Feeling really good, he got up and stretched. There was another rap on his door, this time harder.

"Hold your horses, whoever you are," Ernie shouted. He started smiling and couldn't stop. He hadn't felt this good in a long time.

When Ernie opened the door, he found himself facing twelve men, ten in full combat gear and body armor. He snapped to attention. "Sergeant Ernest Santos retired."

The pilot stamped his feet. "At ease, Sergeant. It's friggin' cold out here. Can we come in?"

"Sure," said Ernie.

Half the men piled into Ernie's small cabin, while the other soldiers set up a perimeter outside. Ernie just watched. For some reason, none of this seemed to bother him. "You boys want anything?"

"Got any strong coffee?" asked the copilot.

The pilot elbowed him in the ribs. He stepped forward. "See anything unusual last night, soldier?"

Ernie kept smiling. "No, Sir."

"You were out walking around last night, right?"

"Why would I do that?"

The pilot glanced at the copilot, and then continued. "Do you remember anything out of the ordinary last night, like some strange lights?"

"No."

"You sure?"

"Fell asleep in my chair after the Lakers game."

The copilot leaned forward. "I almost forgot! What was the score?"

The pilot pushed him back. "Soldier, you need to concentrate!" he shouted at Ernie. "We took a picture of you walking around the marsh last night!"

"No, Sir," said Ernie, calmly. "Must have been somebody else. Spent the night sleeping in my chair." Ernie was telling the truth, at least as he now remembered it. "It snowed like crazy last night. No way I left this cabin."

"Can I talk to you for a minute, outside?" said the pilot to the copilot. They stepped outside.

"He isn't going to tell us anything," said the pilot, his breath already steaming in the cold.

"Yeah, but he's lying," said the copilot. "I'm calling in." He took a portable radio out of his jacket. "Rapier One to Black Cloud, over."

"Go ahead."

"We're at the subject's cabin now. He says he was asleep in his chair all night, and didn't see anything. What do you want us to do?"

"Stand by." The photo-analyst turned to General Westlock. "The guy on the ground denies that he's seen anything."

"Then haul his ass in!"

"Excuse me, General, but…why?"

The general spun around. "Remind who you are again?"

"Major Dan Frankel, Air Force Special Ops," said a man in Air Force blue. He saluted smartly and remained at attention. "May I propose another course of action, Sir?"

The general moved closer to Frankel, until they stood almost nose-to-nose. "You have ten seconds."

"What do we gain by picking up Santos now?"

"We make him talk!"

The photo-analyst smirked. "He's an army ranger with a distinguished service record. How're you going to get him into

Guantanamo?"

"When the security of the US of A is at stake, soldier, you throw the rule book away!"

"Why don't we just follow him…Sir?" Frankel interjected.

"Because? Five seconds, soldier."

"We don't know where he fits into this yet. Either he's an accomplice to whatever's going on, or he really doesn't know anything. Either way, let him think we bought his story and keep watching him. Maybe he leads us to something useful."

"Wait, maybe I've got something," interrupted another analyst.

The general joined him at the computer screen. The contours of an audio file danced by, which of course meant nothing to the general who still hadn't figured out how to use his VCR. "Speak, soldier," said the general.

"I cross-referenced the Santos guy against all the databases and came up with something at FBI. He called them a few months ago."

"Why?"

"Listen." The analyst began playing the audio file:

"What is it, if I may ask?"

"An exoskeleton."

"A what?"

"A suit that gives the wearer super powers. A teenager has it, about sixteen years old. Used the thing to toss a whole tree across a creek, like it was a twig…and he crushed a rock in his hand like it was an egg! His name's Mickey. Nice kid. Lives in Los Angeles."

"Sounds like a kid named Mickey was playing superhero dressed up in a costume. Kids love that stuff," said the analyst. "My son sleeps in Spider-Man pajamas every night. Won't take 'em off in the morning."

"Yeah, my kid won't take off his Super Man cape," chimed in another analyst.

The general cleared his throat and silenced the room. "Except, according to Santos, he's throwing trees like twigs, which none of our exoskeletons can do. Anybody here see the connection?"

"Maybe this Mickey is an alien in disguise."

"More likely he picked up something they left behind," the general said. "Find the boy and place him under surveillance."

"Yes, Sir," the analyst responded.

"Keep him on a tight leash. I don't want to lose him." He pointed at Frankel. "And keep tabs on Santos, sounds like he's in on it."

Frankel snapped to attention and saluted again. "Will do, Sir!"

The general sneered at Latham. "If you want another stripe, take a lesson from that Air Force guy."

"And, gentlemen," the general added more loudly, "Don't fuck this up, or else…" His men all swallowed hard.

Frankel nodded at Latham and left for the men's room.

Chapter Twenty-Two

A week after their trip to the Moon, Mickey and David were lying on Mickey's bed.

"This sucks! I've been on the Moon like Neil Armstrong, and I can't tell anybody about it!" David whined.

"Dude, who's gonna believe you?"

"Good point."

Mickey sat up with his feet over the side of the bed. "We've got to figure this whole thing out."

"You still think it's some kind of test?"

"Has to be."

"Heard any more buzzing?"

Mickey turned and glared at him. "The Moon trip was one big buzzer."

David nodded his head. "What do you make out of all those war movies in the empty saucers?"

"Like I said, they checked out the planets we saw on their star charts. When they got there and saw what was going down, all the shit blowing up, they turned around and left."

"Then why did our saucer land? We've got wars all over the place too."

"Haven't figured that part out yet."

"What do we do now?"

"Like we've been doing, Dude. Just keep playing along. Something's bound to happen."

It had been a month since Mickey and David got their driver's licenses—they were born on the same day—but David preferred to let Mickey do the driving. Besides, his father never let him use the car. It was early November, and the weather in Southern California was unseasonably warm with blue skies. On Friday night, Mickey asked his father for permission to take his mom's

SUV and drive David to Venice Beach to check out the babes. Max was reluctant. He considered his son a safe and courteous driver, Mickey even had a gold star from Driver's Training, but up to that point, he hadn't driven much farther than the market or school. Max was about to say no when Jerry sealed the deal by stating it was time the boys learned how to socialize with girls, and the beach was a great place to do it.

Saturday morning, David arrived in shorts and a baseball cap. He looked glum.

"What's happening?" Mickey stuck out two fingers, another secret handshake between postpubescent males.

David extended two of his fingers in the same manner and headed into the house without saying a word. They went to Mickey's bedroom.

David tossed his baseball cap on Mickey's bed. "They're putting my dad on furlough. He told my mom last night. My folks really went at it after that."

"What does being furloughed mean?"

"It means my dad got pink-slipped, lost his job. Said the city's running out of money."

"So he can just sign on with another police department."

"Said there aren't any jobs. The whole state's going broke. He told my mom to stop spending money or we'll end up on the street."

"Jesus, what did she say?"

"Nothing. While my dad was storming around the house yelling, she ran into the bedroom and locked the door. He gets real mad when she does that. Started pounding on her door, like he was trying to break it down. That's when I bugged out."

Mickey noticed that David's eyes were tearing up. "Where's your dad now?"

"Hauled ass on his Harley. Don't know where he went."

"Where's your brother?"

"Hasn't been home in weeks. Hope the A-hole never comes

back...except he always does."

"Should we check on your mom?"

"She'll get over it. Probably went into the kitchen and poured herself a glass from the bottle she keeps behind the dishes." David grabbed his hat. "Let's go check out the Venice girls before I have to move to Nebraska."

Mickey looked stricken. "You think it'll come to that?"

"If my dad can't get another job around here, it's adios. We'll probably live with his sister in Nebraska. I'll have to learn how to milk cows and grow tomatoes."

Pam and Vickie were sitting in the local Burger Shack waiting to pay their bill. Several of the local cool guys were at the counter making dumb gestures to gain Vickie's attention. In days past, she'd be into this kind of flirtation big time, but recently, it seemed to annoy her.

Pam looked toward the two boys at the counter. "Two of your fans are trying to get your attention. Isn't one of them Jimmy, the quarterback?"

Vickie frowned and pretended not to notice. She angled her chair away from them. "Yeah."

The two boys began hamming it up even more.

"I thought you and Jimmy were tight," said Pam.

"He's a dufus."

Pam picked up the last one of her french fries and smirked. "Since when?"

Vickie glanced at her watch. "Where's your mom?"

"On her way." Pam looked up. "Jimmy and his sidekick are coming over."

Vickie stood. "I'll pay. Let's get out of here."

Pam levered herself up onto her braces. "What's with you?"

"Nothing!" Vickie replied too loudly.

Jimmy approached their table and stopped, rocking back and forth on his heels. He wore his jeans so low on his pelvis that the top of his undershorts showed—it was considered cool. "Hey Vic," he said smiling.

"Hey Jimmy." Vickie grimaced.

"Me and Al are cruising down to Santa Monica in my dad's car. Want to join us?" Al had his hair spiked like a porcupine and stared at Vickie with lust written all over his face. Since Jimmy was the alpha male, Al didn't say anything. Naturally, both of them were ignoring Pam, but she was accustomed to it and didn't care. Besides, lately she'd been talking to David and really liking him.

"Can't do it today. Gotta study," said Vickie. She turned her back and walked toward the cash register, leaving Pam with the two boys.

Jimmy looked annoyed. "What's with her?"

"She's a serious student," Pam replied.

Al thought that was funny and snickered. He had more emblems on his letterman jacket than a grand prix car.

"Since when?" asked Jimmy.

Pam saw Vickie waiting at the front with her hand on the door. "See you guys," said Pam.

"Whatever," muttered Jimmy, acting unperturbed. He looked at Al who was shaking his head. Jimmy yanked up his jeans an inch. "Tell her to call me when she changes her mind, and she will."

Pam joined Vickie outside at the curb. "Now you going to tell me what's going on?" she asked.

"Nothing!" Vickie snapped.

"I'm your best friend. Don't hand me that crap! Something's bugging you."

"I'm just tired."

"Tired of what?"

"Everything…life!"

Pam gawked at her

"I don't mean it *that* way."

She really liked Vickie, although her queen bee routine wore thin at times. "Then what's wrong?"

"It's just..."

At that moment, Pam's adoptive mom, Phyllis, pulled up to the curb and honked the horn.

The girls got in and Pam turned to her friend. "Will you tell me what's wrong now?"

Vickie looked sullen. "I'm tired."

"Tired of what?"

"Tired of being pawed by guys with single digit IQs."

"Even when they've lettered in three sports?"

"It takes more than muscles to be a man."

Pam nodded. "Like brains..."

"That's right."

"Like manners."

"Yeah."

"Like Mickey."

"What?"

"Mickey," Pam repeated. "Biology class?"

"What about him?"

"His IQ is definitely north of two digits, and he's polite."

"He's a dork."

"He likes you."

Vickie gazed out the window. "What makes you say that?"

"Davie told me."

Vickie smirked. "Now he's *Davie*?" She drew out his name.

Pam blushed. "We talk once in a while."

"What did he say?"

"Davie?"

"No! Mickey." Vickie blushed.

Pam smiled at her. "He thinks you're cute."

Vickie took out her compact, stared at herself in the mirror, and pouted. "He's right. What else did he say?"

"Talk to him and find out."

"So, have you done it with Davie yet?"

Pam looked shocked. "We talk on the phone!"

"It's called phone sex."

"Stop!"

As the car pulled away, Jake and several of his biker buddies were just arriving in the parking lot behind the restaurant.

"Ain't that the crip and the blonde your little brother and his buddy hang out with?" said Ralph, one of Jake's biker acolytes. Ralph always wore a vintage World War I German Army helmet with a spike on top, even when he wasn't riding his bike. Might have been squeezing his brain a little too tight, that is, if he had one, as Jake often quipped.

Jake sat back on his bike and leered at the car as it drove away. "That blonde's sure got a tight little ass, doesn't she? Maybe I'll have a chat with her." He jumped on his motorcycle starter and revved the engine.

"I thought we were cruising for your brother and his friend for payback," said Rob, his usual partner in mischief. Either Rob's Harley-Davidson tee shirt had shrunk, or he'd gained more weight.

"Definitely, but first I think I'll get cozy with the blonde."

"She's a little young for you, isn't she?" Rob asked.

"The younger the better," Jake spit back and took off after Pam's car.

Two blocks from the Burger Shack, Pam looked at Vickie. "Shit, I forgot."

"Forgot what?" said Vickie.

"My notes for the history test."

"So, it's your turn to have a brain fart," Vickie said with a grin.

Pam leaned forward to speak to her stepmom. "Can we stop by the school for a minute? I need to get something from my locker."

Chapter Twenty-Three

Mickey's mom's car was a late model SUV. The boys jumped in and buckled up.

"You sure you're in the mood to hustle babes?" asked Mickey. "We could do something less intense, like go to the movies."

"The boardwalk, Dude. Just tell me you brought the suit in case we run into Jake."

"It's in my locker."

"Let's get it."

"Really?"

"It's Saturday. Trust me. He's looking for trouble."

A few seconds after Mickey's white SUV drove by, a black SUV with tinted windows pulled out of the alley and followed them.

The boys entered the school's back parking lot just as Pam and Vickie were getting back into their car. Pam spotted David and smiled.

"Hey, that's Pam," said David with a huge grin on his face. "Pull over."

Mickey eyed his best friend. He could read him like a book. "Sure thing, Davie." He pulled into the space next to Pam's car.

David rolled down his window. "Hi," he said, making eye contact with Pam.

Pam started blushing, a fact not lost on Vickie. "Hi Davie," she answered. "What are you guys doing here?"

"Mickey's gotta get something out of his locker. You?" said David.

Mickey and Vickie exchanged glances.

"Me too," said Pam.

"Where you heading now?"

"Home," said Pam. "You?" Vickie glared at her.

"We're going to Venice Beach," said David. "Wanna join us?"

Pam glanced at Vickie, who seemed tense. "Gotta go home

and study," replied Pam, sounding disappointed.

"Oh yeah, the big history test is on Monday," said David. He looked at Pam sheepishly. "We could study together." Mickey stared at him.

"No!" whispered Vickie under tight lips.

Pam looked at her, disappointed, then back at David. "Wanna borrow my notes? I just got them out of my locker. Drive us home, and we can stop off at FedEx and copy them."

Pam glanced at Vickie. Finally, Vickie shrugged. "Mom?" said Pam.

Pam's stepmother Phyllis looked at Mickey behind the wheel of the SUV. "Ever get any tickets?"

"No Ma'am," he replied. He didn't mention he'd only been driving for a month.

"It's not far. The store's at the mini mall," Pam hastened to add.

Mrs. Joyce smiled. "I guess it's okay."

"You okay with this?" David asked Mickey, under his breath. "It'll only take a few minutes."

"Hop in," was Mickey's answer. He forced a smile. "Hi, Vickie."

"Hey," she replied, half-heartedly, as the girls slid into the backseat. Mickey hopped out and quickly walked across the yard to the lockers. When she thought Pam wasn't watching, Vickie gave him the once-over.

In a few minutes, Mickey returned with his rolled up "motocross" suit and helmet. He opened the rear hatch and put them in the back.

"You going dirt biking later?" Pam asked

"Never know," Mickey replied, as he got back in the car, buckled up, and pulled out of the parking lot.

David had been reading Pam's notes. "This stuff's really good."

Pam blushed. "History's my second favorite subject."

"What's your first?"

"Astronomy. I got a set of binoculars for Christmas. When the sky's clear, I'm outside every night looking at the stars.

"I like science too," replied David, smiling at her. "What can you see?"

"The Moon, of course. Constellations, like the Big Dipper. Sometimes you can see Jupiter. It's a little red dot."

"Mickey has a real telescope," said David.

"You do?"

"Haven't used it in a while," Mickey replied.

"I'd love to look through it some time," said Pam.

Vickie cleared her throat, ending the exchange. Mickey eyed her through the rear view mirror.

When they arrived at FedEx, David hustled inside, copied the notes, and hurried back.

"Where did you say you live?" Mickey asked, looking at Pam in the rearview mirror.

"Not far. Take Buena Vista up past the promenade, then a left on Church Lane."

Vickie lowered the window part way and lit a cigarette.

"My mom doesn't allow smoking in her car," said Mickey, frowning.

"Sorry!" Vickie rolled her eyes and tossed the cigarette out the window.

Unseen behind a hedge that bordered the school grounds, Jake and his buddies watched the entire exchange. When Mickey drove away in the SUV, Jake motioned to his posse, and they drove after them.

A few blocks later, the four teenagers heard the growl of motorcycles. Mickey looked in the rear view mirror and saw Jake closing in behind them. Jake was grinning and using hand signals to vector three more bikers toward the car.

David spun around. "You have to lose them!" he shouted. "There isn't enough time to pull over and put on the suit!"

"Relax. They're just trying to give us a hard time. Too many people around for them to try anything," said Mickey.

Vickie looked through the back window at Jake and his buddies. "What're they doing?" she asked nervously.

Jake pulled closer to the back of the SUV, leaned over, and smashed the wrench against the rear window, cracking it. The girls screamed and grabbed for each other. Mickey veered quickly to the right to get away. This put them on a freeway on-ramp heading south. Mickey accelerated onto the Golden State Freeway. Jake and the three bikers followed behind.

The DIA agent riding shotgun with another agent in the black SUV dialed his cell phone. Both wore black suits and dark glasses. Every time they stopped at a doughnut stand for a cup of coffee, they heard Men in Black jokes.

"Dark Cloud, this is Mobile One. The two subjects are in motion, driving a white Chevy SUV, license number…"

General Westlock interrupted. "Just tell me where they're going, agent."

"They just took the on-ramp to the Golden State Freeway heading south," said Frankel.

The general turned, saw Frankel, and nodded. "To where?"

The conversation was on speaker now. Inside the van, the DIA agents glanced at each other. "I don't know. But, the second turnoff is to Griffith Park."

"Follow them!" growled the general.

"They're being hassled by some motorcycle thugs. Should we intervene?"

The general glanced at Frankel who shook his head no. The general swore under his breath. "Do not engage. Maintain surveillance only." Frankel nodded. Watching their silent interchange, Latham looked chagrined.

"Yes, Sir," answered the agent over the speaker.

The general terminated the connection. "Get me Ops at Area Fifty-One!"

One of the analysts handed the general a phone.

"This is Westlock. I've got a mission for Aurora."

"Would a week from Tuesday work for you, General?" replied the dispatch at Area Fifty-One.

"I need a bird over Los Angeles now, soldier!"

"But General, all the missions are booked. Aurora One is heading up the West Coast toward Alaska and the Bering Strait. The other's in the hanger for maintenance."

"Then divert Aurora One to L.A., *now*!"

"He's a thousand miles away," the dispatcher pleaded, and then gave up. "Where in L.A.? What's he looking for?"

"A white Chevy SUV heading for Griffith Park with two alien contactees."

"Really?" asked the dispatcher in disbelief.

The general handed the phone back to Frankel. "I need to know if they're going to meet up with that saucer again!"

"Sir, they could be heading lots of places, like downtown to Staples Center, or west to the beaches," Frankel said.

"If I had 'friends' in 'high places' and was being hassled by motorcycle goons, who do you think I'd call?" said the general.

Frankel nodded his head. "Friends with a flying saucer. I'll pass it along, General."

When the general left the control center, the ambient stress level immediately decreased. Frankel waited a few minutes. After checking to ensure everyone was occupied, he called back one of the DIA agents in the van on the agent's cell phone. "Did you remember to get hangers for my shirts?"

"Hi, honey, sure did." He smiled at the other agent driving the SUV. "The little woman. Wants to make sure I remember the dry cleaning."

"Grabbing a cold one with the guys after work. See you about eight." Frankel hung up. In code, the DIA agent in the van confirmed to Frankel that he'd tagged Mickey with a nano-recorder.

Mickey continued driving south, constantly glancing in his

rearview mirror. Jake's posse stayed close behind the SUV, waving their arms like they were out joy riding.

"Those are the same toughs from the dance!" yelled Pam, hanging onto Vickie.

"It's David's brother!" Mickey shouted back.

"Pull over and let us out!" screamed Vickie. "It's you two they want, not us!"

"Don't stop!" yelled Pam. "The guy with the wrench is crazy! When we see a Highway Patrol guy, we'll flag 'em over… Wait, here's a better idea! Pull into the next police station. I'll look it up on my iPhone."

"The woman's got brains!" shouted David.

"Control yourself," muttered Mickey.

For a split second, Pam fought back a smile. Then she used her iPhone's GPS to locate a police station. "Keep going!" she hollered from the backseat. "There's a Highway Patrol station one mile on the right!"

They sped down the freeway with the bikers close behind. After a mile, Mickey saw the sign for a Highway Patrol station off the next exit. He steered into the right lane, but Jake and his buddies surrounded the car blocking his exit. The SUV was forced to drive past it.

Mickey hunched over the steering wheel. "Shit! They blocked me!"

Pam looked back and saw Jake leering at them. "I'll find another one!" She began searching on her iPhone again.

Mickey saw a familiar sign and half-smiled. Trying to catch Jake by surprise, he veered off at the last possible moment, hitting the off-ramp. The rear of the SUV started to lose traction. For an instant, it seemed they might topple over.

"You're going too fast!" wailed Vickie, hanging onto Pam.

Mickey regained control. "Yeah, and let's hope a cop sees us and gives us a ticket!"

"Maybe we lost them!" David shouted. He turned around and

looked back. Jake and his buddies were still behind them. "Guess not."

"Are you turning the car around?" asked Pam.

"Got a better idea," Mickey replied, calm and determined.

The SUV sped up the road toward Griffith Park's Planetarium.

David recognized their location. "This road's a dead end!"

"Trust me," encouraged Mickey. He could see Vickie staring at him in the rearview mirror. She seemed less panicked now.

They continued up the hill with Jake and his buddies trailing after like a pack of wolves. Jake made no move to flank or pass. He knew where the road ended.

As they rounded a curve, Mickey stepped hard on the gas. In the few seconds, they were visually separated from the bikers, and he swerved down the dirt road leading to the clearing. Unfortunately, they were driving too fast. Halfway down, the SUV started to skid and fishtailed sideways. "Hang on!" Mickey yelled, as he fought for control.

"Not good!" hollered David.

The girls hugged each other with their eyes tightly closed.

Mickey slammed on the brakes. The SUV spun around and slammed into a tree, rear-end first, at the edge of the clearing. The tree was at the precipice. If it hadn't been there, they'd have gone over, and it was a long way down.

Mickey pushed the airbag away from his face. "Anybody hurt back there?" He turned to David. "You okay?"

"I think so," David replied. He'd bit his lip, and the airbag had pushed his glasses into the bridge of his nose causing a small laceration. Blood dripped down his face onto his shirt. He wiped at it with the back of his hand and frowned. "Nice bit of driving, Dude."

"Didn't have a lot of options," said Mickey irritably.

Vickie started screaming. "Get me the fuck out of here!"

Pam had a bloody nose, but otherwise was fine. She reached

over and unfastened Vickie's shoulder harness. "You're okay." She tried to sound soothing. "Let's get out of the car." Vickie had a laceration over her left eye. It was bleeding briskly. She daubed it with the back of her hand and stared at the blood. "Oh my God!"

Mickey turned around and saw how close they were to the precipice. "Everybody out!" he shouted. He had trouble opening the door. It finally yielded with the sound of tortured metal.

"I'm hurt," cried Vickie from the backseat. Pam applied pressure to Vickie's eye staunching the bleeding. "Give us a moment," she called out. "I'm trying to stop the bleeding."

David looked outside, realized where they were, and scrambled out. He stared at the tree. "Jesus! The tree's pushed half out of the ground!"

Mickey ran to the back of the SUV and grabbed Vickie's arm. "Hurry! You gotta get out!" He yanked her arm, pulling her onto the ground, then lost his balance and fell on top of her. He looked into her eyes, and for a second she stared back. Then, after an awkward silence, he blushed and helped her up. Neither of them said anything.

David helped Pam out. Then they all hurried away from the SUV and slumped to the ground. Mickey looked back at his mother's car. Smoke poured out from under the hood and the windshield was smashed.

"We have to get Vic to a doctor," said Pam. She looked at her cell phone. "No signal. Forget calling a cab."

Mickey started to speak, but then he heard something. "We have bigger problems." He pointed toward the dirt road. They heard the sound of motorcycles fast approaching. Mickey jumped up and ran to the back of the SUV to grab the suit, but the hatch was jammed closed by the tree. "Damn!" he yelled.

David ran over, opened a side door, and crawled over the seats to the back. He couldn't see the suit. The rear seat had been crumpled by the impact, blocking his view. He pushed it back and saw the black cloth of the suit, but not the helmet. "I can't find the helmet!"

An ominous cracking sound came from the tree. As David moved around inside the SUV, the sound repeated, this time louder.

"Get out of there!" yelled Mickey.

Pam was panic-stricken. "Davie, get out!" she screamed.

David tossed out the suit, and then he dove back inside to search for the helmet. He used his legs to kick frantically at the seat. This rocked the SUV and caused an even more ominous cracking sound. "If I don't find the helmet, we're all going to die! Somebody's got to be a hero!"

Pam looked puzzled. "What's he talking about?" Before Mickey could answer, she cupped her hands and yelled. "Who gives a crap about some motorcycle suit! Get outta there!"

"They're coming!" screamed Vickie. The rumbling of motorcycle engines sounded like thunder.

"Found it!" shouted David. He scrambled out of the SUV and thrust the helmet at Mickey.

Pam glared at him. "You risked your life for that? Don't ever do that again!" David responded with a sheepish grin.

Mickey jumped into the suit and put on the helmet. After zipping up, he and David chest bumped each other.

"You're fucking kidding me?" shouted Vickie. "You're dressing for Halloween now?"

Pam struggled to stand. David reached down to help her. "Okay, I give up. Why's Mickey dressed like that?" Pam asked.

"You gotta trust us on this one," said David.

"This is getting weirder by the minute," said Pam, shaking her head.

"Just wait," said David. "There's more."

Vickie stared at Mickey with an odd expression.

Mickey smiled at her and closed the visor. When he did, each of the five buttons lit up. He touched them all and waited.

Chapter Twenty-Four

Jake and his buddies eased their bikes down the dirt road into the clearing. On level ground, Jake stopped and gunned his engine. He looked over at the SUV, shook his head, and smiled. When he saw Mickey wearing the familiar black suit, his smile turned to a frown. He turned off his motor, dismounted, and took the familiar metal wrench out of his saddlebag. "Looks like you kids have a serious problem." He pounded the wrench once against his gloved hand making a loud, threatening thud.

"Leave us alone," demanded Mickey, with the radio voice.

Vickie panicked. "Pam and I just hitched a ride!"

"Don't worry, cupcake. I don't have any problem with you, or your crip friend," said Jake. Pam glared at him. Jake faced Mickey. "But I have a serious problem with these two losers."

"Let the girls go," Mickey said calmly. Vickie glanced at him again.

"They can leave. In fact, me and my buddies will personally give them a ride home, that is if the crippled chick can mount a bike." Jake laughed, and so did his friends.

"Fuck off," said Pam, glaring at him.

"Oh, oh. She's a feisty crip!" They laughed again.

David moved to stand in front of Pam. He stood defiantly with his arms crossed over his chest, glaring at his brother.

This caught Jake by surprise. "Well, well…what do we have here?" Before Jake could continue, the ground of the clearing started to shake. But the tremor didn't stop after a few seconds like the usual earthquakes in California. The force of the vibrations kept growing. Then, a gust of wind hit the clearing, strong enough to make the dust and leaves fly about, accompanied by an ear-splitting whining sound.

"What's happening!" screamed Vickie over the din.

Mickey tilted his helmet toward the sky. "Jakey, this would be a good time to split." Everyone else looked up and saw the silver disc right above them, descending down to the clearing.

David pulled Pam away from the path of the descending saucer. Vickie froze where she stood, transfixed.

"Vickie!" screamed Pam. David ran back for her and hustled her out of the way.

Mickey turned toward Jake. At that moment, Jake wasn't faring much better than Vickie. "I suggest you move now," Mickey said.

"Dark Cloud, do you copy?"

"Go ahead, Aurora," said the technician inside Cheyenne Mountain. He handed General Westlock the phone.

"Did you track that white Chevy SUV?" asked the general.

"Just arriving over the LA area now, but we've got something else…bigger."

"This better be good, soldier."

"It's a flying saucer!"

The general glared at everybody in the room. "I knew it!"

"The *fucker* just took off from Mammoth Lakes in California and blew by us like we were standing still!"

The general looked over at Lieutenant Latham. "Aurora, are you still tracking it?"

"Yes, Sir! In fact, it just landed!"

"Where?"

"In Los Angeles, a clearing near the Griffith Park Planetarium."

"General," said Lieutenant Latham excitedly.

"Yes, Latham. I'm always right." The general pushed the speaker button. "Aurora, you're to maintain surveillance." The general turned back to Latham. "Get us eyes on the ground, now!"

Jake snapped out of it and started running for the road with his buddies right behind. Halfway there, they stopped and watched as the disc settled in the clearing. It landed on Jake's motorcycle squashing it flat as a pancake.

With the disc at rest, the tremors, the wind, and the whining ceased. Mickey touched the red button and his visor popped open. Smiling, he turned to the other three kids huddled off to the side. Vickie appeared to be in shock. David was perfectly calm. Oddly, so was Pam. "It's okay," David said reassuringly. "It's a flying saucer. Mickey called it." Vickie gaped at him. Pam stared at the saucer.

Mickey pointed at the disc. "Check it out." A rectangular area was darkening. Then the ramp formed and descended to the ground leaving an opening in the side of the disc.

"This is our ride out of here," said Mickey.

"You're joking, right?" said Vickie blinking.

"Don't worry, we've done it before," said David.

"You *what*?" shrieked Vickie.

Mickey walked briskly to the top of the ramp where he gestured for the others to follow.

"I'm not getting in that thing!" yelled Vickie.

"You might want to reconsider," Mickey called down. He pointed toward the dirt road. Jake and his friends were walking back down the road. Jake was holding a gun.

David grabbed Pam by the waist and started pulling her up the ramp. "It's okay! We've done it before!" he said, urging her. "It's here to help us!" After glancing at Jake, Pam used her legs as much as she could to help David maneuver her up the ramp.

Vickie still hadn't moved.

"Vickie, come on!" yelled Pam.

"Hurry!" yelled David, motioning with his arm.

Vickie looked back and saw Jake lifting the gun. Terrified, she bolted up the ramp.

"Get inside," Mickey said calmly.

Pam glanced at David. "Trust me," he said. She nodded and followed him inside.

Vickie stared at the door and started to tremble. "I can't!"

Mickey was at her side. "Yes you can," he said in a soothing voice.

Something about his voice calmed her. She turned toward the doorway. "I can't believe I'm doing this!" Her voice trailed off as she disappeared inside the saucer.

Mickey pulled down his visor. The green button was especially bright and pulsating. He pushed it.

Sneering, Jake raised the gun and pointed it at Mickey. "Game's over, GI Joe!" He pulled the trigger. This was followed by a loud bang, and his hand jerked back. Almost simultaneously a flash of light burst near Mickey's head, along with a sound like an electrical short circuit—a *pffzt* sound. Nothing happened to Mickey. He remained standing at the top of the ramp, unscathed and unperturbed.

Enraged, Jake fired two more times in rapid succession. Again, two pffzt sounds were heard, followed by two flashes of light along the trajectory of the bullets. The smell of ozone permeated the air.

"See ya!" Mickey waved to Jake and walked into the saucer. Shortly after, the ramp flowed back up, and the side of the disc resumed its unblemished silvery shape. Jake dropped the gun and stared at the disc, dumbfounded.

The ground trembled again. Dirt and leaves billowed into the air forming a vortex over the disc. Jake started backing away. Slowly, the disc began to rise about a hundred feet off the ground. Then, with a popping noise, it shot straight up and disappeared from view.

For a few moments Jake remained staring into the sky. Then he shook his head, as if trying to clear it, and looked around. Besides the crashed SUV, a pancake of multicolored metal was all that remained of his beloved motorcycle.

"Black Cloud, this is Aurora. Are you getting this?"

The Special Ops Room in Cheyenne Mountain was packed, and every pair of eyes was on the video monitors displaying the imagery uploaded by the Aurora spy plane orbiting over Griffith Park. "Five by five," replied Latham.

"Fucking amazing!" exclaimed the pilot of Aurora.

"Keep it professional," said General Westlock menacingly.

"Sorry, Sir."

"Follow that saucer, son!" instructed the general.

"Maybe if we were the space shuttle."

"What do you mean?"

"It's gone, that's what I mean, Sir! Took off and blew out at Mach…I don't know, twenty-five or something. Ask the radar guys. My gauges don't register that high."

General Westlock turned to another soldier at one of the monitors. "He's right, Sir. It's already past the Moon."

"Where's it going?"

"No way to tell. We don't track objects in Outer Space. That's NASA's gig."

"I ID'd the two girls and the biker who fired the shots," Latham said, a little too eagerly. "We've been following the boys for the past week."

"Who are they?" asked the General.

"The shooter's name is Jake Walker, the older brother of David Walker. He's a real dirtbag and suspected drug dealer. The girls are schoolmates, both A-students. The kid named Mickey appears to be the ringleader."

The general looked around at his astonished staff. "Can somebody tell me how four teenagers just moseyed onto a flying saucer and took off for parts unknown?"

Everybody shrugged their shoulders with puzzled expressions.

"Gentlemen, you've got forty-eight hours to find out."

Latham responded first. "Yes, Sir!" He turned to the others. "Time to pull out all the surveillance stops—tap all their phones, do work-ups on everybody, including the old guy at Twin Lakes, and park a satellite over L.A."

"Call somebody at NASA," continued the general. "I want to know where that saucer is going, and when it's returning. And follow everybody who gets off!"

"No intervention, Sir?" asked Latham.

"Not until I have some answers!"

Latham saluted. "Yes, Sir!" He felt in charge again, and it felt good. He glared at Frankel who was holding his stomach, heading for the door. "Where are you going?"

Frankel appeared to be in pain. "To the men's room. Must be something I ate."

Chapter Twenty-Five

The teenagers huddled together inside the lighted interior of the saucer.

A section of the wall in front of them darkened and then became clear.

"What's happening?" yelled Vickie. She was clinging to Pam.

"It's just the window," said Mickey. The four teenagers looked out. Clouds raced by at incredible speed.

"What does that mean?" Vickie pointed at the clouds.

"It means we've taken off," replied Mickey.

"Taken off…as in flying?"

Mickey smiled at her. "That's right."

"Oh my God!" she shrieked.

Mickey grabbed her by the shoulders. "It's okay. I know it's hard to believe, but David and I have flown in this thing before."

David tried to sound reassuring. "We're just going for a little ride." He left out the part about "the little ride" being a quick trip to the Moon.

"And then we go home?" Vickie asked.

With wonder on her face, Pam strained to examine the interior of the saucer. "Cool," she said.

"That's right. Now we sit back and enjoy the ride."

Vickie looked around. "Sit on what?"

Mickey pointed. "Lean against one of those silver pillars and push the white button that's blinking." There were four pillars now.

"Then what happens?" asked Vickie without budging.

"It's like riding on a rollercoaster. The bar has to come down to hold you in the car."

Vickie remained standing in place. "What bar?"

Pam pushed Vickie toward one of the pillars. "C'mon, Vic! It's not like we have a lot of choices at the moment. Just do it!" She glanced at Mickey. "The guys aren't afraid."

"Why does it have to be me?" Vickie walked slowly to one of the pillars. Mickey and David knew what was about to happen, and with a glance, silently agreed not to say anything.

"Now what?" Vickie asked.

"Just lean back and push the white button," said Mickey.

Vickie looked at Pam for support. When Pam nodded, she sidled up to the pillar and pushed the button. It more or less grabbed her. As the silver substance quickly flowed around her, Vickie screamed. "What's happening? Get it off me!" The process quickly continued, cocooning her entire body up to her neck. "Oh my God!" she cried.

David gripped Pam's hand.

Mickey grimaced. He knew what was coming next.

The clear bubble formed over Vickie's head finishing the process. She continued screaming, but now her voice had the radio quality. The intensity of her protest was initially earsplitting, but then the loudness modulated, as if the sound had been turned down. They could hear her bellowing, but now at a tolerable level. It was loud enough to hear her cursing like a sailor.

Pam gawked wide-eyed at Mickey. Before she could say anything, David stepped in front of her. "It's just the chair. It's really comfortable inside. Don't worry, you can get out anytime you want by pushing the white button."

Vickie heard this and frantically stabbed at the white button. Nothing happened. "Get this fucking thing off me!"

"We all better get in our chairs," said Mickey. He pointed at the window. It was filled with the blackness of space.

Pam stared at it, dumbfounded. "Are we…?" her voice trailed off. "Are we in…space?"

"Yep, but this is just the beginning of the ride," said David. "Better sit down before this baby really gets going."

The stars blurred into silvery streaks across the window.

"Now would be an excellent time!" said Mickey.

The three teens hurried to the remaining silver pillars, the two boys carrying Pam. Pam took the one next to Vickie, pushed the blinking white button, and watched transfixed as the silver material flowed up her body.

Soon all four reclined in their chairs with bubbles covering their heads.

"See, Vic, it's okay," said Pam. "We're all okay!" Vickie could hear Pam's voice clearly inside her bubble. She started to calm down. She didn't realize it, but part of this change was due to the pillar.

The teens stared at the blackness of space with the stars zipping past. They were too engrossed to notice that the laceration over Vickie's eye was disappearing. David's cut and Pam's bloody nose were healing too.

"Listen up!" Mickey called out. "You might want to hang on. There's a little maneuver coming up that feels like a roller-coaster!"

"Hang on to what?" yelled Vickie. "I can't even wiggle my toe in this straightjacket!"

The saucer went through one of its sudden gyrations causing the view out the window to whip around in a blur. Now the Moon was centered in the window.

"I think I'm going to puke," Vickie moaned.

"Don't worry. Whoever built this thing already thought of that," said Mickey, who didn't feel well either.

The Moon continued to grow steadily larger. Even Vickie was becoming interested in the view, as opposed to terrified.

"Mickey, can you hear me?" asked Pam.

"We can all hear you," Mickey replied.

Pam heard his voice in her bubble, as if it came over an intercom without distortion. "Where is this thing taking us?"
"You're looking at it."

"This is some kind of practical joke, right?" Vickie asked.

"It's no joke," said David. "We'll be landing soon, and then we'll see some cool stuff before heading home."

"What if I want to go home now?" moaned Vickie.

"Stop worrying," replied David. "I told you, Mickey and I already took this trip, and it's beyond cool."

Pam sighed. "I'd like to say I don't believe any of this, that we're on some ride at Disneyland, except it sure feels real."

"It's real, all right," said Mickey, "and just like Disneyland, you can't hop out until the ride is over."

Vickie started jabbing at her white button again. Nothing happened, but then she started to feel more relaxed, even comfortable, as if the bubble read her anxiety level and compensated. She settled back and watched.

The flying saucer accelerated and the image of the Moon in the window grew larger with every passing second.

"I hope this thing's got brakes!" exclaimed Vickie as the Moon's craters filled their view.

Just when a crash landing seemed imminent, the disc made an abrupt course adjustment and continued past the Moon.

"What just happened?" asked David. Mickey didn't respond. David thought he heard the sound of retching. "Mickey?" he asked again.

"Yeah," said Mickey finally, in a husky voice.

"What just happened?"

"I puked."

"Before that. Why'd we zip around the Moon and keep going?"

"Not a clue."

"Maybe we're not landing this time," said David. "Maybe we're just taking a joyride and then going home."

"We're going home?" asked Vickie. She seemed almost conversational now, as if she didn't have a care in the world.

"I don't think so," said Mickey. "See that red ball out there that's getting bigger?"

"Yeah?"

"Pretty sure it's Mars, Dude."

Pam stared in rapture at the growing red orb in the window.

All Vickie said was "Oh."

For the next thirty minutes, the reddish orb in the center of the window kept growing larger. Soon it appeared exactly like the photos of Mars everybody was accustomed to seeing. Mars had been covered extensively in the news lately, especially as one of the two rovers was still motoring around taking pictures, and the Polar Lander was digging holes looking for water. It really did look reddish in color with irregular white areas at both ends marking its polar ice caps.

"Oh my God. Is that really Mars?" asked Vickie in awe.

"Mickey, what happens now?" asked David.

"Not a clue."

"Can't you find something else to say?" Pam sounded irritated.

"Sorry," Mickey answered. "I'm new to this astronaut gig. I've only flown to the Moon."

Mars grew ever larger in the window. They could see surface features now, including mountains and a vast valley, the solar system's largest rift. It was the so-called Grand Canyon of Mars, a remarkable slash in the surface of the planet twenty-five hundred miles long and up to four miles deep. The earth's Grand Canyon would easily be swallowed up in its depths.

"Do you think we're going to land?" asked David.

"Don't say it," Pam interrupted before Mickey could respond.

It looked like the disc planned to land, or maybe crash, but it made another sharp turn and continued past the planet. After that gyration, the view stabilized to the blackness of space.

"Not again," said Vickie.

"Everybody okay?" asked David.

"Yeah," said Vickie, sounding more annoyed than stressed.

"Where do you suppose this joyride is going next?" asked Pam.

"If I had to guess, I'd start looking for a planet with a big red dot," said Mickey.

"He means Jupiter," said David.

"Duuhhh… You're not the only one taking science this year, and I've got an A so far." Vickie sounded relaxed and more like her old self.

They couldn't see anything that looked like the planet Jupiter. Instead, looming ahead were countless rocks of various shapes and sizes, from beach balls to mountains—the asteroid belt between Mars and Jupiter. The disc accelerated straight toward it, making one wild turn after another to avoid collisions.

"I feel like I'm in a pinball machine!" yelled Pam as the craft banked around another massive rock. The scene in the window changed so rapidly, they all squeezed their eyes shut.

"NOT GOOD!" yelled David.

"Mickey?" yelled Pam. He didn't reply.

"He's sick!" yelled Vickie, "and he's not the only one!"

There was the sound of retching. Whose, it wasn't clear.

After several minutes of wild gyrations, accompanied by a duet of visceral sounds, the disc cleared the asteroid belt. While two of the bubbles were busy with housecleaning, the other two teens stared out the window into the blackness of space with its sprinkling of stars.

They continued on this trajectory in a straight line. The passage of time was difficult to gauge. The cocooned chairs felt warm and comfortable, with fresh air circulating. Somebody dozed off and started snoring.

"Who's that?" asked David.

"It's Vickie," Pam snickered. "She keeps me awake when she sleeps over."

"Why do you hang out with her?" David asked. "She's not

very nice, and she smokes."

"Yeah, what's with her?" Mickey chimed in. "Why's she so stuck-up?"

Vickie was still snoring, so Pam answered the question. "Her life's tough. Her parents are divorced and don't get along, and money's tight. She's wearing her sister's clothes."

"That's no excuse," said Mickey.

"How does judging us make her life any better?" asked David.

Pam hesitated for a moment. "When I transferred over last year, some of the kids gave me a hard time. Maybe you guys didn't notice."

"I…didn't know," said David. "We didn't have any classes together."

"Me neither," said Mickey.

"I'm not blaming you guys. It was some of the girls in Vickie's group, Lacey and Sharon—that bunch. They really hassled me, until Vic made them stop."

"She did?" said David.

"That's right. Vic barely knew me, but told everybody we were friends and to knock it off. Gotta tell you, life got a lot better after that, and now we're best friends. In fact, most of the time Vic lives at my house. My mom loves her."

"Why did she help you?" asked David. "I mean, she acts like such a hard-ass all the time."

"Because that's not the *real* Vic. I know her now, and I know she's hurting too, maybe not the same as me, but just as deeply. Being a hard-ass is how she hides it." Pam sighed. "Sometimes we build walls around ourselves to keep out the pain, but end up making ourselves prisoners. I let my busted-up legs do that to me, until I met Vic. She keeps telling me I'm special in other ways and won't let me get down on myself. She's my greatest fan. That's why I love her." Pam paused, as if collecting her thoughts. "Deep down, she's more insecure than all of us. Her bleached hair and all that makeup—that's her suit of armor, to prevent others from looking too closely."

David listened to her explanation closely. He could see a little of himself in Vickie now, how he buried his anger over his father's rejection and his older brother's bullying. That's why he took refuge at Mickey's house, like Vickie escaped to Pam's. But unlike Vickie, he never took his pain out on anybody else…just himself.

The three of them hadn't noticed: Vickie wasn't snoring any more.

Chapter Twenty-Six

Sometime later, a new sphere appeared in the center of the window. It had broad bands of color—grays, blues, and a giant swirling red spot.

"Ready or not, here comes Jupiter," said Mickey.

As they traveled closer, they could see more detail. A halo of smaller spheres circled the planet, not like the rings of Saturn, just dots here and there. These were Jupiter's moons, sixty-three total. Galileo discovered the four largest in 1610 which are still referred to as the Galilean moons—Io, Europa, Ganymede, and Callisto.

As the saucer continued toward Jupiter, the features of these moons became visible. Io, the one closest to the planet, had geysers with plumes of gas shooting outwards. The teens learned in science class that the plumes were eruptions of sulfur from Io's volcanoes. Odder still, this rocky moon was surrounded by an electric blue cloud of plasma that seemed connected to Jupiter. As the saucer drew closer to Jupiter, this plasma glowed like bright blue neon.

"That's awesome!" shouted Vickie, genuinely captivated now.

The most imposing of the moons was Ganymede, a sphere as large as the planet Mercury and the largest moon in the solar system. Compared to Io, its surface was bland—wholly covered with ice and scarred by impact craters. Closer to the planet, the moon Callisto appeared to be the same size as Ganymede, but Callisto stood out because of an absolutely gigantic impact crater punched into its side—the largest crater in the entire solar system, five hundred miles across.

As they passed the innermost moon, the disc decelerated and settled into orbit around Jupiter, but made no attempt to land. It had traversed the 350 million miles between Mars and Jupiter in a few hours. Mickey appreciated how truly incredible this was.

"Now what?" David whispered.

They continued circling the planet allowing the teens a fantastic view of its surface. Jupiter is a gas giant, just like Saturn, Uranus, and Neptune, with its overall mass about one one-thousandth of the Sun. Its most distinctive features are its colored bands—gigantic storms of hydrogen and helium, the main components of its atmosphere. The most famous is the so-called Great Red Spot, a cyclonic storm with a red color. This was first seen from Earth in the 17th century, and the cyclonic storm has been raging ever since. The four could also appreciate a small ring system around Jupiter. It was reminiscent of, but much smaller than the famous rings of Saturn. The space travelers wondered if they'd be seeing Saturn next.

For an hour, the saucer neither approached Jupiter nor left its orbit. The only perceptible change in course was its gradual approach to another of Jupiter's moons, Europa.

"We seem to be moving toward that smooth-looking moon," said Vickie. "Anybody know which one it is?"

Pam beamed. "It's Europa!"

"How did you know?" asked Mickey.

"Look how smooth it is, and the lines all over its surface."

"Wasn't Europa in that old sci-fi movie, *2001*?" asked Vickie.

"It was in the sequel, *2010*, with Roy Schneider," said Mickey. "In the movie, the aliens gave everybody a warning, *'Don't go near Europa!'*"

"Tell that to our ride," muttered Vickie.

"I have over a hundred sci-fi flicks on DVD!" interjected David.

"Cool! My favorite is *The Day the Earth Stood Still,*" said Pam. "Do you have that one?"

"Both versions! Klaatu barada nikto!"

"You two are perfect for each other," said Vickie.

The moon grew steadily larger in the window. Mickey was right—it was Europa, the smoothest object in the solar system.

However, its most distinctive feature is the presence of lines running all over its surface called "track ways."

"I read about Europa," said Pam. "It's covered with a layer of water ice several miles thick. The track ways are thought to be fissures that form and reseal as the ice periodically melts and refreezes, like the lines in an ice sphere."

"You think there's life on Europa, like in the movie?" asked David.

"If you land on Saturday night," Vickie snickered. Nobody else found this funny.

"It was just a movie," said Mickey.

"Maybe they were onto something," added Pam. "Life requires three ingredients to develop—energy, organic molecules, and liquid water. Right?"

"Yeah," said David.

"I slept through that class," said Vickie.

"Let her finish," said Mickey.

"Sources of energy and organic molecules occur commonly throughout the galaxy," Pam continued. "Liquid water, on the other hand, is exceedingly rare. If liquefied water does exist under Europa's icy mantel, along with organic molecules, and the sun's light or a molten core are sufficient sources of energy, then it's conceivable that life in some form could exist there."

"Show off," muttered Vickie.

Europa filled the window. Unless they swung around the moon and headed somewhere else, it seemed they would land. As the saucer approached, it changed orientation again, this time more slowly, and the window revealed Europa's horizon. They were definitely descending. This continued until, after a slight tremor, all motion ceased.

"Well, guys, we're now the first humans to land on Europa," announced Vickie. "So what the fuck do we do now?"

Simultaneously the other three yelled, "Shut up!"

A few minutes later, the floor shivered and a white vapor rose in front of the window. The vapor thickened until they couldn't see through it.

"I think I know what's happening," David whispered.

"Don't hold back, what?" said Mickey.

"Europa is covered by ice, right?"

"Right."

"I'm guessing we're melting our way down, and that's steam out there."

Nobody replied, hoping he wasn't right.

The view stayed the same for about half an hour. Occasionally the floor vibrated; otherwise, nothing else happened. Then the sensation changed to an uncomfortable rolling motion, as if they were floating on water like a bobbing cork. Fortunately it lasted only fifteen seconds before anyone became seasick. Lights shot out from the rim of the disc confirming that they were floating on water. They saw an ice ceiling above. Here and there tongues of ice projected downward from it like the underside of an iceberg. The disc navigated around the projections, heading somewhere.

"Speaking of movies, did anybody see *Titanic*?" asked Vickie.

"Stow it, Vic," said Pam.

"Do you see something?" David asked his friend.

"Maybe," replied Mickey.

"Jesus, I see it too! Some kind of structure!" exclaimed Pam.

"You're imagining things," said Vickie.

"I think Pam's right," said David.

Ahead in the foggy gloom, the lights of the disc reflected off a round bubble-like object with something inside. As the disc drew closer, they detected several similar bubbles in a cluster. Transparent horizontal and vertical tubes connected the bubbles and the structures inside them. The size of the bubbles was absolutely immense.

"Holy shit! What are those?" exclaimed David.

"I have a feeling we're about to find out!" said Pam excitedly.

The disc floated directly toward one of them, and its speed slowed.

While the bubble obviously excluded a large volume of the water around it, its surface was perfectly clear without any visible substance of its own—no wall, no sense of thickness, no internal supporting structure. The water inside appeared to be missing.

"I wonder what's keeping out the water?" David asked.

The disc coasted to a stop right before it. They were close enough to see inside it now. It was unmistakably a city, complete with thoroughfares, oddly shaped structures that were possibly buildings, and flat areas divided up by fence-like structures, the purpose of which was not apparent. Missing were any signs of life.

"That's got to be a city!" said Vickie.

"But where are the aliens?" asked Pam, straining closer to the window.

"Looks like nobody's home," said David.

"Works for me!" Vickie said gaily.

Before them, a circular section of the bubble darkened until it matched the approximate diameter and width of the disc. When this area coalesced, the disc trembled and moved forward, passing through the bubble's wall.

Once inside, the disc resumed forward motion, stopping near the tallest structure. As the disc settled to the ground, the teens' bubble helmets lifted and the substance of their pillars withdrew into the floor leaving them standing. Without her pillar for support, Pam slumped to the floor. David rushed to her side and helped her up. The teens peered out the window.

"Now what?" David asked.

"ET phone home?" Vickie replied.

A clear tube extended from the tall structure's side directly toward them. A soft thump heralded its contact with the disc. After that, a rectangular area in the wall darkened to the now familiar pewter color. No one moved.

"It's weird, but I feel like I've seen this before," whispered Pam. She shook her head, as if trying to clear it.

"Maybe in a sci-fi flick," David whispered back.

"Anybody know where Baggage Claim is?" asked Vickie. Nobody laughed.

The darker area drooped to the floor of the disc, formed a puddle, and was absorbed. In the rectangular portal left behind stood two silvery beings.

"Oh shit!" exclaimed Vickie.

"Great," said Mickey. "The human race finally makes first contact, and that's the only thing you can think of to say?"

The two aliens remained stationary. The teens stood their ground too, waiting to see what would happen next. What choice did they have? They couldn't fly the saucer back to Earth by themselves. More than that, they were becoming immune to surprises. Besides, except for getting space-sick, nothing terrible had happened.

One of the silver beings glided forward and stopped a few feet from Mickey. Its shape was roughly humanoid, but nothing else about it seemed organic. Its head was shaped like an inverted flask. That structure perched on a stalk above a still larger inverted flask. The most remarkable feature was its face, if that's what it really was, a flat screen alive with constantly shifting patterns of colored light. Both aliens stood on two appendages similar to legs, but neither had anything that looked like arms.

Mickey extended his hand.

"Jesus, what are you doing?" whispered David.

"What's it look like? I'm saying hello."

The light show on the nearer of the two aliens became even more chaotic. It moved closer to Mickey. Mickey held his ground. A thin projection began to extend from the alien's side. It stopped a scant two inches from Mickey's outstretched hand and took on the shape of a hand which then closed into a fist. Having no idea what would happen next, Mickey held steady and waited. The silvery fist edged closer, finally grazing Mickey's hand. As they touched, the kids heard a sound. While quite odd in timbre, it was unmistakably the word, "Dude."

Chapter Twenty-Seven

"I feel sick," moaned Vickie as she slumped to the floor. The second alien, who'd been standing in the doorway, moved forward with the same fluid grace and stopped close to her unconscious form. It inclined its head with lights flashing across its face. After a few seconds, it spoke with the same odd voice. "This female unit is defective." Next, it glided toward Pam. A silver projection grew from its side stopping a few inches from her chest. The lights on its face flashed faster.

Unafraid, Pam held her ground. The tip of the alien's appendage flared into the shape of a disc and held steady, pointed at Pam's legs. After another light show, it spoke again. "This female unit is also defective. Shall I begin repairs to the female units?"

The first alien had remained motionless with its arm extended toward Mickey. The pattern on its face changed, becoming uniformly yellow with a black circle in its center. Its projection flowed back into its torso and was completely absorbed. "Proceed," it replied with an identical voice.

David ran over and stood protectively in front of the girls. He held out his arms. "No!" he yelled.

The alien near the girls swiveled its head completely around and faced the alien in front of Mickey. Lights flashed across both aliens' faces. The alien near Mickey spoke again. "There is no cause for alarm. There will be no pain."

"No way, José!'" said David sounding determined. He stiffened his stance.

"There is no José unit here," said the alien. Each time it spoke, it became easier to understand. "The female units are defective. They should be repaired."

Vickie regained consciousness, scrambled to her feet, and huddled behind Pam.

"What does repaired mean?" asked Mickey.

"Make them well," replied the alien.

"You can do that?"

"Yes."

"How?"

"You would not comprehend."

"I know what you guys do!" shouted Vickie. "You abduct people and conduct weird experiments on them!"

The alien's face played with colored lights. "It would be useful if the unit known as Pam could ambulate more efficiently. There will be no pain."

Pam looked suspicious. "Wait a minute. You can help me walk again?"

"Within the City."

Her pain, the years of harassment, the parade of doctor visits, her dashed hopes and unresolved sadness all welled up. Pam found herself stepping toward the nearest alien.

"Pam, you're not thinking about…?" said David incredulously.

"We're millions of miles from earth, and the only way we're getting home is if we trust these guys. Somebody has to make the first move. Might as well be me." Pam stared at the alien. "What do I have to do?"

"Hold up your hand," it replied.

"Hold up my hand?"

The alien extended its appendage. The tip of it morphed into the shape of a hand with the palm facing up. "Like this," it said.

"What happens next?" asked Pam, warily.

"We will touch."

"That's all?"

"Then you will be repaired."

Pam glanced back at David, and then slowly held up her hand.

The alien's appendage morphed again, changing back into a long projection. There was nothing sinister about the shape, nothing that looked sharp or knife-like. A disc about the size of a nickel formed at the end. Briefly, it touched Pam's palm, and then withdrew.

Pam turned her hand around and stared at it. Then she showed it to everyone else. The alien had implanted a flat silver disc in the center of her palm. It appeared to be made of the same silver substance as the two aliens. She flexed her hand several times and scratched at the disc with her fingernail. It appeared perfectly flat, now part of her skin.

"It's like a silver sticker, but I can't remove it."

"Does it hurt?" asked David, examining it closely.

"I see it, but I can't feel it. It's like it's not even there." Pam flexed her hand again and asked the alien, "What's this thing supposed to do?"

The alien swiveled its head away, colors played across its face, then its torso flowed in the opposite direction toward the doorway. The first alien spoke again—at least that's how it seemed. Their voices were identical, so it was difficult to recognize which one spoke. "She is connected to the City now. We may leave."

"That's it?" said Pam.

"Pammie, are you all right?" asked Vickie with concern.

"Yeah." She flexed her palm a couple more times and then looked at her legs. "Wait…I'm starting to feel some strange sensations in my legs!"

David touched her shoulder. "What do you mean?"

Pam took a step. David reached over to help her, but smiling, she gently pushed his hand away. "I have dreams where I can walk again. My legs start to feel all warm and tingly…the same as I feel now!" Excited, she removed her braces. She took a few steps, beamed at everyone, and then lithely pirouetted several times like a ballerina. She finished with a curtsy and a bow.

Vickie put her hands over her mouth and gaped. "Oh my God, Pammie!"

The two silver beings glided toward the door. One of them swiveled his head completely around while maintaining its fluidic motion forward. Its face coruscated with multicolored lights. "You will come with us now. We must communicate further about the Choice."

Mickey started following them. "What choice, silver Dude?"

"First you will observe," replied the alien. It swiveled its head back toward the direction its torso moved with no further comment.

Mickey turned to face his friends. Pam stood tall and steady. Vickie's eyes brimmed with tears.

After a glance at Pam, David walked confidently toward the doorway. "Okay, let's go," he said.

"Works for me," said Pam, smiling. With a bounce to her step, she caught up with David and took his hand. They laughed and skipped through the doorway, two carefree children at a Sunday picnic.

As they approached the end of the tube, the wall before them darkened and flowed into the floor leaving a round opening. The two aliens moved through without slowing their fluidic stride. The teens followed right behind, and they entered a cavernous room with a ceiling that soared hundreds of feet into the air, something like the atrium inside an expensive hotel. Adding to that impression were several striking fountains scattered about. Crystal clear water sprayed outward from the center of each which then cascaded downward in a spherical pattern as though constrained by an unseen bubble. Several more silver aliens stood motionless in the room. Their faces seemed alive, which is to say that the flat panels of their heads were all lit, but each displayed the same unchanging pattern—a pale blue background with a black circle at its center. It might have been a room full of televisions all stuck on the same channel.

"Somebody should change stations," said David as they walked by a motionless pair.

In their transit across the open area, the two aliens made no effort to interact with their inert comrades.

Mickey stopped next to one and stared at it. “Hello?” he said. He rapped on the top of the alien’s head with his hand. “Anybody home?”

“Kind of crude, don’t you think?” remarked Vickie, standing next to him.

One of their pair of aliens swiveled its head around and said, “They will not respond.”

“Why not?” asked Vickie.

“All questions will be answered.”

“When?” asked Mickey.

The alien swiveled its head forward and didn’t reply.

Pam kept dancing ahead. “The other aliens aren’t paying any attention to us,” she said to David when he caught up to her.

“Maybe we aren’t very interesting,” he whispered back.

Mickey remembered the dead saucers on the Moon. “Or maybe they’ve seen aliens like us before.”

“Pretty eerie,” said Vickie, sidling closer to him.

A section of the far wall morphed and flowed into the floor. Still moving forward, the lead alien’s head swiveled back with yellow and red lights playing across its face.

Pam stopped walking and put her hands to her ears. “Did you hear that?”

Vickie looked puzzled. “Hear what?”

“It was in my head! I heard it say something in my head!” Pam searched the faces of the others. “You didn’t hear it?”

The alien responded, “She is connected to the City.” It swiveled its head back around, and with its companion, disappeared through the doorway.

Mickey looked at Pam. “I didn’t hear anything. What did it say?”

“It said I will have rest and nourishment. I heard it clear as day!”

Mickey stared at her with a blank expression.

Pam frowned. "You guys didn't hear anything, did you?"

"Nope," said David. "Did it say what's for dinner?"

They entered a smaller chamber with six silver pedestals positioned around its periphery. In the center hovered a large silver sphere six feet in diameter without any visible support.

After putting on a brief light show, one of the aliens projected its monotone voice. "It would be efficient if the units known as Michael, David, and Victoria received their connections to the City." It extended a silver appendage with a small silver disc on the end toward Vickie.

Pam touched Vickie's shoulder. "It's okay. Let him touch you." She nudged Vickie toward the alien.

"Are you sure?"

Pam smiled and winked at her.

Vickie held up her hand, palm forward, and scrunched her eyes closed. The alien's appendage grew in length, touched her, and then withdrew. Vickie quickly pulled back her hand and rejoined Pam. She opened her palm and saw a silver disc in the center, just like Pam's.

Vickie smiled and touched her ear. "I can hear them too! It's as if I'm wearing ear buds."

Next Mickey stepped forward. When he did, another silver disc formed on the silver being's appendage. Mickey allowed it to touch his palm. Soon after, David did the same.

Lights flashed across the alien's face, and each of the teens heard a voice in their heads. "In order to complete the diagnostics, you must stand next to one of the City ports. Then you will rest." The teens heard the alien individually address them by their first name.

"How do you know our names?" asked Mickey.

"Stand next to one of the City ports," the alien repeated.

Mickey moved to the nearest silver pillar. "This is a port?" It looked no different than the chairs in the saucer. "If it is, we know the drill." He leaned against the pillar, and it began to enfold and encase him with a clear bubble over his head. Mickey grinned at his friends. The couch then reclined and pivoted to face a globe at the room's center. The globe's surface, a bright red, rhythmically changed in intensity while it spun with increasing speed.

"Disco!" said Mickey, smiling.

"What is disco?" asked the alien voice in his head.

"You know, dancing, the 70s, John Travolta?"

Lights flashed furiously across the being's face, but it said nothing further.

Following Mickey's lead, the three others soon reclined in front of the spinning red globe. Simultaneously the couches attached themselves to the silver dots on the teens' palms, immobilizing their hands. A surge of warmth began to suffuse their bodies emanating from the discs. It was a thoroughly pleasant sensation, like waking up in the morning on a warm summer day with the window open. They heard the voice in their bubbles. "Do not be alarmed. The diagnostics will now commence."

Mickey noticed a tingling sensation spreading from his hand up to his head, then down to his feet. He could sense the blood moving through his arteries and feel the muscles of his back and legs rhythmically contract. He felt more aware than he could ever remember, as if he could see without his eyes and sense his surroundings in other ways. After this strange surge of awareness, he started feeling adrift in a warm sea of drowsiness. Soon he fell asleep and began dreaming. Strange colored images cavalcaded across his slumbering vision—alien vistas replete with unfamiliar sounds and odd smells. Then he awoke.

Mickey opened his eyes, alert, and remarkably refreshed. The bubble withdrew from his head and the couch tilted so he faced the hovering globe. This happened to the other teens who also felt refreshed and calm. Vickie smiled at Mickey in a way that made him feel warm inside.

The two aliens positioned themselves on each side of the globe facing the teenagers with their torsos flush with the floor. The heads of the aliens swiveled to face each other with colorful flashing lights. The teens then heard the familiar monotone voice in their heads.

"Repairs to the organic units have been completed. The spinal support of the Pamela unit has been strengthened. This will be adequate for locomotion while she is in contact with the City field. The ocular organs of the David unit have been realigned. External lenses are no longer required. The Michael unit arrived intact and required no repairs. His metabolism has been adjusted to more efficiently process nutrients. We detected oxidized organic residue within the respiratory organs of the Victoria unit. The contaminants have been removed. We have not detected similar toxic residue within the respiratory organs of the other organic units. The reason for this disparity is not yet clear."

"Okay. I get it. I won't smoke anymore." Vickie sounded contrite.

"I feel positively great! I'm not hungry either," said David.

"What happened? How long did we sleep?" It was Mickey speaking.

"You have been inactivated for five of your Earth minutes, Mickey unit. During that time you received a complete diagnostic, nourishment for one cycle, and a reset of your neural processor. Your species refers to this organic function as sleep."

One of the aliens moved closer to Pam. "Permanent reconstruction of the Pamela unit's spinal support cannot be completed at this time." It paused for a second. "We are…sorry." It swiveled its head to face her directly. "The energy grid will provide support for adequate locomotion within the City. Please enjoy your stay." It glided toward the center of the room.

The faces of the aliens displayed an absolute chaos of lights without any discernible pattern. This abruptly stopped and the voice continued. "We will speak of the Test and of the Choice. When this task is completed, you will be returned to your sphere."

"Our sphere?" said Mickey.

"You call it Earth."

Chapter Twenty-Eight

The surface of the globe blossomed with light, and then resolved into a moving picture. It reminded Mickey and David of the saucers on the Moon. They could see a city with the similar buildings and interconnecting tubes as they were in now. However, numerous silver aliens were moving about with faces alive with color, light, and differing patterns.

The voice resumed. "Cycles in the past, the organic process you call life developed in the waters of this sphere which your species calls Europa. When the organic units that evolved from that life developed the ability to live outside the fluid, they constructed living places to live on dry land. As their evolution progressed, they developed the ability to travel beyond Europa, to gather knowledge from distant spheres. This became their passion, being explorers."

"Where are those guys now?" asked David.

The voice continued. "The sole limitation to their ability to travel the stars was their organic bodies. They put them aside and adopted a form not constrained by time."

"Put them aside?" said Mickey.

"They became what you see now—us."

The teens looked stunned.

"My God!" exclaimed Pam.

"You're not robots?" asked David.

"What are you?" demanded Vickie.

"Non-organic beings."

"You're cyborgs!" exclaimed Mickey.

"What's a cyborg?" Vickie asked Mickey.

"Half man, half machine, like *The Six Million Dollar Man* on TV," answered David.

"We were once such beings, but no longer. We completed our evolution to a nonorganic form. We became immortal."

"Why would you do such a thing to yourselves?" Pam sounded horrified.

"Our new forms allowed us to travel the distances between star systems unfettered by time."

"What does that mean?" Pam asked.

"I think I understand," said David. "It would take thousands of years traveling at less than the speed of light to reach even the nearest galaxy, Andromeda. Flesh and blood beings can't live long enough to see the end of the journey." He turned to the alien. "Is that why you did it?"

The alien moved closer to David, studying him with a furious light show on its face. "Yes."

"And you've been testing us?" asked Mickey.

"It was necessary."

"Why?"

"After eons of travel throughout the universe we have learned to completely control matter and energy. With that knowledge, we created the City to supply our needs. Unfortunately, we failed to understand the fundamental property of all life, the process of evolution." The voice paused and the picture on the sphere melted away. "We failed to understand that the inevitable result of our achievement of physical perfection would be our extinction. That, Mickey unit, is why we have administered the Test."

"You keep referring to a test? What is it?" asked Pam.

"And what does it have to do with us?" said Vickie.

"One of our vehicles has been observing your species."

"Is that how you knew our names?" asked Mickey.

"Yes. The time had come to administer the Test again."

"You've done this before?" asked Mickey.

"What's the friggin' *Test*?" asked Vickie.

"Hang on there," interrupted Mickey. "Okay, alien Dude, time to come clean about this Test you've been putting David and me through."

"Not just David and you, Mickey unit, all four of you," the alien corrected.

Pam shook her head. "I'm so confused."

The second alien's face came alive again. Their heads swiveled to face each other and began flashing back and forth similar patterns. The voice continued. "Diversity must be maintained. Without it, extinction is inevitable. Physical perfection must be avoided. Evolution must not be allowed to stop. Connected to the power of the City, our thoughts alone were sufficient to provide everything we wanted. When there was nothing left to want, there was no reason for us to be. That is why you were brought here."

"Which tells us what?" asked David.

The silver globe activated again and a new scene appeared. They saw a smooth sphere with a lacework of lines on it. It was Europa. From its surface, or perhaps from inside it, silver saucers shot into space in multiple directions.

"For a number of cycles, we carried on as we had before, but then, members of our civilization began deactivating."

"They died?" asked Vickie.

"We cannot die."

"Got sick?" asked David.

"We cannot become defective, David unit. We cannot suffer the same material demise as an organic being. We are constructed differently. Our forms will remain until this universe has ended."

"What do we have to do to return home?" Vickie sounded scared.

Both aliens swiveled their heads to face her. They displayed the same blue face with a black circle in its center. "Our race must reacquire uncertainty. We require...*Dude*."

"What did you say?" asked Mickey.

"Dude."

"I hear you, but what do you mean...*Dude*?"

The two beings communicated through light patterns. The teens neither heard nor sensed their discussion. Afterwards both aliens swiveled to face Mickey.

"To stop the extinction of our race, we must reacquire two things: First, we require uncertainty. We need new problems to solve. For a time, our entire purpose was to explore the universe, to amass knowledge and learn all that we could. Eventually we learned that everything in the universe is the same in function, if not in form; further travel for its own sake became illogical. We returned here and occupied ourselves with problems only of thought. For several cycles we busied ourselves calculating what you call Pi, but then found the answer. Other mathematical puzzles proved unsatisfying. The answer was to acquire the company of unpredictable organics, beings constantly offering new problems to solve—to become their mentors."

"You're saying you need a project, because you already know everything?" asked Mickey.

"Yes."

"You need some reason to be alive!" Pam exclaimed.

"Dude is what we need. Dude is better than Pi. Dude does not compute. Your species has discovered Dude. Your species has perfected imperfection."

"Because we're both creative and unpredictable, because we can talk Dude and science at the same time, we have what you need?" asked Pam.

"Yes."

"I find it impossible to believe that, in the whole universe, we're the only species that isn't perfect," David said.

"Many sentient organic species in the galaxy are unpredictable, although none more so than yours, but only your species has passed the Test."

"You still haven't told us what the Test is! I want to go home!" Vickie sobbed.

Mickey reached to comfort her. "You can't drag us millions of miles from home and not tell us why!"

"You mentioned two factors of importance, and being dumb is just one of them," prompted David.

"Not dumb, as you define it, David unit. Your species is guided by purpose, but is infinitely unpredictable in its choice of strategy to achieve that purpose."

"All right, '*unpredictable*' —but there's something else that's important to you, besides being unpredictable. Does it have something to do with the saucers we found on our Moon?"

Two silver heads swiveled to face each other. Their light show went into high gear, and then both faced David. "The neural diagnostic failed to accurately compute your processor capabilities, David unit. You are most unpredictable."

"Just tell us about the saucers on the Moon," said Mickey impatiently.

One of the aliens swiveled its head to face Mickey. The other remained fixed on David. "When we computed the solution to the problem, saucers were sent throughout the galaxy to locate sentient organic species to repopulate Europa."

Vickie's face turned ashen.

"You found a few, didn't you? We saw some of the saucers on our Moon," said Mickey.

"There are numerous sentient organic species in star systems throughout the galaxy. All that are required for such evolution are energy, organic molecules, and liquid water, such as on Europa, Earth, and Mars in this system."

"There's life on Mars?" David blurted.

The alien ignored his question. "We brought back members of several species to attempt repopulation, but realized our calculations had been flawed. Sentience is not enough. We require a second trait, and that trait is rare. The equations that describe this trait are precise, but it is difficult to find a word in the database that is equally precise. We calculate with ninety percent confidence that the word '*benevolence*' is accurate." The voice paused for a second. "The power of the City could not be efficiently managed by the species that we brought here because they lacked…benevolence."

The whirling globe blazed again with the familiar image of a building's atrium, perhaps the one they just transited. Sudden flashes of light erupted on the screen. One of the fountains exploded releasing a geyser of water. Through the curtain of water, a running humanoid emerged. It took several strides closer to the screen and disappeared in another blinding light. The globe dimmed to a uniform black for a few seconds, as if trying to recover, and the image reformed with no sign of the humanoid. Then the screen went completely black.

"What just happened?" asked Vickie. She sounded ill.

Lights flashed across one of the alien's faces. "We failed to account for a fundamental property of organic life. Organics must consume more organic material in order to grow and multiply. This is accomplished by gathering, or by consuming other organics. It requires less energy to consume than to gather. If one organic being acquires the power to be stronger than another, it will find it more efficient to consume the weaker."

"When you brought other species here and connected them to the power of the City, they misused it," David said.

"You are correct, David unit. We have conducted this experiment forty-two times with identical results. After sentient organics acquire the power of the City, they inevitably turn the power against each other until there is only one individual remaining. This behavior is not suitable to repopulate."

"Repopulate?" asked Pam. She glanced at Mickey.

"You kidnapped them to breed, didn't you?" said Vickie. Her lips trembled. "Is that what you're planning to do with us?" She buried her head in Mickey's shoulder.

"We learned that organic sentience, which is inherently unpredictable, is not enough. We require a species with the trait of benevolence. We calculated with an eighty-three percent probability that there is at least one species in the galaxy with this trait. To find that species, we devised the Test."

One of the aliens moved near David. Yellow lights flashed rapidly across its face.

"With limited time remaining," continued the voice, "saucers were sent to many star systems seeking organic species suitable to administer the Test."

"The Test for benevolence?" asked Pam.

"Because the location of your sphere is proximate to the City, the Test was administered to your species twelve thousand of your orbital cycles ago, and again at six thousand cycles. The results were unsatisfactory."

"What does unsatisfactory mean?" asked Mickey.

"Your species was immature. Several of your cultures exposed to our presence devolved into superstition and worshipped us as gods."

"So you waited and tried it again…on me," said Mickey.

"Yes."

"How do you test for benevolence?" asked David.

The alien swiveled its head to face David and paused before speaking. "The saucer does not interact with the organic species, or the environment, until it detects a single organic unit suitable for the Test. When such a unit is identified, it is given a small sample of our power. This is done with limitations. We cannot allow the unit to use the power to establish a hierarchy. The results of the Test are monitored. That is the Test."

"It's the suit!" Mickey blurted out. "That's the power you're talking about!"

"The suit, as you call it, when applied to the body of an organic allows that unit to experience a small measure of this City's power. If that unit chooses to use the power with benevolence and does not seek to establish a hierarchy over other units, then a mating pair of units from that species will be given the Choice to live here and rebuild our organic population."

"So the *choice* means they can decide to live here or not, but they don't have to?" asked Vickie.

Mickey tensed. "I'm the dude who passed the Test, so I'm the one who has to decide—right?" He turned to his friends. "Why would I do it? I mean, leave my family…" His voice trailed off.

"Because of the gifts," said the alien.

"Jesus, now what!" exclaimed Vickie. "A Test, a Choice, and now a deal? Okay, here's my choice. Send me home!"

"Hang on there," said Pam. She looked down at her legs. "What do you guys mean by gifts?"

"If the mating pair chooses to return to Europa and rebuild our organic civilization, the pair will be provided with a carefree life and certain enhancements. In return, Earth will be given knowledge that would require at least one hundred additional cycles to acquire, provided the biosphere can survive your specie's current mismanagement, which is unlikely. "

"Such as?" David asked.

"A source of limitless clean energy, the cure for many diseases, an end to famine."

The teenagers took a collective deep breath.

"You said the two 'units' who remain here will receive enhancements and a carefree life. What did you mean?" asked Vickie.

"You will follow me now," said the alien moving toward a portal that had appeared in the far wall.

"Where are we going?"

"To the garden," replied the Europan.

Chapter Twenty-Nine

They entered a completely empty large bubble. One Europan had remained behind. Unlike the other chambers, this one had an opaque round ceiling. The place had the feel of an auditorium after the show was over, but without any empty popcorn containers on the floor or discarded theater tickets lying around. After they entered, the portal closed behind them. The Europan moved to the center of the chamber and the teens gathered around.

"Where's the other guy?" asked Mickey.

"It is no longer active," replied the Europan.

"Where's the garden?" asked Vickie. "This place is empty."

"As is the universe," said the alien. It extended its appendage upwards and a blinking dot of golden light appeared at the tip. The chamber plunged into total darkness. Mickey felt Vickie's trembling hand grab his. "What's happening?" she moaned.

"Behold," boomed the alien's voice, which echoed about them. They could see the single point of golden light burning in the air. It was difficult to remain standing, so intense was their disorientation. They were in a void with no up or down. Mickey sensed he was losing his equilibrium and steadied himself by widening his stance. At least he could feel the floor beneath his feet. He dropped his arm around Vickie's waist to steady her and felt her move into his arms. He felt the wetness of her tears.

The point of golden light exploded without a sound, filling the chamber with blinding light. The experience, however brief, was terrifying, like being trapped in a fire except there wasn't any heat.

"What was that!" yelled Mickey.

"What's going on!" shouted Pam.

Within seconds, the blazing light in the chamber began to coalesce. Islands of greater density appeared as clumps of light surrounded by blackness. One of the clumps expanded in size, and the teens realized their perspective was like peering through a microscope—they were zooming in closer.

"I think I understand," said David.

"The Big Bang," whispered back Pam.

The island of golden light shot toward them at incredible speed. Reflexively, Mickey turned away, but then turned back again, forcing himself to look. Soon, the golden light surrounded them, a cloud of scintillating luminescence that moved through their bodies as if they had no substance. As the teens peered closer, if that's what they were doing, the golden light's substance dispersed into a fog, and then into a canopy of starry lights. The sequence ended when the lights collapsed into a single point and disappeared leaving them in darkness again.

"In the beginning," continued the alien voice, "the matter in the universe consisted of what you call hydrogen atoms, one proton surrounded by a shell containing one electron." The point of light reappeared and positioned itself in the chamber's center. Around the wall of the chamber, a shadow raced around them; sometimes they could see it, and then it would wink out. Mickey tried to make sense of the shadow's movement, but couldn't.

"The matter of the universe is predominantly hollow," continued the Europan. "In terms that your neural processors can understand, the volume of a hydrogen atom is 99.999999999 percent empty. The kernel of matter within it, the nucleon, is infinitesimal in proportion to the size of the atom's structure. The substance of the atom is an electrostatic field, nothing more. To use your words, the atom is "empty." The matter of the universe that makes up your reality is comprised of atoms. Therefore, the universe is empty, as is this chamber."

The single point of light representing the proton of a hydrogen atom retracted until it was smaller and surrounded by a spherical haze. As seconds passed, more appeared until a lattice of hydrogen atoms dancing in place surrounded them. Collisions between them occurred, each causing a brief blinding flare of light, and the complexity of the lattice grew. Some atoms now contained two nucleons, and their hazy shells seemed denser.

"Helium atoms are forming," said David.

"Fusion," added Mickey.

Collisions continued, and the complexity of the atoms increased.

"The periodic table finally makes sense," whispered Vickie. Mickey squeezed her hand.

The atoms retracted again—the latticework became smaller and smaller, until nothing but a black void surrounded them with points of light.

"The universe contains little substance," said the alien voice, "yet to us, it exists." Their field of view, their virtual microscope, continued reducing its magnification at a dizzying speed, until a familiar blue orb hovered before their eyes. It was Earth. "What is real?" repeated the Europan. "The answer is our sensory inputs."

The light turned on, and they were standing again in the empty chamber with the opaque ceiling.

"That was interesting," remarked Pam, "but what was the point?"

"Yeah," said Mickey, "we're still waiting to see the garden. Why would anybody want to stay in a place like this? There's nothing here."

"Do you hear something?" asked Vickie.

"I hear it," said David. "It sounds like a bird's chirping."

"A mockingbird," noted Pam. "I could hear them from my bedroom window when I was growing up…makes me think about home." She fought back tears.

"Do you feel that?" asked Mickey. "I just felt a breeze."

"Somebody turned on a fan," said David.

"No, it's more than that," said Vickie. "I smell something…I can taste it too. It's salty, like being near the ocean."

They could hear the crashing of waves and feel the wind on

their faces, yet they were still standing in the empty chamber. The shrill cry of sea gulls replaced the mockingbird's song.

"It's a nice trick, but so what?" said Mickey.

"Whoa!" exclaimed Vickie. Now they were standing in sand that definitely hadn't been there moments earlier.

"What is real?" repeated the Europan.

They could hear the sound of crashing waves, feel the wind buffeting their bodies, and taste the salty spray peppering their eyes. Then the ceiling vanished. Suspended above their heads, the Europan sea roiled with miles of angry water whipped into whirlpools the size of cities without visible barriers holding it back.

As the maelstrom of sight, sound, smell and taste grew, Vickie dropped to the sand and covered her head. "Make it stop!" she screamed. Mickey crouched beside her, gathered her into an embrace and stared up at the ceiling, waiting for the waters to crash and drown them. David and Pam stood holding hands, their hair whipped about by the wind. David looked defiantly at the silver alien. Pam closed her eyes and smiled.

It ended and they were in the silent empty chamber again. Before the teens could react, the floor beneath their feet morphed to soft grass. The opaque canopy changed to a blue sky dappled with white fluffy clouds. Flowers and trees appeared, along with a waterfall and the scent of honeysuckle on a gentle breeze.

"What is real?" repeated the alien as it moved toward an open portal on the horizon.

"Wait!" yelled Vickie.

The alien's head swiveled around to face her while its torso continued moving. "For what purpose?"

"You can't stuff a couple of kids in this fishbowl and expect them to play virtual reality games all the time and be happy! Kids need to stay connected! We need to text. I have two thousand friends on Facebook. I need to keep up with them. That's a full time job!"

"That is what cell phones are for," the alien said.

"You don't want to actually talk to anybody."

The alien's face turned a uniform grey. "What form of technology do you employ for more urgent communication?"

"We tweet."

"You mimic birds? This is a custom we are not aware of." Lights flashed furiously over its face as it consulted its Earth database.

"Tweeting is a form of communication, like emails," said Vickie, shrugging. "You want everybody to know what you're doing as fast as possible."

"But not speak to them with your voice?" asked the alien.

"Right."

"Why?"

Vickie looked at Pam with a perplexed expression. "You explain it to him."

The alien interrupted. "We will study this avian technology and adapt it to our systems." It stopped its forward motion and turned its head to face the area of the wall next to the portal. A rectangular shape changed to the now familiar pewter color, and then changed into the semblance of a large video screen. The screen momentarily displayed a field of jagged lines, and then an imaged resolved with a bizarre scene of unfamiliar-looking animals. They had legs and sort of a head, but no neck, and their torsos had divided segments like a caterpillar. The teens heard an odd keening sound. Then something like a bird, or maybe it was a machine, swooped down toward the animals that scampered away. Right afterward, an alien face moved to the center of the screen and waved its tentacles. "Wrong channel," said the Europan, and the image on the screen changed to Monday Night Football.

"Fourth and forever from the three yard line," said the frantic announcer. "Not even Joe Montana could get out of this one, folks!"

The alien's head tilted toward the teens. "We have observed a custom amongst your people of naming individuals for their place of origin—Joe Montana, Dakota Fanning, Paris Hilton, to name a few. This does not occur on Europa."

"Why not?" asked Mickey.

"We would all be named Europa. Numbers are more efficient."

"I see," replied Mickey. He poked David in the ribs.

"TV is cool, but it's not enough if you're still by yourself," said Pam. Vickie nodded in agreement.

"You may place calls without restrictions," said the alien.

"You mean like a phone call?" asked Mickey.

"To where?" David asked.

"Anywhere with sentient life advanced enough to have communication capabilities," replied the alien.

"Anywhere?" said Vickie, dumbfounded.

"The universal translator is efficient, but the world view of organic races in other star systems may differ significantly from what you are accustomed to. Caution is advised to avoid…headaches."

"We can call Earth from here?" asked David.

"Observe," replied the alien. It spoke a series of numbers, the screen went blank, they heard the unmistakable sound of a phone ringing, and then…"

"Domino's Pizza. Lay it on me," answered a male voice.

The kids' faces broke into smiles.

"Lay what on you?" replied the alien with a New Jersey accent.

The man at Domino's Pizza hesitated. "What a minute! Melvin, is that you?"

"My designation is not Melvin."

"That's enough crank calling, Melvin! I know your mother, buddy boy!"

"I would like to order a large pepperoni pizza," stated the alien.

"But you don't eat!" shouted Vickie.

The alien spoke to the teenagers in their heads. "I am demonstrating our telephone capability."

The man's voice on the phone sounded wary. "Okay, if you're not my deadbeat nephew Melvin, where are you calling from?"

"Europa."

"We don't deliver past 23rd Street!" The line went dead.

"You can call anywhere you want on that, wherever it is?" asked Vickie.

"Correct. Unlimited calling, anywhere, anytime—a one million G network. "

"Very cool!" said Vickie. "What about email?'

"Observe," said the alien.

The video screen changed to the home page for AOL, and then the email login page appeared. The user name box filled in with vickiesastar.

"Vickie's a star?" said Pam, gawking at her friend. "Jeez Louise, Vic!"

Vickie's cheeks turned beet red, but before she could reply, the password box began filling in.

"Hey!" exclaimed Vickie. "How'd you get my password?"

"The number of permutations containing references unique to you, Vickie unit, is quite limited."

Before Vickie could respond, they heard the familiar "You've got mail," and Vickie's inbox appeared. It reported two hundred and twelve new messages.

"Two hundred and twelve messages in one day?" said Mickey incredulously.

Vickie cocked an eyebrow. "I have a lot of friends."

Chapter Thirty

Mickey turned to the Europan and frowned. "What if we get tired of being cooped up in this *Star Trek* holodeck, even with phone service and email?"

The Europan moved toward the portal. As it did, the video screen dissolved into the wall. "Follow me," the teens heard in their heads.

"Now where?" asked Mickey.

"In your frame of reference, it would be called a marina," replied the alien.

Mickey and David stared at each other. "What?" they exclaimed simultaneously.

They entered a small spherical chamber with several machines resting on cradles. The chamber's transparent walls and the sea of Europa encircled them, as though they were fish in a bowl.

Mickey walked up to one of the machines. It resembled a jet ski. "What's this thing?"

"The database indicates an acceptable descriptive name would be…an Aquaski," replied the alien.

"You can't jet ski under water," scoffed Vickie.

"You stated your belief that there would be insufficient opportunities to create neural stimulation after exhausting the possibilities of the holographic world. This is not correct."

"You will explain," requested David.

"You're sounding like the silver dude," whispered Pam behind her hand. He smiled.

"Those remaining here would not be confined to the City. There is a world to explore," replied the alien.

"It's under water," said Mickey.

"Sit on the saddle of the Aquaski, Mickey unit."

Mickey obliged, and soon a silver bubble suit flowed up from one of the Aquaski's seats and covered him. He grabbed the handlebars. "Cool. What do I do now?"

"Engage the thruster by depressing the throttle."

"I'll hit the wall!"

"Engage the thruster," repeated the alien.

Mickey shrugged. "If you say so." He depressed the throttle and the Aquaski shot through the habitat's wall into the Europan sea. The teens could see him floating outside and could clearly hear his voice. "Wow!" he exclaimed. He engaged the machine's thruster and somersaulted in wider and wider arcs. "Hooeey!" he yelled. "This is seriously fun!"

A light beam shot out from the Aquaski's cradle, touched the ski, and then reeled it back through the wall.

"Hey!" yelled Mickey. "I was just getting started!"

With the Aquaski nestled in its cradle, the bubble suit dissolved away from Mickey.

"There is insufficient time, Mickey unit. You must soon be returned to your sphere."

Mickey gazed through the wall at the churning currents of the Europan sea. "What's out there besides water and ice?"

"The world that gave birth to my race. You would not be…disappointed." The Europan began moving away.

"We're still not convinced," called out David. Pam look surprised.

The Europan stopped. They heard it say, "Explain," in their heads.

"Don't get me wrong," David continued, "intergalactic phone calls and email, the holographic room and water toys are all seriously cool, but they're not real enough for me."

The Europan swiveled its head with its usual light show. "Continue," it said.

David looked to Pam for help. She smiled at him and nodded. "I think I can explain," she said. "When I want a lemon, I don't care how real it looks or smells. If it's an illusion of force fields with a chemical odor, it's not real to me."

"All atoms are 99.999999999 percent force fields, therefore, so are lemons."

"No! You're not getting it. When I hold a lemon in my hand, I want it to have germinated from a seed in the ground that became a tree, and then the tree sprouted lemons that ripened and fell to the ground. It's not the same as my saying 'poof' and having a lemon magically materialize in my hand!"

"Poof?" said the alien.

"Never mind poof! A real lemon has a history, a life of its own. It's real! Don't you get it?" Pam searched the faces of her friends, silently begging for support.

"She means an object isn't real unless it exists in all four dimensions," said David.

Vickie stared at Mickey. "What did he say?"

"The fourth dimension is time," said Mickey. "Something that just pops into existence doesn't go back in time. Pam needs that dimension for it to be real."

Vickie nodded. "Okay, I get it."

"How many lemon trees would you like?" asked the alien.

"Forget the holo-room or whatever clever descriptor you've come up with," said Pam. "It's not real."

"Follow me," said the alien, and it started moving again.

"Are we going home now?" asked Vickie.

"There is one more thing to see," replied the alien.

They entered another empty bubble, this one much smaller than the holo-room, and with transparent walls. Once again, the Europan stopped in its center. After his display flashed a few times, a container budded from the substance of the floor. This container, about the size of a car, held rich brown soil.

"Another trick?" said Pam, sounding impatient.

"It was collected on your world, along with a library of flora and fauna…including lemons. Whoever agrees to live on Europa can plant the seeds in this room and have four dimensional lemons."

"One lemon tree in this little bubble of yours ain't gonna cut it for me," said David.

The alien's face flashed furiously with a myriad of colors. Then the bubble they were standing in began expanding. The walls shot away from them at a dizzying speed until they stood in a vast chamber, so enormous the sea seemed miles away.

"Holy guacamole!" exclaimed Mickey. "How big is this place now?"

"Several of your earth miles, Mickey unit. How many lemon tree seeds do you wish to plant in this space, Pam unit?"

Pam seemed flustered. "How much real dirt do you have? How many seeds? You need sunlight and water!"

"Real dirt, as you call it, can be replicated from raw materials in the planetary core. It is a simple process. Seeds can be replicated by using synthesized DNA, or from original matter gathered on your planet. Water is all around us." A hole appeared in the bubble's wall close to them and a trickle of water flowed down creating a puddle.

"It can't be salt water," cautioned Pam.

"The water is filtered as it passes through the force field. It is appropriate. You may taste it."

David allowed some of the water to fill his cupped hand and tasted it. He smiled. "Tastes like the High Sierras."

"What about sunlight?" Vickie asked. "We're a long way from the sun, and we're under the ice."

Another light show erupted across the alien's face. Soon after, a glowing orb appeared high above. It cast a pale yellow light and permeated the air with a clean, fresh fragrance. "The light source you require," said the alien.

"What about animals?" David asked.

"We have collected a complete library of DNA spanning your entire geological period. We can clone whichever animal species you desire."

"Even something that's extinct?" said Mickey, "such as a

dinosaur?"

"Yes."

"Charming," said Vickie, "a T. Rex stomping down all the lemon trees to make lemonade."

"This place could make a serious amount of lemonade," said Mickey looking around.

The alien started once more toward the portal. "We will leave now, unless there is something more you require."

"You have an answer for everything, don't you?" said David.

There was a flash of lights across its console. "Yes."

Chapter Thirty-One

They returned to the chamber with the disco video ball and the other, now inactive Europan.

"How many times have you administered the Test, the one for benevolence?" asked David.

"The Test has been administered forty-three times. You are the first species from any planet to pass."

"Way to go, Mickey!" exclaimed David. "Remember all the dead saucers on the Moon?"

"Of course."

"Those were from the species who flunked the test." David turned to the silver alien. "Weren't they?"

"That is correct, David unit."

Mickey stood straighter. "Why are all those dead saucers parked there and not someplace else?"

"There is one more variable within the equation of the Test. That variable is time. The inactivation of my species is proceeding at a logarithmic rate. Ten Earth days remain before the process is complete. There is insufficient time remaining to send more saucers to other organic civilizations. Earth is…the last stop."

"Why can't somebody switch you all on again?" asked Mickey.

"One of our kind must remain active to initiate the process." The alien swiveled its head to face the second alien, but its fellow now displayed the same lifeless pattern as the other inactive aliens. "The extinction of our species is not yet certain. There is an eight percent chance of sufficient time remaining to repopulate Europa with organics from your sphere. Only the Choice remains."

"You hope two of us will choose to live here?" asked Pam.

"One aspect of your species' unpredictability is the concept of hope. Hope is illogical. Hope does not compute. I have tried to incorporate hope into my equations. I cannot."

The alien began moving toward the door. "You will be sent home now. In ten of your sphere's rotations, the saucer will return. Then the Choice must be made."

"You want two of us to return here with the saucer in ten days?" asked David. He shook his head in disbelief. "That's not much time to make such an important decision."

"Ten Earth days," repeated the alien.

"What if nobody wants to?" Vickie said, sounding desperate.

"This civilization will end. Without our technology, perhaps yours as well." The alien swiveled its head to face the opposite direction and moved through the doorway. They heard its voice one more time. "You will be returned to your sphere now."

David raced after the alien. "Wait!" he shouted. "I'm not buying it."

"The City will provide your every desire, David unit. Money is irrelevant."

"David's right," said Pam. "Your plan won't work."

"Explain," said the silver alien.

"You can't repopulate with a single male and female breeding pair," she replied. "There's not enough genetic material to support a stable population. Adam and Eve are a myth."

"Incorrect," replied the Europan. "A maternal ancestor to all living humans lived two hundred thousand Earth years ago."

"Mitochondrial Eve," said Vickie. "We learned about her in science."

"Who?" Mickey asked.

"The DNA in our mitochondria is passed down through our mothers. They traced it back to one woman who lived around two hundred thousand years ago."

"Doesn't matter," said Pam. "You still need at least forty breeding pairs to repopulate, given the normal mutation rate."

"How did you know that?" asked David.

She shrugged. "When you can't hop, skip and jump, you read."

"You are incorrect, Pamela unit. You make assumptions that are not valid here."

"Now you can explain," Pam replied.

"All necessary genetic diversity is synthesized. All necessary mutations can be engineered. There is no nucleotide degradation within the City. One complete genome from each sex is enough to create the necessary genetic material."

"I thought mutations occur naturally, and at a steady rate."

"On Earth, mutations are variations in the genetic code that occur through damage. There is no damage here."

"Why not?"

"Your species calls them nannites. Microscopic machines that float around in the blood and repair things."

Mickey faced the Europan. "You have stuff like that? I mean, what do you need it for? You guys are machines."

"There was a time when we were both, Mickey unit. We used such devices to extend the life of our organic forms. Each of you has them in your bodies now."

"What!" yelled Vickie. "You injected me with microscopic machines!" She frantically shook her hands. "Get them out of me!"

"That is how we made repairs to your bodies, Victoria unit. You will remain healthy now."

"For how long?" David asked.

"The estimate is two hundred of your Earth years," replied the alien.

"Jesus!" said Vickie.

"Still want to give the little guys back?" asked Mickey.

"Well…"

"Wait a minute," said David. "You said 'create' a minute ago. Are you talking about cloning, like growing babies in vats?"

"A combination of natural biological processes and nucleotide optimization will be sufficient. There will be no mass production of organic units."

"But if you let good ole Mother Nature set the pace, even with genetic jiggling, won't it still take forever to reach a population of any substantive size?"

"Assuming a reproductive age of twelve earth years to seventy, and twenty children per female, it would only take one hundred earth years to achieve a population of one thousand individuals."

"Twenty brats for each woman? Are you kidding?" exclaimed Vickie. "Might as well be rabbits!"

"Wait a minute," said Mickey. "Time isn't irrelevant. There's only one of you guys left with any juice. You said Earth is the last stop."

David glanced at Mickey. "He's right. You're holding out on us."

"I fail to comprehend."

"You want something else, and I figured out what it is," said David.

"Explain."

"You can't feel anymore! That's what this is really about. You're trying to be alive through us."

Mickey looked startled. "What?"

Pam smiled at David and hugged him, then turned towards the alien. "The basis of the unpredictability you're so desperate to reacquire is our emotions! You can't feel any more! That's what's really wrong!"

If it was possible for a panel of lights to show emotion, the remaining alien looked sad. For a moment, its panel displayed the same monochrome blue field with a black circle at its center. Then it lit again, with cascading red and yellow lights conjuring up the image of a sunset, something Europa would never see.

Vickie was astonished. "Oh my God! You're not machines! You're people stuffed into metal boxes!" She stared at the alien with glistening eyes. "Maybe all you need is to feel again."

"We have long ago lost touch with what you identify as emotion. We do not believe that it can be reclaimed," said the alien.

David frowned. "The price of being immortal is too high."

"You told us you know everything, so give it up…become flesh and blood again," Mickey said.

"It cannot be undone."

The one remaining active alien returned to the previous room and came back with Pam's braces. "You will need these," it said. Then it escorted the four teenagers back to the saucer.

Once inside, they silently took their places next to the pillars that would become their couches for the trip home. The alien remained in the doorway.

Before leaning against her pillar and pushing the white button, Pam turned to it. "How many other Europans are still active?"

"I am the last."

Chapter Thirty-Two

Day Ten

At dusk, the saucer touched down in the clearing at Griffith Park. The teens spent a good part of the return trip discussing their adventure to Europa and concocting a plausible excuse for their absence. They unanimously agreed to avoid the larger issue until they could wrap their heads around it. According to their watches, they'd only been gone ten hours or so. Mickey explained the collapsed time as the result of traveling at near-light speeds, which was far simpler than what he would have to do when he returned home—explain how he smashed his mother's SUV. Wasn't going to be pretty.

As soon as the teens stood on solid ground, the saucer's ramp retracted and the craft ascended, disappearing into the twilight. For a moment, the teens silently gazed at an empty sky. They couldn't see the Aurora spy plane circling overhead.

Pam took a few more steps. "Well, it feels better than before, but not like walking without my braces." Tears welled in her eyes. "It felt amazing to walk like a normal person."

Vickie hugged her. "Pammie, I'm so sorry!" she started crying too. Pam forced a smile.

David glanced down at the silver disc on his palm. He came over and put his hand on Pam's shoulder. "You're walking a little better."

"Yeah," she sighed. She wiped a tear from her eye.

"I wonder if this gives us any super powers like Mickey's suit?" said David, flexing his palm.

"Don't try throwing trees around," Mickey replied. He now surveyed the clearing, stopping with his gaze fixed on his mother's SUV. He took a deep breath. "Well gang, let's get organized. I'll call my parents to pick us up. Who's got a cell phone?" Vickie fished hers out of her pocket and tossed it to him.

Mickey caught it and grimaced. "No signal. Wait here while I hike up to the highway and try calling from up there."

"What will you say happened?" asked David.

"We crashed the car trying to catch a ride on a flying saucer to Europa," Mickey replied matter-of-factly.

"Say what?"

"Get real! I'll tell them we came here to view the stars, crashed the car in the dark, but everybody's okay. That's partly true. I'm leaving out the rest."

Vickie shrugged. "Like anybody would believe us." Mickey started up the path. "Hang on, Mickey. I'll join you."

As they hiked up, a black SUV with a whip antenna turned around and quietly drove off.

Day Eight

Two days later, Mickey sat alone on the steps behind the science building eating his lunch. This was his usual lunchtime perch, except now David was off with Pam. He looked up.

"I have a PB and J. What do you have?" asked Vickie.

Mickey pushed his books aside and made room for her. He held up half a bologna and Swiss.

She wrinkled her nose and sat down. "Gross." They sat silently for a moment. "So what are you thinking?" she asked, not making eye contact.

His smile faded. "About what?"

"You know."

He sighed. "The big decision."

"And?"

"Maybe today's the day."

She tensed. "You decided?"

"Saturday."

Vickie looked shocked. "You're making an announcement? Why? Nobody else knows!"

"They will after we go..."

Vickie's pulse was hammering "I haven't..."

"Bowling," Mickey interrupted.

"What?"

"I have my own ball."

Vickie broke into a smile.

Mickey looked down. "Maybe I shouldn't have told you that I have my own bowling ball."

"Why not?"

"Makes me sound like a dufus."

"A dufus who has super powers and can save the world."

Mickey blushed. "Not me, it's the suit." He summoned his courage. "So would you...I mean, go bowling...or, you know...something like that?"

"I've already toured the solar system with you...why not?"

He reached for her hand. She didn't stop him. They sat like that, holding hands, until the bell sounded.

Day Six

Two days later, the four teens huddled together in Mickey's bedroom. Jerry had cooled down by then, mollified by the fact that nobody was hurt, and excited that her car would get a new paint job along with the bodywork—sky blue. White had become passé.

Jerry baked a fresh batch of oatmeal cookies for today's get-together. She passed Max on her way to Mickey's bedroom carrying a tray with four glasses and a carton of milk under her arm. The aroma of the freshly baked cookies made Max's mouth water. He tried to snatch one, but she yanked the tray away.

Max looked annoyed. "How many cookies do you think two teenagers can knock off in one day?"

"Four teenagers. Two girls are with them."

Max raised an eyebrow. "Oh?"

Jerry looked pleased. "I think our son finally has a girlfriend! So does David. Isn't it sweet?" She pushed her way into Mickey's bedroom, set the tray and carton down, and then closed the door, leaving the cookies' tantalizing aroma lingering in the hallway. Max muttered something and headed for the refrigerator.

After Jerry left the bedroom, the teens polished off the cookies and resumed their discussion, the same one they'd been having for the past four days. Pam and David were on the bed with Pam's braces lying next to her. They were holding hands. Mickey sat on the floor while Vickie sat in the chair next to his desk with the helmet in her lap.

They noticed that Mickey appeared sullen. They also knew that he was the one who passed the aliens' Test. The unspoken question in the room was which of the girls would accompany him to Europa, that is, if he made the Choice to go. With four days already crossed off the calendar, the pressure was mounting.

"The power to end famine, a cure for cancer, who knows what else," marveled Pam, staring at him with a determined expression. "Not even Moses had that much clout."

Mickey's face turned red. "I have to leave my family, move to Europa, and live with a bunch of machines—not sure I'm prepared for that."

"You have to," persisted Pam.

"No I don't!" snapped Mickey.

"One person can't stand in the way of the whole human race!"

Mickey rose to his feet, shaking. "Is that what this is about, or is it a new pair of legs?"

"Mickey!" Vickie glared at him.

David stepped between them. "Your father's a newsman."

"So?" Beads of sweat dripped from Mickey's brow.

"Been watching the news lately?"

Mickey felt pummeled from all sides, even by his best friend. "What's that supposed to mean?"

"The world's totally messed up," David replied. "The silver dudes said they could show us how to fix it."

"Then *you* go!" Mickey shouted, losing control.

David saw his friend's distress and lowered his voice. "I didn't pass the Test. You're Batman, I'm Robin, remember?"

Mickey faced Pam. "Okay, Joan of Arc, if I go, will you join me?"

Pam locked eyes with David. "Vic, what about you?"

Vickie kept turning the helmet over in her hands. "I was only along for the ride. Pretty sure they don't want me." She avoided eye contact with Mickey.

David cleared his throat, trying to change the subject. "Am I the only one who feels different since we've been back?" He glanced down at his palm.

They knew what he meant. Since they'd returned, each one of them had felt different. Pam and David had clearly become an item, and everyone at school knew about it. But it was more than their social interactions that had changed. David, who once needed glasses to see, now had twenty-twenty vision, and he not only finished a race in gym class, but also came in second. Coach Dunivant had him drug tested. Mickey climbed all the way up the rope in gym class without wearing the suit. Vickie's transformation was even more dramatic. She seemed like a different person now: quiet, often introspective. She openly allowed herself to be seen with Mickey. The school's in-crowd was in shock.

By far the greatest transformation was Pam's. Before the trip, she was intelligent, understandably shy and wounded by her disability, even heroic at times in how she ignored it. Otherwise, Pam was a normal teenager with the usual frailties and yearnings. Now, she was something more, not physically, but emotionally. Mickey started referring to her as Joan of Arc. In Pam's eyes, Mickey didn't have a choice: he had an obligation—a sacred duty. Though she'd given her heart to David and received his in return, she would go to Europa if Vickie refused. Pam returned a zealot of the Choice, but it had nothing do to with her walking again. Vickie had never seen this side of Pam. It was as though a new personality had emerged. At times, Vickie found her frightening.

Mickey stood. "You know what guys? I'm done discussing this for today."

"Let's go to a movie," Vickie suggested.

"I hear the new James Bond movie is the best yet," Mickey said. He looked at Vickie.

"Sure," said Vickie.

"We only have six days!" Pam and David reminded them, in unison.

Max sat in the den listening to classical music, his preferred method of relaxation.

Mickey joined him on the couch and listened for a moment. "Mozart?"

"Vivaldi, *Four Seasons*." Max had his eyes closed and rhythmically waved one of his hands, as though he were conducting the orchestra.

"Dad, is it tough being a newsman these days? I mean, all the news is pretty bleak…war, global warming—those kinds of things."

Max stopped conducting and turned down the hi-fi's volume. "Been that way for years. Maybe it's improving a little…I don't know." He studied his son's face. "Something on your mind, Mick?"

"Nope."

"Trouble with your girlfriend?"

Mickey bristled. "She's not my girlfriend. We're just seeing each other."

Max smiled. "Dating, seeing, hanging out—in my day it was all the same."

Mickey fell silent for a moment. "Dad…if you were given the opportunity to do something really important, something that might save countless lives, but you had to give up everything you loved to do it, would you?"

Max stared at his son. "Are you thinking of joining the Army?"

"No. But I'm going to leave home someday."

"We all do, when we're ready—otherwise we just become grownup kids."

"Yeah, I get that."

"You sure nothing's on your mind?"

Mickey looked lovingly at his father. "I'm still a kid. What could be on my mind?"

Mickey closed the door to his bedroom and stood by his dresser. On top were some of his favorite toys, those youthful mementos a boy hangs onto even after he's left childhood behind—a Millennium Falcon spaceship, his favorite action figures carefully posed in battle array, and the model airplane he and his dad built years earlier. He picked up the model airplane, enjoying the familiar feeling of it in his hand and stared at himself in the mirror. He remained that way for several seconds studying his reflection, wondering which side of the glass he was really on. Was he the Mickey who got As on tests but kept to the social shadows with his equally nerdy friend Davie, or a superhero with the fate of the world in his hands? With a heavy sigh, he went to his closet. Before opening the door, he glanced around his bedroom taking in the comforting sights and smells. Then he saw the black matte suit under his bed, and he turned to open the closet door.

Inside were more memorabilia: his skateboard, a baseball glove, and propped up in the far corner, his fishing rod. Flooded with memories, Mickey reached for it, but in the darkness, he saw the bright silver disc on his palm and froze. He stared at his hand as if it belonged to someone else. With growing urgency, he pawed behind his clothes until he found what he was looking for and left his bedroom.

Mickey walked through the kitchen carrying his telescope.

Max gave it to him when he was seven years old. Many a night they'd studied the heavens together and talked. Tears welled up in his eyes as he recalled. He quickly wiped them before anybody noticed. The aroma of his mother's cooking filled the kitchen, which didn't help. She was sitting at the table. He turned his head away from her as he walked past.

"I haven't seen that telescope in a while," she said.

Mickey shrugged. "Not tired yet. Thought I'd do a little stargazing. Never know…might see a UFO."

"Where's your sidekick?"

"Over at Pam's."

"Vickie's a nice girl too."

Mickey looked annoyed. "Don't worry, she didn't dump me."

"Vickie is such a sweet girl. Something else bothering you?"

Mickey opened the door to the backyard. "Nope." He stepped out into the dark.

He walked to the farthest point in the yard, set up the telescope's tripod, and pointed the tube at the full moon. He had no idea where to find Jupiter in the night sky. As he touched the eyepiece, he noticed his hand was shaking. Soon, he was trembling all over. In frustration, he kicked the telescope's tripod, sending it crashing to the ground, and slumped down on his knees in the wet grass. He pounded the ground with his fist. "Why does it have to be me? I'm not a Star Trekee like David!" He was shaking and fought to control it.

"Mickey?" called his mother from the kitchen. "Who are you talking to?"

Mickey slowly got up and brushed the grass from his jeans. He held up his cell phone. "Davie's on the phone. He says hi."

"Tell him I think that he and Pam make a cute couple!"

Mickey started trembling again. "I will." He turned and stared at the moon.

Across the street, an unmarked van was parked under a tree with a directional antenna on its roof pointed at Mickey's bedroom window. Two DIA agents inside wore headphones in front of an impressive array of electronic equipment.

"Did you get any of that?" one asked the other, trying not to yawn. They'd been in there monitoring the entire day.

The second agent took off his headphones and rubbed the bridge of his nose. "Classical music, current events, only the Mickey suspect could pass some test at school, the David suspect is into Batman, and they all went to the movies—James Bond. Did I miss anything?"

"What does it all mean?"

"If you had a teenaged kid, you wouldn't ask."

"They said something about silver dudes. What do you suppose that means?"

"Must be a rock band."

"One of them said something's happening in six days."

"Maybe a school test, but given their last ride, I think we need to report it."

Day Three

The teens walked down the corridor toward the cafeteria. Several of their classmates stared at them.

"Why's everybody gawking at us?" asked Vickie under her breath. She looked annoyed.

"Forget about it," replied Pam, lumbering along in her braces. "We've got bigger fish to fry." She smiled at David. He blushed. The closer they were to "Decision Day," the bossier she became. Pam seemed more like a coach now than a friend.

Mickey smiled and looked down, as if he was embarrassed to say what was on his mind. "I think I get it," he said.

"Okay what?" asked Vickie.

"We're an anomaly."

David chuckled. "What's so unusual about us? I mean, we've been to Europa on a flying saucer, have silver Day-Glo palms, and you're the proud owner of a superhero suit. All seems pretty normal to me."

Pam poked him in the ribs and chuckled. "Nobody knows any of that stuff."

"Mickey glanced at Vickie. "That's not what I meant."

"Okay, what?" she said, now louder.

"You're with us...David and me. A few days ago you and your crowd treated us like lepers."

Pam tried not to laugh.

"Yeah, well..." Vickie's voice trailed off.

They reached the cafeteria and sat down. Vickie saw two girlfriends eyeing them, talking behind their hands. She stuck out her tongue at them and they turned away.

"This is all fun, but it's time to get back to a certain pressing topic," said Pam.

"Like figuring out what's safe to eat here?" said Mickey, doing his best to delay the conversation.

David closed his eyes. "Jesus, Mickey, get serious! We have three days left!"

"You mean I have three days," said Mickey a little too loudly. Several people stared at them. Vickie glared back.

Pam took Vickie's hand. "And one of us."

David glanced at Pam. His heart pounded in his chest.

Vickie broke the awkward silence. "What's beef burgundy?" she asked, noticing the day's menu posted above the cafeteria line.

"Leftovers from yesterday swimming in brown gravy," replied Mickey, glad for a break in the tension. Their group discussions had been like this ever since they returned from Europa. They were skating on thin ice, and everybody knew it.

"What about pizza?" Vickie offered.

"Pizza again?" replied David, sounding disgusted.

Mickey smirked. "Are you afraid of clogging your arteries?"

"Big deal! Our nannites will clean them out," said Vickie.

Pam stared at Mickey with her arms crossed. "If *you* want to fix *everything…*"

"Give it a rest for a few minutes, okay?" Mickey blurted out.

Nobody dared say anything else.

Chapter Thirty-Three

Day One

Two days later, David's father was in his garage polishing a vintage Harley Davidson motorcycle. A cigarette was hanging out of the corner of his mouth, and a half-finished beer bottle was on the bike's saddle. Several more empty bottles were scattered around the floor. He paused as the growl of another motorcycle echoed up the driveway. It was one of Jake's biker friends who approached with Jake riding on the back. Jake hopped off holding a grocery bag and watched his friend ride away.

"Where've you been?"

"Staying with Rob. Needed to unplug from the domestic scene."

"Where's your bike?" asked his father. He continued polishing the chrome of the Harley's tailpipe.

Jake pulled a bottle of beer from the grocery bag. "Totaled." He popped the top and took a swig. His father raised an eyebrow but didn't say anything. Jake looked at the empty beer bottles on the floor. "How many have you downed, Pops?"

"Not enough. How'd you total it?"

Jake leaned against the workbench and shook his head. "Now that's an interesting story." He looked away, as if trying to decide what to say next.

"You can ride this baby until I sell it." Dick frowned and continued polishing.

Jake snapped out of it and stared at his father in astonishment. "You're going to sell the Harley? You love this machine!"

"Got canned. We need the money."

"You're shitting me!"

Dick continued polishing. "The Department's cutting back due to the state's damn budgetary crisis. I got thirty days before

I have to clear out my locker."

Jake finished off the last of his beer. "Any cop jobs around?"

"Nothing. Already checked." He stared at the floor, lost in thought.

"Pops, what are you going to do?"

"Try to cut back, sell the house…sell this bike. Maybe move in with my sister until I can find another job."

"What did Mom say?"

Dick chuckled. "You mean when she doesn't have her nose stuck in a bottle?" Jake glared at his father. "I tried talking to her," Dick continued. "Tonight I'll give it another try, if she's sober." He sighed and continued polishing. "But right now, I think I'll just finish polishing this old beast, and we can take it for one last spin."

"I got a few bucks saved. Maybe I can find a way to get more."

"Keep your money. Won't make any difference." Dick opened up another bottle of beer. His face was flushed, and his speech was becoming slurred.

Jake held out his hand. "Give me the keys, Pops. You're not riding anywhere tonight." Dick tossed him the keys. "Maybe I know where there's something real valuable, something that probably has a big reward on it," Jake continued.

"What're you talking about?"

"I saw some high-tech military hardware. The guy who has it is a kid! No kid is supposed to have shit like that. I'm betting he stole it. I've seen what it can do too. It's pretty mean shit! There's got to be a big-ass reward on it!"

His father ignored him.

"Pops, listen to me! I'll bet the Army, or wherever that stuff came from, would pay pretty good to get it back."

His father stopped polishing, threw down the cloth, and started walking toward the house. Jake yelled after him. "The kid who has it is Mickey! Davie's in on it too!"

"You're watching too much TV." Dick shook his head and shut

the door.

Jake stood staring at the closed door for a moment, and then jumped on his father's Harley. After gunning the motor so loudly the windows rattled, he roared down the driveway, skidded with a screech of the rear tire, and accelerated down the street.

That night, after he sobered up, Dick knocked on his bedroom door. He and his wife had a huge screaming match that afternoon and she'd locked herself in. She'd done it before. "Open the door. We gotta talk," he called out.

She didn't answer. He pounded on the door.

"Linda, open up the door! We can't ignore this." He knocked on the door more frantically, but without any answer.

"Damn it, Linda! We'll just start over someplace else. Hell, we've done it before! I can't do this alone." He waited for her response, but nothing was forthcoming.

Alarmed, Dick threw his shoulder into the door. After a second thrust, the molding broke away and the door flung open. The bed was rumpled and the pillows were strewn on the floor. The bathroom was empty too. Linda wasn't there. He saw an empty bottle of vodka on the nightstand. He picked up the phone and called Linda's sister. "Linda there with you?" he hurriedly asked.

"No." Beth sounded alarmed. "Why?"

"She's drinking again, and she's not here." He hung up. After thinking for a moment, he grabbed the keys to his truck and took off running for the garage.

The boys were in Mickey's bedroom in their usual position—lying on their stomachs on top of his bed, propped on their elbows. "So what do you think?" asked David. The suit was rolled up under the bed. Mickey instinctively reached down and touched it.

"About what?" asked Mickey, as if he didn't already know what David meant. The whole Choice thing was a serious crisis, the biggest of his life, but he'd finally made up his mind.

"About *what*? Duh! About going back to Europa," replied David. "There's only one day left before the saucer comes back."

Mickey turned over and sat up on the edge of the bed, which usually signaled he had something important to say. "I've made up my mind."

"Okay?" David sat up too.

"I'm not going."

"Have you thought about..."

Mickey interrupted him. "I'm not going to spend the rest of my life away from my family...and friends!"

"Maybe you shouldn't put yourself first this time, not with the fate of the whole human race at stake!"

Mickey looked shocked. "What the fuck does that mean?"

"You know damn well what I mean!" David said. "Always the perfect son with the perfect parents, never does anything wrong!"

"Wait a minute! Is this about me, or you?"

David started shouting. "It isn't fair! Why is it always you? Why does the suit only fit you?" He began shaking. "I went in the flying saucer too! I did everything you did! So why do you get the chance to make everybody proud of you, and not me!" He stopped, shocked at his own outburst.

Mickey stared dumbfounded at his friend. "Then *you* go!" he finally managed to say.

"They don't want me!" David muttered. "Nobody does."

They were quiet for a moment, letting their emotions subside.

"I wish it *was* you." Mickey held up his palm. "I don't want this thing! I want everything to be the way it was." He flashed back on their years as friends. "I want us to go bike riding. I like driving a car. I want to lie on my bed and talk about girls. And I want to go out with Vickie..."

David seemed more composed. "It's okay. I get it now."

"What?"

"Doesn't matter that the silver dudes showed up—everything

was going to change anyway."

"What do you mean?"

"The only constant in a biologic system is change. Nothing ever stays the same. Trying to stop that is what screwed the Europans."

"That's pretty profound. Where'd you read it?"

"Didn't."

Mickey stared at his friend with a newfound respect. "Trying to stop what?"

"Evolution. You can't stop it. That's what all this is really about."

"And if I choose not to go, that changes things too."

David nodded his head. "Evolution waits for no…boy."

"Then you go."

"Can't. I didn't pass the Test."

"If I go, I have to take one of the girls with me. If Vic won't go, it has to be Pam!" Mickey's eyes glistened and he looked away. "How could I do that to you?"

David struggled to control his emotions. "Even when we're together, it's all she talks about…how important the Choice is. She gets this look on her face like she sees something we don't…a vision or something." David shook his head. "I'll lose Pam if Vic won't go."

"Not if I don't go!"

"No! That would be worse! Like Joan of Arc telling God to find someone else and having to think about it for the rest of her life!"

Mickey thought before responding. "Maybe none of this matters."

"Sure it does!"

"No. Think about it. The saucer brought all four of us to Europa and gave all four of us silver discs, not just me. Maybe the suit was just the entrance exam. I passed, but the Test is still going."

Before David could reply, they heard the screech of tires, and then a loud crash when Dick lost control of his truck and skidded into the side of a parked car.

"Holy crap!" shouted David. They tore out of the bedroom and ran for the front door.

Jerry had the door open. "Oh my God! He's hurt!"

"What?" cried Mickey as he and David arrived.

Jerry looked frantic. "Call 911!" She hurried down the brick walkway with the boys right behind her.

"What's going on?" yelled Max from the top of the stairs. He saw his wife running across the street and ran down the stairs after her.

Dick was slumped over the steering wheel of his truck with a gash on his forehead. He struggled to sit upright and wiped the blood out of his eyes with his sleeve.

Jerry reached him first. "Don't move! You're hurt!"

He backed the truck up.

"What are you doing?" Jerry shouted.

Mickey and David arrived. David stared at his dad. "Dad!" he screamed.

Dick glanced at his son and drove off, peeling rubber down the street.

Jerry grabbed for David. Max looked at the dented car and the glass fragments on the street. "What happened?"

"Dick hit a car with his truck and took off," Jerry replied.

"Where's Linda?" asked Max.

David pulled away from Jerry and ran to his house.

They caught up with David in his parent's bedroom. Max eyed the empty vodka bottle on the nightstand. Jerry noticed it too.

"What's going on?" moaned David.

Jerry hugged him, and then stared at Max. "Maybe your mom and dad had a disagreement and they've gone somewhere to cool off, you know, to think things over."

"My dad's hurt!" exclaimed David. "I saw the blood."

"He probably took himself to the hospital."

"Where's my mom?" David was trembling.

Jerry glanced at Max again. "Probably at your Aunt Beth's house."

"I need to find her!"

"Then let's get in the car and drive over to your aunt's house," said Jerry.

"I'm going too," insisted Mickey.

"You're staying home with your father," Jerry replied.

"But…!"

"No buts!" Jerry glanced at Max for support.

Max put his hand on his son's shoulder. "Mom will call when they find Linda."

"What's going on?" asked the DIA agent who was monitoring the boys' bedroom conversations. The van with Fred's Plumbing painted on its side was parked a few doors down the street.

"Get anything?"

"Lot of teenage boy testosterone stuff, something about robots, and that rock band again, the Silver Dudes, and something about going to Europe."

"Anything about the saucer?"

"Yeah, it's coming back in one day."

The older agent shook his head. "And you're telling me that now?" He started texting on his cell phone.

"What are you doing?"

"Reminding my wife to pick up the dry cleaning."

Chapter Thirty-Four

"What's going on?" Mickey asked his father.

Max shrugged. "My guess is they had a fight and both of them took off. All we can do now is wait." He paused. "Hey, there's some leftover roast beef in the fridge. I could make us some sandwiches?" He smiled at his son.

"Not hungry. You go ahead. I'll play some video games in my room until Mom calls."

"Okay."

Mickey hugged his father and disappeared into his room.

The teenagers had planned to meet online later that night when their parents were asleep. Europa, the silver aliens, and their plight needed to wait.

Mickey collapsed on his bed and reached for his Game Boy. He noticed his palm. The silver dot in its center, the one he'd been careful to not let his parents see, flashed brighter than ever. He cupped his hand over it but could still see it, like when he'd put his hand over a flashlight in the dark.

He sat on the edge of the bed and stared at his hand. The intensity of the disc had noticeably decreased. He waved his arm around and its brightness modulated depending on the position of his hand. Remembering the map gizmo in the visor, he lay down again duplicating the position he'd been in when he first noticed the flashing. The disc returned to its higher intensity. "Wait a minute!" he voiced aloud. He began to use his hand like a direction finder, waving it around in ever-wider arcs. The closer he was to his bed, the brighter and faster it blinked. When he reached for the ceiling, it dimmed. When he stretched all the way down to the floor, it blazed and lit up the floor like a laser. The disc was pushing him toward the suit!

Mickey reached under the bed with his hand near the suit. All the buttons were lit on the sleeve, illuminating the floor with multicolored lights. Something was definitely happening, but what? The Test had ended, and the saucer wasn't due back for another day. He hadn't heard any buzzers going off recently. The only way to figure it out was to put on the suit and see what happened next.

He slipped into the suit and lowered the helmet. With the visor down, the buttons on his sleeve stopped blinking, but remained brightly lit. The visor display became active too, just as it had when it led him to the saucer the first time. Mickey stared at a glowing map, and he thought the pattern of streets looked familiar. The curser appeared at the end of one of the streets blinking furiously, as if urging him to travel there. It would have been nice if there were a readout explaining why!

He took a step toward the door and stopped. He had two problems. First, he was anxious to hear about David's mother. Second, he needed to sneak out of the house wearing the suit without his father noticing him. Of course Max didn't know what the suit really was. He thought it was some motocross suit he and David discovered at the lake and for some reason couldn't part with it. Torn with indecision, Mickey took off the suit, stuffed it under his bed, and left his bedroom. He hid his hand in his pocket so his father couldn't see the flashing disc.

Max was sitting at the kitchen table halfway through a roast beef sandwich. He made quite a mess of it but seemed to be enjoying himself.

"Would you mind if I waited over at Pam's house?" Mickey asked. "I'll take my cell phone." Pam lived six blocks away.

Max looked at the kitchen clock. "Kind of late, isn't it?"

"Who's going to sleep tonight?"

Max put down the half-eaten sandwich. "Okay, but take a jacket." He noticed the mess and mopped it up with his napkin. "You sure you don't want to eat something first? This cold roast beef is pretty darn good."

"I'll grab a snack at Pam's. When you hear something about

Mrs. Walker, call me."

"Okay." Max dabbed at the ketchup on his chin and resumed eating.

Mickey hurried to his room and grabbed the suit, quietly walked down the stairs, snuck into the kitchen without his dad seeing him, and opened the side door to the garage. He ran in and donned the suit. As soon as he pulled the visor down, the glowing map and blinking cursor reappeared. Mickey started to ease his bike out of the garage trying not to make any noise, but the blinking cursor light went crazy. He decided to exit through the back door and walk the bike one street over, just in case. There he pushed his bike into motion and hopped on. When the power of the suit took over, pedaling became effortless. As expected, the cursor on the visor began moving too. The challenging part was not pedaling a hundred miles an hour. He kept glancing at cars to keep his speed down to a reasonable pace.

He followed the map: first down the street, right on Burbank Boulevard, and then left on Buena Vista. Because of the visor, he saw everything quite clearly, like it was high noon. He turned on his bike's light so drivers could see him.

He rode north on Buena Vista Street. After a couple of blocks, near Victory Boulevard, the visor indicated a left turn. Just as he was passing the entrance to a strip mall, the cursor stopped blinking and remained stationary. He wondered why the suit brought him here. He found himself in front of a small commercial center with only a few stores, a pizzeria, a drycleaners, a small dress shop, and a liquor store. Only the liquor store appeared to be open. He got off his bike and looked around. Since no other shops were open, he started toward the liquor store. For a second he stopped and stared at the clock on top of its neon sign. It read 11:45, less than fifteen minutes to the tenth day.

As Mickey moved down the row of dark stores, the image on

the visor changed. First he was looking at the door outside the drycleaners, and then he was seeing inside, as though he had X-ray vision. It was really weird! He could see racks of clothes in plastic bags hanging from the ceiling, the front counter, the cash register—objects he shouldn't be able to see. It reminded him of awakening after the nap on Europa when his senses seemed extra sharp. He wondered if this could be the same thing. But why now, and why was he directed here? He should be home with his father waiting for his mom to call about David's mom! Of course, he'd been to Europa in a flying saucer. Unusual occurrences had become the norm now.

As Mickey continued down the row of stores, he saw the details of each of their interiors. Past the dress store, he arrived at the sidewall of the liquor store, the last store in the row. Around the corner of the building, light poured out of the liquor store's double glass doors. He stopped and used the X-ray vision to look through the wall, and then froze. He saw a man wearing a pirate's mask standing in front of the counter pointing a gun at the clerk! The clerk had his hands raised and was shaking so violently he was having difficulty standing. The man in the mask was yelling and gesturing with the gun. He seemed as nervous as the clerk. A third man wearing a ski mask stood behind the man with the gun. That guy held a bag and anxiously glanced out the glass doors.

With his pulse hammering, Mickey kept to the shadows and continued watching. Suddenly the view through the visor changed again. Now he could clearly see the face of the man behind the pirate mask. It was Jake!

Mickey's blood started to boil. He had to put a stop to this. Feeling invincible, he started toward the front of the liquor store. Jake was finally going to get a real lesson in the use of power! This time, it wasn't about him and David. The clerk's life was in danger! Mickey had visions of seeing Jake's useless bullets bounce off the suit while he moved around and formed a barrier in front of the defenseless man.

A step away from bursting through the glass doors, Mickey stopped. This wasn't right! What if Jake panicked and shot the clerk? He watched enough cop shows on TV to know this wasn't the right move! No matter what Jake had tried to do to him, the right action was to call the cops and let them handle it. That's when he realized he forgot to take his cell phone! A second later, all five buttons on the suit darkened and the visor popped open. Mickey stared down at his forearm and stabbed at the dark buttons. Nothing happened! He was exposed, bathed in the light coming through the glass doors, without super powers! Not good!

Sensing movement outside, Jake spun around. He recognized the suit and locked eyes with Mickey. In a panic, Mickey ran back around the corner of the building and dove for the shadows. Lying on the ground panting, he stabbed at the suit's buttons, but nothing happened! His eyes were drawn to the clock above the liquor store. It was after midnight, the tenth day.

Chapter Thirty-Five

Jake knew he'd seen Mickey and his cursed suit! His level of anxiety ratcheted up. With his gun still pointed at the clerk, he strained his neck to look outside, but couldn't see anyone through the doors. He yelled to his accomplice to look outside. He'd seen somebody, somebody he knew!

Mickey hid in the shadows, camouflaged by the matte black of the suit and helmet. The man in the ski mask ran outside, spun around several times, but couldn't see him. He ran back into the liquor store shaking his head. "There's nobody out there!" he shouted at Jake. "Grab the money, and let's get out of here!"

Fighting back rage, Jake faced the frightened clerk. Without taking his eyes off him, he called back over his shoulder. "Check again, you idiot! I told you. I saw somebody! I think it's my kid brother's friend. Find him!"

The masked accomplice propped the door open and peered outside. "I told you, there's nobody out here!" he yelled back. "Come on! Get the fucking money!"

"All right, all right!" Jake shouted. He was certain he'd seen Mickey, but now wasn't the time to chase after him. Besides, he knew what Mickey could do with that suit. Brandishing his gun, Jake screamed at the clerk. "Do what I tell you, buddy, and just maybe you'll live!" He motioned to his accomplice to bring the bag. "You see this bag, dufus?" Jake yelled at the cowering clerk. "Fill it up with everything in that cash register as fast as you can! You get that?" The terrified clerk nodded and struggled with unlocking the cash register. His hands shook so much he kept fumbling with the key. Jake glanced over his shoulder into the darkness of the parking lot. His hair was plastered in sweat beneath his mask.

Feeling helpless, Mickey watched the scene unfold. He looked at his arm. The buttons were dark, but he had to help! He remembered seeing a pay phone when he'd first entered the parking lot and started running for it.

Graffiti covered the payphone kiosk. Since the advent of cell phones, payphones were becoming an endangered species. Mickey lifted the receiver and noticed the severed cord. Just then, the red and white buttons on the suit lit up! What was going on?

Mickey had one option—to trust the suit. He put on the helmet and pulled down the visor, hoping for the best. Instantly he could see what appeared to be the circuit diagram of the phone box projected before his eyes. Not certain what it all meant—he hadn't studied electricity in science class yet—and still holding the severed receiver in one hand, he reached over and touched the phone box with his other hand. Just as his gloved finger touched the cold metal, he heard an unmistakable dial tone in the helmet. When he removed his finger from contact with the box, the tone stopped. He touched the box again and heard the dial tone. Somehow the suit completed the circuit! Why not? A few minutes earlier, he experienced X-ray vision. He left his hand in contact with the phone box, dropped the severed headset, and dialed 911. After two rings, he heard a female voice inside the helmet.

"This is Emergency Services. How can I assist you?"

Mickey yelled, "There's an armed robbery going down right now! You have to send the police!"

"State your name and location, please," responded the 911 operator with a calm and professional voice.

"My name's Mickey, and I'm right around the corner at Starlight Liquor…I saw the gun!"

"How old are you?" The 911 operator sounded more alert now.

"I'm sixteen," Mickey shouted.

"This isn't a joke, right? Because if it is, you could be in a lot of trouble."

"I'm telling the truth!" Mickey yelled back. "You have to send the cops now, before somebody gets hurt!"

"Are you in any danger?"

"No, I'm around the corner, and it's dark. They can't see me! You have to hurry!"

"Okay, calm down, son. Stay on the line. Don't hang up, no matter what! Do you understand?"

"Yes, Ma'am, I understand. I won't hang up!"

"I'm going to connect you to the police. Don't hang up while I make the connection."

"Yes, Ma'am. Please hurry!"

"Good. Okay, here goes..." The phone clicked a few times, and then Mickey could hear the 911 operator talking to someone else.

"Police Emergency, this is Harris."

"Foothill Emergency, this is 911 Operator 13. I have a young man on the phone who claims an armed robbery is in progress at Starlight Liquor Store, Buena Vista and Victory."

"Put him through," said the male voice.

"Go ahead, Mickey, tell Officer Harris what you saw."

"It's a robbery! I saw two guys wearing masks. One of them has a gun!"

"Okay, kid, now listen up. Did I hear your name's Mickey?"

"Yes, Sir, it's Mickey."

"Okay Mickey. My dispatcher is sending four black and whites to your location. Should arrive in a few minutes. Watch for them, because they're going to be on silent approach—that means without their lights and sirens. They're going to park around the block right behind you. We know exactly where the public phone is you're talking from. Just stay where you are and wait there. Don't move! Do you get that kid?"

"Yeah, I get it!"

"Okay, now I'm going to hang up, but the 911 operator will remain on the line. Stay put!" The officer then disconnected.

"What's your parent's number, Mickey?" requested the operator.

"It's okay! I already called them!" Mickey hung up, which is to say he took his hand off the phone box. He had no intention of calling his folks. Feeling safe inside the suit again, he was determined to move closer to the action. He pulled down the visor, but nothing happened. He looked at his sleeve. The buttons were dark again. Jesus! Now what?

Chapter Thirty-Six

In two minutes, four police cars came roaring up without their lights on. Twelve policemen jumped out. Six of them were strapping on body armor and clutching assault rifles. After suiting up, they began to deploy toward the lighted liquor store. The others wore bulletproof vests. Two of the officers ran over to Mickey. The rest fanned out to approach the liquor store from different angles.

Mickey removed the helmet, putting it under his arm.

"Kid, are you all right?" asked one of the officers. He was holding a bullhorn.

"Yes, Sir. Maybe a little scared, but I'm fine."

"Tell me exactly what you saw—how many guys are in there, that kind of thing. Don't be scared."

"Sure officer. I stopped to get a Coke at the liquor store and saw two guys holding it up."

The officer gave Mickey the once-over. "You think it's smart to ride around in that black suit in the dark, kid?"

"I was hanging with friends and lost track of the time. Got thirsty."

"How old are you?" asked the second officer.

"Sixteen."

"Ever hear of the curfew, kid?"

"Yes, Sir! Won't happen again."

"We don't have time for this," said the officer holding the bullhorn. He looked older than the rest, with gray hair. His nametag read Captain Stevens. "Did you see if the guys in there have guns?"

"I saw two guys wearing masks. One of them was pointing a gun at the clerk."

"What about the second guy?"

"I didn't see any gun. He was wearing a ski mask and holding a bag."

"Did they see you?"

"Maybe one of them did, but as soon I saw what was going down, I got the hell out of there!"

Officer Stevens spoke into a hand-held radio. "Unit Two, this is One, do you copy?"

The small radio crackled to life. "Copy One. We're in position. We confirm two males wearing masks inside the liquor store. They know we're out here. One male wearing a Halloween mask is holding an employee hostage with a handgun to his temple. The other male, wearing a ski mask, is hunched down behind the counter. I don't see a gun on the second guy, but one of his hands is behind the counter out of sight. Do you copy, One?"

"Two, how do you know they saw you?"

"The guy with the gun got behind the clerk and dragged him to the glass doors so we could see him."

"I copy, Two. A hostage situation, two male suspects in masks, no ID possible at this time, at least one handgun. The eyewitness is here with me. He's a sixteen-year-old male who was going to the liquor store to buy something. Says he never got inside. I'll stash him in one of the cars and come to your position. We'll try some talking. Maybe we can get out of this mess without any heavy stuff. One, out."

Officer Stevens dropped the radio to his side. "Son, I'm going to ask you to go sit in one of the squad cars until the shindig's over. Okay?" Mickey nodded.

Under the watchful gaze of Officer Stevens, Mickey slowly walked to one of the squad cars. He took a seat in the back, but left the door open. Officer Stevens nodded to him, and then ran back toward the liquor store. Mickey waited until Stevens was out of sight and put the helmet back on. Damn! The suit was still dead! He slumped back against the car seat. Wouldn't matter much longer, anyway, he thought. When the saucer arrived, he wasn't going. His days as a teenage superhero were over.

After a moment, Mickey sat upright. Even without the protection of the suit, he had to see how things were playing out. When he was sure no one was watching him, he slipped out of the squad car and ran around the complex to the opposite side. From across the parking lot, he positioned himself behind a tree and watched.

Having lost the element of surprise, three of the squad cars turned on their headlights, activated their roof-mounted flashing lights, and pulled into the parking lot directly in front of the liquor store's glass doors. Their reinforced car doors swung open, and the officers crouched down and used them for cover. Rifle barrels extended through open windows aimed at the liquor store. One officer positioned himself in the alley with a shotgun blocking any rear-door retreat.

Officer Stevens raised the bullhorn and called out to Jake. His amplified voice could easily be heard inside the liquor store where the interior was brightly illuminated by all the headlights.

"This is Burbank PD. We have you surrounded. Throw your guns out the door and come out with your hands up. No reason for bloodshed. You boys made a mistake. Don't make it any worse for yourselves."

Inside the liquor store, with his gun hand shaking, Jake turned to his accomplice who was hiding behind the counter not holding up very well either. "This was a bad idea, Jake!" Rob yelled. "We better give up like the man said. I'd rather go to jail than get shot!"

"I'm not going to jail, asshole, and neither are you! We got ourselves a hostage, remember?" He shoved the barrel of the pistol against the clerk's chest causing him to stagger and cry out. "Shut up!" Jake yelled, and grabbed him again. He put his masked face in front of the clerk with their noses almost touching. "Where's the fucking phone?" Jake shouted. Spittle shot out from the mouth hole in his mask.

"Under the counter!" The clerk pointed and then covered his

head with his hands. Jake threw him to the floor, and then picked up the phone and dialed 911.

"This is 911 Emergency Services. What is the nature of your emergency?"

"You get me the police right now, lady. Tell 'em it's the guy in Starlight Liquor holding a gun to the face of the clerk! You got that, lady? You get the cops on the phone right now or I waste him!"

"Please don't leave the line," said the 911 operator. "I'll connect you to the police immediately."

A moment later, Officer Steven's cell phone rang. "Stevens," he said.

"Shut the fuck up and listen!" yelled Jake. "You and your boys get the hell out of here right now or I waste the clerk! You hear me, cop? This ain't no game we're playing!"

"Yeah, I hear you, buddy. Just calm down, okay? Nobody has to get hurt. I'm going off-line for a minute to talk things over with my men. Stay cool, and keep the line open, okay?"

"Ya got five minutes to clear out, asshole, or this guy's toast!" yelled Jake again.

"I'm just going to put down the phone for a minute! You can wait a minute, can't you?" Officer Stevens covered the phone with his hand and motioned over the leader of the assault team. A man in body armor and a helmet ran up to him. "It's amateur night in there, Ken," Officer Stevens said. "Do you have a shot if I have to go that route?"

"Those two dipshits are standing behind double glass doors! At this distance, my boys could hit 'em with sling shots."

"Have your snipers take up position, but take no action unless I give the word."

"My guys already have them in their crosshairs. Just say when."

Officer Stevens looked at the assault team captain square in the eyes. "You will NOT shoot unless I give the command, and if

I do give the command, you will NOT shoot to kill. Is that understood! For Chrissake! They're probably a couple of kids! Nobody dies tonight—not on my shift! Got it?"

"Okay, boss. Non-lethal, we just mess them up a little. I need three minutes to pass along the orders and finish getting into position." The officer jogged away.

Officer Stevens put the cell phone back to his ear. "Hey, man, don't you think it'd be better to throw down the gun and walk out of there? Where do you think you're going to hide? You know we're going to find you."

"You got three minutes, cop—three minutes until I blow the clerk's head off!" Jake threw the phone at the glass doors, and the phone broke into pieces and clattered to the floor.

Dick Walker drove up in his truck. He had a bloody bandage on his forehead and a portable police radio in his hand. Staying low behind the police cars, he got out and ran to Officer Stevens. "What's going down?" he asked.

"I thought you were off today."

"I'm about to be off permanently."

"What happened to your head?"

"Little mishap in the garage. I heard you guys squawking."

"You don't need to be here. Go to the hospital and get your head fixed."

"Rule 110. Any on-duty officer in the vicinity of a Code Four will come to the aid of his fellow officers. I'm not a night watchman yet. What have you got?"

"Have it your way. Two perps, one with a gun and a hostage. Probably two dumb kids. The guy with the gun says if we don't drive away in three minutes he'll waste the hostage. I tried to talk him out, but he smashed the phone."

"I see you got a SWAT team here. Sounds like you don't have too many options."

"The guy with the gun is just some stupid ass kid! Dammit…I can't shoot a kid! I gotta give him another chance." Officer

Stevens picked up the bullhorn again. Dick drew his gun and hunkered down beside him.

"I think we should talk about this," said Officer Stevens using the bullhorn. "You're just making things worse for yourself and your buddy."

"You got one minute now, Cop. I'm not bluffing!" bellowed Jake from inside.

Officer Stevens dropped the bullhorn to his side. He and Dick exchanged glances.

From across the parking lot, Mickey watched the whole thing. Jake had the clerk by the throat with the barrel of his gun near the clerk's ear. The clerk was weeping. It was awful! He saw Jake talking to somebody using a phone before he smashed it against the door. It had to be to the cops. He heard Officer Stevens on the bullhorn trying to reason with him. The guy behind the counter in the ski mask looked to be every bit as terrified as the clerk!

Two shots rang out, the glass window imploded inward, and Jake and his friend went down. Dumbfounded, Mickey stood up. "Oh my God, they shot Jake!" he yelled to no one. The assault team rushed inside with their rifles at eye level. Walker and Stevens followed right behind with their revolvers drawn.

Without thinking, Mickey ran closer. He saw Jake and his buddy lying in spreading pools of blood. Jake had been shot in the chest, and his friend was hit in the shoulder. Blood spattered the wall and counters. The clerk lay prostrate on the floor, convulsing with terror, his face and clothing mottled with Jake's blood.

Jake gasped for breath as blood trickled from his mouth. One officer approached leading with the muzzle of his rifle. He kicked Jake's handgun away from his outstretched hand. "One down. Clear!" he shouted.

The second officer approached Jake's accomplice on the floor behind the counter. He didn't see a second gun. "Two down. Clear! No weapon!"

Mickey heard sirens approaching. A paramedic ambulance and a fire truck with their red lights flashing pulled into the parking lot.

Officer Stevens bent over Jake and pulled off his mask. Dick stood inches behind him.

"Jake? Oh God, it's my son!"

Mickey fell to his knees. Jake had been shot! He felt guilty. If he hadn't called the police, Jake probably could have taken the money and run. Nobody would have recognized him behind his mask! Then Mickey realized that the suit had directed him here and allowed him to see it was Jake behind the mask. Somehow this was part of a larger scheme of things, except right then, none of this made sense!

The paramedics lifted Jake onto a stretcher. Ashen-faced, Dick stayed at his side. He gently wiped the sweat from his son's forehead and watched the paramedic working on him. "How bad is he?" Dick asked, his voice rasping.

"It's a chest wound. The bullet hit the lung and there's a lot of internal bleeding. We have to get him into surgery in a hurry. That's the only chance he's got."

Dick bent down over his son. His hands trembled so badly he grabbed onto the stretcher's rail to brace himself. "Why'd you do it?" he whispered in Jake's ear. Officer Stevens stood back and bit his lip.

Jake smiled at his father, and then grimaced with pain. Dick tensed, like he'd been struck a blow. "You needed the money, Pops," Jake whispered back. He started coughing up blood.

Dick's legs threatened to give way, but he steadied himself. He looked down at his son with tears in his eyes.

The paramedic touched his shoulder. "We gotta move!"

Dick nodded and stepped back.

Jake used his hand to beckon his father closer. Dick glanced at the paramedic who nodded.

"It was that brat Mickey who fingered me." Jake coughed

again. "He was wearing that military shit I told you about."

The paramedic gently pried Dick away from the stretcher. "We're running out of time!"

Dick touched his son's forehead with his hand and moved back from the stretcher. Moments later, with its siren blaring, the ambulance sped away toward Burbank Memorial.

Officer Stevens put his hand on Dick's shoulder. "I'm so sorry."

"Yeah," Dick said quietly.

"I'll drive you to the hospital."

Dick ignored him and ran out to his truck, his boots crunching on shards of glass. He backed up and peeled rubber out of the parking lot. Officer Stevens stared at the pool of Jake's blood congealing on the tile floor and sighed. He walked to the doorway but stopped, as if he'd just remembered something. He looked around. "Hey, where's that kid?" he yelled. "Somebody go check on him, now!" A moment later, Mickey approached him out of the dark.

Officer Stevens was startled. "What the hell are you doing here? I told you to stay in the squad car!"

"Sorry, officer," said Mickey. "I had to watch, and when I saw the ambulance pull away, I figured it was safe."

Officer Stevens briefly closed his eyes. "Yeah. I'll have one of the guys drive you home. Where do you live?"

"Can I call my mom?" Stevens handed him a phone and he dialed.

"Mom?" said Mickey, tentatively.

"Mickey? I don't recognize the number. Whose phone are you using?"

"Tell you later. It's complicated. I need to tell you that Jake's at the hospital. He's hurt bad. His dad's with him. Did you find Mrs. Walker?"

"She wasn't at her sister's. I'll bring David to the hospital now."

"Okay," he said, and hung up the phone before his mother could say anything. He handed the phone back to Captain Stevens.

"My mom's going to Burbank Memorial with David Walker, Officer Walker's son. Would it be okay if you took me there?"

"You're a friend of the Walkers?"

"I'm David's best friend. I live across the street."

"This whole thing is fucking unbelievable!" Officer Stevens exclaimed. "Sorry, kid. I'll drive you there myself."

Chapter Thirty-Seven

2:00 AM, PST, Burbank Memorial Hospital

Dick hadn't left his son's side. A blood soaked bandage was half off his head. When the stretcher carrying Jake disappeared through the operating room's double doors, Dick stood with his hands balled into fists, paralyzed by a combination of grief and rage. Jerry entered behind him.

She glanced at the OR doors. "Is that Jake being wheeled into surgery?"

Dick didn't make eye contact. "Yes," his voice cracked.

"Oh my God!" Jerry exclaimed. "Mickey didn't say it was that serious."

"He wouldn't," Dick said through clenched jaws. "Did Linda show up?"

"She wasn't at her sister's. Any idea where she might be?"

"No," Dick muttered.

Jerry stared at the OR doors. "This isn't fair!"

Dick laughed out loud. "Since when did fair have anything to do with life?"

They walked in silence back toward the ER waiting room. When they arrived, Dick saw David but made no move to speak to him. Jerry was about to say something, when a doctor approached them. "Okay, officer, let's get that head of yours stitched back together." He gestured toward one of the exam rooms.

David rushed over to them. Dick walked away with the doctor without speaking to his son.

A minute later, Mickey hurried into the ER waiting room.

Jerry was startled to see him. "Where's your father?"

"He's not here. I came on my bike."

"You *what*?"

"I didn't tell him I was coming! He thinks I'm at Pam's."

Mickey sounded panicky.

Jerry was horrified. "You rode all the way here in the middle of the night on your bike? What's the matter with you? Don't you think two people in ER are enough for one night?"

David looked puzzled. "Two?"

Jerry felt helpless and struggled with the right words. "Your father and Jake."

"Jake? What happened to my brother? I thought we came here for my mom?"

"There's been an accident. He's in surgery."

David looked ashen. Jerry grabbed him and steered him to a chair. She sat beside him. "We'll wait here for your father, okay?"

David didn't reply.

Jerry left David, grabbed Mickey's hand, and pulled him where David couldn't hear.

"I saw what happened to Jake!" Mickey said before his mother could say anything further. His hands were trembling.

"I know. It's terrible! He was in an accident on his motorcycle."

Mickey looked down. "That's not what happened."

Jerry looked confused. "That's what Dick said."

"He got shot while holding up a liquor store!" Mickey blurted out.

"What?"

"I was there! I saw the whole thing! I'm the reason he got shot!"

"Oh my God! What are you talking about?"

"I was riding by Starlight Liquor Store and saw two guys holding up the place. I was the one who called the cops!"

Jerry shook her head in shock. "What were you doing by the liquor store?"

He lied. "I was on my way to the hospital. Thought his mother might be here. It's on the way. It was just a coincidence!"

"I can't believe this!" Jerry stared wide-eyed at her son. "Why do you think you caused the situation?"

"If I hadn't called the cops, the clerk would have given Jake the money and he could've gotten away. He was wearing a mask! Nobody knew it was him! After the police arrived, Jake wouldn't come out, so they shot him and his buddy. It's all my fault! How am I going to tell David?" Mickey could barely hold back his tears.

Jerry grabbed her son. "Listen to me. It wasn't your fault! Jake's been heading down the wrong road for years. It was just a matter of time!"

Dick walked out with his head freshly bandaged.

"David's over there," said Jerry, inclining her head towards the waiting room.

"You watch him." Dick walked away.

"Where's David's mom?" Mickey asked.

Jerry's eyes began to glisten. "I don't know."

"We have to find her! Maybe we should call the police!"

"Her husband's a cop!" Jerry snapped. She immediately felt sorry and grabbed him into a bear hug. "We just have to wait, for Jake and for Linda. That's all we can do—that, and pray."

Mickey panicked. "I can't tell David about Jake. I can't tell him what I did!"

She held onto his shoulders. "You did the right thing! For God's sake, it's not your fault, Jake was holding up a liquor store! I knew that boy would come to no good!" She took a deep breath to calm herself. "We have to think about Davie."

Mickey implored. "Please, don't tell him what I did!"

She let go of her son. "You didn't do anything wrong, but don't worry. I won't say anything. Your friend has enough on his shoulders right now."

Mickey sat down in one of the waiting room's chairs and put his head in his hands.

After surgery, Jake was moved to the ICU. Dick followed the

gurney inside. Jerry and Mickey waited with David in the waiting room.

Thirty minutes later, the ICU's electric doors opened and Dick reemerged with an unreadable expression.

"How's Jake?" Jerry asked with genuine concern.

Dick stared at her, his expression blank. "Stable." He ignored David. "I'm going outside for a cigarette." Then he glared at Mickey. "I know all about it." Suddenly he looked angry. "Jake told me. This isn't over!" He stormed off.

"Knows about what?" asked David.

Before Mickey could answer, Jerry pulled both of them along. "Nobody's making any sense tonight. Just forget it." David was exhausted. Jerry put her hand on his shoulder. "Honey, let's go back to my house and get some sleep. I'll give the nurse our number." She pulled David toward the door. He didn't resist.

On the way out, Jerry stopped at the nurse's station. "I'd like to be called when there's an update on Jake Walker's condition. Here's my number." She passed a slip of paper.

"That's the gunshot wound," said the nurse without looking up.

"What!" David exclaimed.

Jerry looked daggers at the nurse. "This is his brother. He didn't know."

The nurse glanced at David. Her face reddened with embarrassment. "Sorry. Could be hours." David started to tremble. Mickey turned away.

Jerry stared into David's eyes. He was barely holding it together. "I didn't want to tell you."

David was puzzled. "Why?"

"Too many bad things for one night." She looked over at the nurse. "Is his father here?"

"I haven't seen him for a while."

"Do you want to look for your father?" Jerry asked David.

David shook his head no.

Jerry stood. "We're going back to the house." She ushered David toward the elevator. Mickey followed a few steps behind.

Chapter Thirty-Eight

3:00 AM, PST

Nobody spoke a word on the car ride home. Max met them at the door. All he said was, "I heard."

After they entered the house, Jerry hugged David again. "Would you like something to eat, honey?"

"No thank you, Mrs. B. Not hungry. Is my mom home yet?"

Jerry lied. "Your father went to get her."

"Where was she?"

"Took herself to a movie. Why don't you two go to Mickey's room and sack out for a while. When the hospital calls about Jake, I'll wake you. I promise!"

"Can't sleep," said David, holding back tears.

Mickey glanced at his mother. "Me neither."

"All right. I'll bring a tray with some milk and cookies in a few minutes."

"Better make that a double order," said Max, smiling. "There're already two girls in there, Pam and Vickie. Showed up an hour ago and refused to leave."

Mickey glanced at David. "I called Pam from the hospital." David's lips quivered into a smile.

Jerry looked at her watch. "It's after three A.M. on a school night!"

"Can't they stay? Please?" Mickey pleaded.

Jerry smiled at Max. "They're such sweet girls," she said.

Pam and Vickie joined them in the living room. "We really want to stay," said Vickie. Pam moved closer to David with her own eyes glistening.

"Only if it's okay with your parents," said Jerry.

"I already checked with my mom, and Vic's been staying at my house for the past few days," said Pam.

"I'll get a couple of sleeping bags from the garage," said Max.

"Okay, you win," said Jerry. "Looks like it's going to be a sleepless night. I'll whip up a double batch of cookies." She started for the kitchen.

"Don't forget to share some with your husband," Max muttered.

They went into the kitchen.

"I assume that crap about Linda going to the movies was for David's benefit," said Max.

Jerry leaned against the kitchen counter looking distressed. "I don't know how much more he can take."

"Her car's still in the driveway," said Max. "What did Dick say?"

"To butt out, and that's putting it nicely."

"Did you see the empty bottle on the night stand?"

"Yes."

"Maybe we should call the police."

Jerry sighed. "I already did. She's not officially missing for twenty-four hours, and—"

Max nodded. "Dick's a cop."

"I felt like they were politely telling me to mind my own business."

"This whole situation is unbelievable," said Max.

"Let's hope it doesn't get any worse."

Frankel stood next to his car in the parking lot of McDonald's a few miles from Cheyenne Mountain. After checking to make sure nobody was watching, he dialed a secure cell phone. "It's on the way back," he said.

The man with the orange signet ring reclined in his chair. Frankel's voice was on speakerphone in a large conference room. "So I've been informed." His associates, each one from the major industrial world powers, were sitting around a massive wooden conference table.

"What's your plan?" Frankel asked.

"We have only two options…capture the saucer or destroy it." The man held up his jeweled hand, silencing the murmurings in the room.

Frankel was startled. "You can't be serious!"

"The president is convening an emergency cabinet meeting in two hours. You'll attend as General Westlock's aide and assist in promoting his plan to capture the saucer. Hopefully he won't fail as miserably as his predecessors in 1947. If the general is successful, we'll take the saucer from him and control its technology. If he fails, we'll destroy it and maintain the status quo."

Sweat dampened Frankel's hair. "Capturing it won't be easy. Who knows what kind of tech it's got, or how the technology exchange will take place?"

Silence momentarily filled the conference room. "The gift of alien technology is indeed the most interesting part of all."

Frankel listened.

"What do our alien visitors intend to offer, and how will it be delivered? It seems to me there has to be an intermediary."

"An intermediary?" questioned Frankel.

"They can hardly leave a hard drive on the front steps of the White House. I suspect they'll insist on a fair distribution of the technology to all countries as well. Of course that's unacceptable… The intermediary might be one of them, but that would be far too melodramatic. No, perhaps the teenage boy, the one who's already been enhanced. Whoever it is, we can't risk the technology falling into the wrong hands! In the event of failure, a tactical nuclear device will be in position."

Frankel was dumbfounded. "You can't detonate a nuclear bomb in downtown Los Angeles!"

"It's low-yield, and you'll have several hours to evacuate the area."

Frankel wiped his brow. "You're still talking about injuring millions of people with the fallout!"

"The general's plan is, in fact, reasonably clever. The civilian astronomical authorities believe the saucer is a meteor heading for the west coast of the U.S. He intends to promote this story to create a panic facilitating the removal of the civilian population. We'll use our considerable media assets to assist him. He can then surround the landing site with his soldiers and whatnot without interference and capture the saucer."

"What if the president doesn't endorse the plan?"

"You'll help the general convince him that the object is truly an alien craft, and that possession of its technology will significantly advance America's interests, as opposed to that of another world power. One of our associates in the president's circle of advisers will assist you."

Frankel's mind raced. "What if the general can't pull it off? We can't murder all his men with a radioactive cloud over Los Angeles!"

"A force of arms should not be necessary. Our information indicates that the teenager named Mickey controls the saucer. Capturing him is key to the operation."

Frankel sounded panicky. "What if he won't cooperate, or the suit makes him invulnerable?"

"Make no mistake. If I can't gain control of the saucer and their technology, I *will* destroy it. I suggest you begin the civilian evacuation immediately."

Frankel stared at his cell phone.

"One more thing," the voice continued. "After you capture the saucer, eliminate the children, the boat mechanic, the policeman, and his son. They know too much." The line went dead.

Frankel dropped the phone to his side and leaned against the car.

1:00 AM, HST, Keck Observatory, Mauna Kea, Island of Hawaii

"It's confirmed," announced the lead astronomer.

"How big is it?" asked another astronomer. Several of them huddled around one of the large computer screens. In its center, a blinking, rapidly moving white box enclosed a single point of light against the star field.

"Not big enough for an extinction event, but it'll make a mess of things depending on where it hits. Best guess, a crater of one hundred meters across, maybe less. We'll know more as it approaches."

"What's its trajectory?"

"Heading right for us. Probably popped out of the ORT cloud and got lassoed by Jupiter's gravity well. The sucker swung right by Mars Express along the way, like it was posing for a picture. Take a look." The picture changed on the computer screen, showing a teardrop shaped streak of light.

"It's already past Mars? Jesus! How fast is the fucker going?"

"Too fast. Never seen anything like it."

The first astronomer picked up the phone. "How soon before you can give me an impact estimate?"

"We're triangulating now with ESO in Chile. As fast as it's moving, shouldn't take long."

"Better call it in."

The White House Situation Room, 6:00 AM, EST

General Westlock sat back in his chair with a smug expression. "It's coming!" he said. Frankel sat next to him trying to appear calm. Under his coat his back dripped with sweat.

The president turned to his science advisor. "Okay, Ralph, what do you think?"

"Anything's possible, Sir."

General Westlock stared down the science advisor. "Stop with the political bullshit, Connors! It's the saucer, and you know it!"

The president loosened his tie and glared back at the general. "Let's suppose, for the moment, you're correct. What are you proposing we do?"

The general's gaze passed around the rapt faces of the entire cabinet. "Capture the damned thing when it lands in L.A.!"

His words stunned everyone at the table.

The president cleared his throat. "How do you know that's where it's going to land?"

"Don't, at least not yet. But it took off and landed from the same friggin' park at least twice. I'm betting that's where it's heading this time too."

"Why shouldn't we leave it alone, wave goodbye when it flies away, and give the press the usual bullshit cover story?"

"You can bet the Ruskies and the Chinese won't if it lands in their backyards next."

The president thought for a moment. "We could welcome it on behalf of the people of the United States of America."

"Makes for a great photo op," said his campaign manager.

The general sneered. "That thing has already abducted five of our citizens and the boat mechanic is acting like an alien zombie. Ever see *War of the Worlds*?"

"How do you plan on capturing it?" asked the president.

"We could nuke it," interjected the vice president.

"Nuking Los Angeles wouldn't be good in a re-election year," the science advisor said with a wry grin.

"We must get control of the thing, and I know how!" exclaimed the general, his expression full of confidence from years of clandestine operations.

"It's six A.M., General," reminded the science advisor. "Why don't you skip the dramatics and tell us."

After a nod from General Westlock, Frankel handed him a manila file folder. The general opened it and held up an enlargement of Mickey's photograph taken from the high school yearbook. "He's the key to this operation."

"Looks like a teenager!" said the vice president.

"He's the one who controls the saucer! In fact, he and three of his friends rode that thing to Europa," the general said. He spread out three more photographs on the table—David, Pam, and Vickie.

"Four adolescent kids hijacked a flying saucer for a joyride to Europe? Get real!" said the vice president in disbelief.

"Not Europe, *Europa*!" snarled the general.

The vice president stared at him blank-faced.

"A moon of Jupiter with ice on it," said the science advisor.

Still no response from the vice president.

"The movie *2010*, the one with Roy Schneider..." the general added.

"Oh, *that* Europa!" exclaimed the vice president.

The science advisor shook his head and smirked at the president. "Gimme a break!"

"It's true! This kid," he thrust Mickey's photo into the air, "has some high-tech gizmo the aliens gave him. It's a suit that gives him super powers. He uses it to control that saucer!"

"Right," said the science adviser, trying not to laugh.

"Here, listen to this!" The general played Ernie's recorded phone call to the FBI, which impressed the cabinet members.

"Who is that guy?" asked the president after the audio file finished playing.

"A former Army ranger named Ernie Santos," replied the general. "He saw the kid using the suit, and as a true patriot, called the FBI!"

"How do you know those teens were on the alleged...flying saucer?" asked the president.

Frankel glanced at the general and raised a finger. "May I, Sir?" The general nodded.

"A DIA team followed them to the park where the saucer took off, and the Aurora spy plane tracked its flight out of the atmosphere. We have photos of them landing and leaving the saucer a day later." He passed around photographs of the teens near the saucer.

"It traveled to Europa and back in one day?" asked the

science advisor. "That isn't possible!"

"That's how I know this isn't some meteorite heading here with our name on it!" stated the general confidently. "Nothing natural can move that fast!"

The president glanced at his watch. "I'm scheduled for a breakfast meeting with the Chinese Envoy at eight A.M. Gotta be on my game to mix it up with that guy. So let's cut through it. Lay it all out, General, and I'll give you my decision by noon."

"About the time it should land, Sir," Frankel blurted out.

"What do you mean?"

"At the speed it's traveling, it'll be here by nine A.M. Pacific Standard Time."

An aide rushed in and whispered something to the president's chief of staff. After the aide left, the chief of staff turned on the television mounted on the far wall. "Looks like we have a problem."

The banner read: CNN, London: Breaking News!

The news anchor delivered the news with a deadpan voice. "The worldwide astronomical network responsible for tracking so-called near-earth-objects is reporting that a meteor is hurtling toward Earth and is expected to impact within the next four to six hours. Information is sketchy at this point, but word has leaked that the projected impact is somewhere in the western hemisphere. The Prime Minister has scheduled a press conference in two hours. He's cautioned the public not to panic. Please remain in your homes. Avoid the highways and don't run to the supermarket for supplies. Stay tuned to this station for further announcements."

The president sighed. "General, are you're absolutely sure that thing's not a meteorite that's going take out L.A.?" He looked at his science advisor who shook his head.

"Absolutely, Sir."

The president turned to his cabinet. "Then what's the harm in playing along?"

"What do you mean?" asked the science advisor.

The aide rushed in again and dropped a pile of online newspaper printouts in front of the president. The first headline read: The Mayans were right! The president held it up for the cabinet members to see. "The public already believes a meteor is coming. You can bet half the citizens of L.A. are already in their cars. I say we go with it. Gives us an excuse to send in the troops, in the name of public safety. If the general's right, we're in position for capturing the saucer and keeping all its goodies."

The secretary of defense nodded his agreement, giving the general a thumbs-up, then winked at Frankel. The general's face flushed with the anticipation of capturing a flying saucer. Not even Eisenhower had done that!

"If the General's wrong and the object is a meteor with L.A.'s name on it," the president continued, "we're getting as many people out of town as we can." The president stood, indicating the meeting had ended. "This is a political gold mine. Make it happen, gentlemen."

Chapter Thirty-Nine

5:30 AM, PST, Twin Lakes, California

Ernie stepped out of his cabin wearing an insulated ski jacket zipped up to his chin and his leather gloves. Nearby, he saw the same two military types who had been camped out in his backyard for weeks. Must be conducting some kind of cold weather training, Ernie thought. The military pair wore insulated army cold-weather jackets and drank coffee from thermos cups, but neither wore gloves. Whatever their official activities were, they kept to the same schedule as Ernie, right down to when he woke in the morning and called it quits at night.

Ernie walked over to them. "You guys ready for our morning walk around the lake?" he asked. They always accompanied him. Not great conversationalists.

One of the agents clapped his hands, trying to stave off frostbite. "Pretty cold this morning. How 'bout giving us a break and dogging it today?"

"You young guys are fit to go, but I gotta jump-start this old body of mine every morning, or one of these days I ain't getting up, if you know what I mean."

The two DIA agents glanced at each other. "Well, if we're going to go, let's go," the first agent said, clapping his hands for warmth.

Ernie held up his gloved hands. "Let me loan you some of these bear-claw gloves. I keep a couple of spare pairs. Keep your hands nice and toasty."

"Great. Appreciate it. Don't take long."

"Gimme a minute. They're in my closet somewhere." Ernie turned and walked back into his cabin.

Once inside, Ernie noticed that the television was on, except he was fairly sure he hadn't turned it on that morning. He stepped over to his easy chair where he found the remote control buried in its usual hiding spot...under the cushion. Then he noticed the television screen. That crazy *Jetson's* show was on again! Before he could click the remote's power button, exhaustion overcame him and he slumped into his chair. Two seconds later, the television scene changed and Ernie began snoring.

No more than a minute later, Ernie roused and headed for the bathroom, although Mother Nature wasn't calling. He gazed at the window over the toilet. He now had a strong compulsion to raise the window and climb through to the outside. A few seconds later, he stood behind his cabin without the slightest notion why, except it seemed like a great idea. After a shrug, Ernie headed off into the woods toward the marina's parking lot at a rapid clip. He didn't have a clue where he was going...he just knew it was important; in fact, it was the most important thing he'd ever done.

One of the DIA agents glanced at his watch. "It's been ten minutes. How long does it take to find a spare pair of gloves?"

"Maybe he had to polish the claws," said the second agent with a smirk.

"Something's wrong. I'm going in."

The agents rushed to the cabin door, and in less than two seconds, picked the lock. Actually Ernie never locked the door, but the whole lock-picking routine did look professional.

The two agents entered Ernie's cabin, searched the premises, and found the open window in the bathroom.

"Son of a bitch!" exclaimed the agent.

Back in the living room, they stared at the television. "If he's skipping out on us, why turn on the TV?"

"This guy has something to do with UFOs, and from our last briefing, things are heating up. Maybe that's how he contacts them."

"Through the TV?"

The other agent flipped through the channels.

"What are you doing?"

"Calling a UFO?"

"Let's go."

7:00 AM, PST, Burbank, California

The girls were lying on Mickey's bed while the boys were sprawled across sleeping bags on the floor.

"What happened to your brother?" asked Vickie. Mickey suddenly looked nervous.

"He got shot!" David cried.

Both girls looked stunned. "How?" Pam finally managed to say.

"He was holding up a liquor store with one of his biker buddies!"

"Unbelievable!" exclaimed Vickie.

Mickey clenched his fists, struggling with what to say. "Dude, there's something I need to tell you…"

Suddenly Max and Jerry opened the bedroom door and stepped inside with long, somber faces. David saw their expressions and tensed.

Pam jabbed Vickie in the ribs. "Ow!" she protested. Pam gestured toward David. "Help me get down!" she whispered. Vickie got the message and helped her slide down onto David's sleeping bag.

While Max remained standing, Jerry sat down on the sleeping bag between the boys. Pam took David's arm. Her grip was firm and steady.

"They found your mom," said Jerry. "She's okay," she hurried to say. "But…" She took a deep breath, and the kids held theirs. It was pretty clear she had received bad news. "She's in the hospital, same one as Jake."

Pam grabbed David and hugged him. He sobbed in her arms. "You said she was at the movies!"

Jerry stared at Max. "That's what we thought. The police

found her. She fell and hit her head on a street curb…but she's going to be okay!"

Vickie started crying too.

"They're going to keep her at the hospital for a while, until she gets her strength back."

"She was drunk!" shouted David, startling everyone. He broke down again.

Looking stricken, Pam rocked him in her arms.

Jerry quickly added, "She's going to get help this time, honey. She'll be okay!"

"There's one piece of good news," said Max. "Your brother's out of surgery and he's going to be okay. Your father's with him now."

Jerry shook her head, an unspoken message, as if to say 'don't speak about Dick.'

"You're staying with us for the next few days, honey," said Jerry. "We'll go see your mom a little later, after she's had a chance to rest, okay?"

David straightened himself up and wiped his eyes. "I'd like to be alone with my friends for a while…if that's okay."

Pam kissed his cheek.

Jerry tried to smile. "I'll go start breakfast. How do pancakes sound to everyone?"

"Great," they replied half-heartedly, all except David.

Jerry and Max left their son's bedroom.

In the kitchen, Jerry set the table. Max slumped on one of the kitchen chairs. "I'm exhausted."

"That's because you haven't had any sleep. Go take a nap." Jerry began moving at top speed, pulling out a box of pancake mix, a bowl, and opening the refrigerator for the milk and eggs.

"You're amazing," said Max, admiring his wife. "Don't you ever get tired?"

"I'm a woman. We're genetically superior. Men just refuse to admit it."

Max smiled. "Want me to help?"

"You're a male, and you're genetically programmed to watch TV." Jerry laughed at her husband's downturned expression. "Just kidding, dear. I've got breakfast covered."

Max looked out the kitchen window. "We're not the only ones up at the crack of dawn."

Jerry furiously stirred the pancake batter. "Who else is up?"

"The street's full of cars all heading in the same direction."

Jerry shrugged and poured pancake batter into a hot pan. "I've never been one for sales. People turn into Neanderthals fighting over so-called bargains."

Vickie sat on the edge of the bed. "I know it's not a great time, but there's another little matter we need to talk about, like *now*, and everybody knows what it is." She held up the palm of her hand. Her silver disc pulsed with a bright white light, brighter than ever. The other three looked at their palms. Their discs glowed as intensely—four teens, four silver discs, and another world expecting a life-or-death answer.

Pam squeezed David's hand, covering his disc with hers. This created the odd effect of surrounding them in an aura, similar to an aurora borealis.

"Whoa! What's that?" exclaimed Mickey.

Startled, Pam and David released their hands. The aura disappeared, and their discs resumed their normal glow.

"Try that again," said Vickie.

Chapter Forty

Max yawned, slumped on the couch, and looked at his watch. It was seven-thirty A.M. He turned on the television. On the screen, the president of the United States was stepping to the podium. Great...more bad economic news, Max guessed. The crawl line at the bottom displayed *replayed* from an earlier live broadcast.

"My fellow Americans," the president began. "NASA has just issued a warning that a moderate-sized meteor is on an impact trajectory with Earth. This finding has been corroborated by sister space agencies in Europe and Russia. Because of the unusual speed of the object, the time of impact is projected at around nine A.M. Pacific Standard Time"—he paused and stared into the camera—"which gives us hardly any time to prepare. While the actual impact point can't be accurately determined at this time, best estimates are that it will impact somewhere off the west coast of the United States...possibly near Los Angeles." He paused again.

Max gasped and shouted to his wife. "Honey, get in here!"

Jerry was sitting at the kitchen table, sipping a cup of coffee and getting a second wind. Hearing Max's urgency, she ran to the living room. "What?"

"The President's on TV! You gotta hear this!"

"So what? If the president changes his shirt, there's a special announcement."

The president continued. "I've ordered all available civil defense assets to mobilize in the Southern California area. Residents along the coast, and in the major metropolitan area of Los Angeles, are asked to begin an orderly evacuation. Please do not panic..."

"Oh my God!" Max yelled. "Get the kids!"

"But they're sleeping!"

"There's a meteor heading straight for us!" Max grabbed her shoulders and shoved her in front of the television.

The screen now displayed a white streak across the blackness of space. The president's voice continued narrating in the background. "This is a live picture of the object taken from the Keck Telescope atop Hawaii's Mauna Kea volcano. The object is estimated to be one hundred meters wide. Its exact weight cannot be estimated without knowing its composition. Unfortunately it's moving at extraordinary speeds, which is why we don't have much time to prepare." He paused. Jerry and Max stood frozen, waiting. The president cleared his throat. It was obvious something worse was coming. "An object of this size and velocity, if it impacts in the ocean close offshore, may trigger a five hundred-foot tsunami, or if it impacts on land, cause significant damage. Therefore, all residents along the west coast of Southern California and in the metropolitan area of Los Angeles are urged to immediately evacuate. The Highway Patrol and the National Guard have stopped all inbound traffic to Southern California. All highways in both directions now lead inland. If you are currently in these areas, you are urged to leave immediately. Do not go to an airport. All air traffic is grounded. If you don't have a car, or access to a neighbor's vehicle, get to the nearest school shelter. Buses are waiting. Citizens outside of the projected impact area are urged to stay inside their homes and await further announcements." The president stepped away from the podium. Immediately, a stunned newsman was on camera.

"Oh my God! Get the kids!" shouted Jerry. Both Max and Jerry sprinted for Mickey's bedroom.

"Playing around with our palm gizmos is cool, but guys, in case anybody's forgotten, our personal UFO is on the way," said Vickie. "It's now or never."

Pam had that peculiar faraway look in her eyes again. "This could be the most important moment in the history of the human race," she said.

Mickey looked glum. "Do I hear violins?"

"No sarcasm, not now!" Pam's eyes bored into Mickey's. "It's time to choose!"

"What if I can't?"

They heard frantic pounding on the door. "Kids!" screamed Jerry. "There's a meteor coming! We have to get outta here, *now*!"

All four teenagers stared at each other.

Max flung open the door, and he and Jerry rushed in. "Let's go," ordered Max, trying to sound calm but clearly not. "In the car, *now*, everybody!"

"What meteor?" Mickey asked.

"The president was just on TV!" shouted Jerry. "Los Angeles is being evacuated! We don't have much time!"

David glanced at Mickey. "Wait a minute. Do you think?"

Jerry began pushing them out of the bedroom.

Mickey yanked his arm away, reached under the bed, and pulled out the suit and helmet.

His mother stared at the suit in his arms. "You're taking that thing?"

"Let's go!" yelled Max.

Chaos reigned on the street. Front doors were open. People were piling into cars with their pets, carrying valuables, and then heading down the street toward the boulevard to join a traffic jam of shrieking drivers and honking horns.

"Get in the car, kids!" shouted Max.

"Come on, come on!" Jerry yelled, opening up the back door of Max's sedan. It was parked in the driveway behind her now shiny blue SUV.

The boys exchanged glances. "Where're we going?"

"The President said everybody's to head inland, away from the ocean. The meteor's going to land in the ocean and cause a five hundred-foot tsunami!"

They heard the sound of approaching helicopters.

"We can't go," Mickey said to his dad.

"Get in the car!" Jerry shrieked.

None of the teens moved.

"We don't have much time!" Max yelled. The street was nearly empty. Most of their neighbors' cars had already raced down the street toward the freeway.

The sound of the helicopters grew louder by the second. Mickey had to shout to be heard. "We can't go!" He held up his palm showing the flashing white light of the disc. The other three teens did the same.

"We don't have time for laser tag!" Max shouted back. The sound of the helicopters was almost deafening now. They looked up and saw two black military helicopters circling directly above their house.

"It's not a meteor…it's a flying saucer!" Mickey screamed over the din.

His father couldn't hear him. "What?"

Mickey put his mouth right near his father's ear and yelled. "There's no meteor. It's a flying saucer, and I've been on it. We all have!"

Max stared at his son, stunned. "You can't be serious!"

"We're serious!" shouted David. "There's no tsunami coming, but we have to get to Griffith Park!" The two girls nodded insistently.

Jerry glanced at Max. "What's going on?"

An amplified voice boomed from one of the helicopters hovering right overhead. "Stay where you are. You're all under arrest!"

Mickey looked up at the black helicopter. With the rotor wash whipping his hair, he handed the suit to David, grabbed his mother's purse from her arm, and emptied its contents onto the ground.

Jerry watched in disbelief, barely able to stand beneath the maelstrom of air. "What are you doing!" she screamed at her son. Max continued to stare up at the helicopter.

"Mom, trust me on this!" Mickey shouted. He found his mother's car keys and motioned to the other kids. "Get in the SUV!" He sprinted for the driver's side door. Still holding the suit and helmet, David grabbed Pam around the waist with his other arm and glanced urgently at Vickie. The two of them carried Pam and lifted her into the SUV's backseat.

Jerry started after them, but Max grabbed her arm. "I trust our son. Let them go."

"You can't be serious!" Jerry shrieked. She tried to pull free from his grip, but Max wouldn't release her.

Jerry glared at him. "Okay, but on one condition!"

David shoved Vickie through the SUV's back door causing her to sprawl on top of Pam, then slammed the door and jumped in the front passenger seat. Mickey was behind the wheel and revving the engine. He glanced at David who grabbed the armrest. Mickey jumped on the accelerator steering the SUV across the lawn, through a flowerbed, finally knocking over their mailbox and out onto the street.

Mickey's parents watched the SUV speed away. Both of them sprinted for Max's sedan.

Chapter Forty-One

Dick stood outside the ambulance entrance and lit another cigarette, ignoring the chaos around him. Patients were being evacuated—something about a meteor. As soon as Jake was out of surgery, they'd be taking him somewhere too—that is, if he survived. Then he'd be going to jail. Linda had a concussion, and her examination revealed a serious liver condition. The doctor said it was caused by alcohol. On top of everything, he lost his job. How much loss could one man face all at once? He could emotionally shut down, or even end it all. Wait for the meteor? Dick Walker wasn't that kind of man. He enjoyed wearing a badge and carrying a gun. He woke in the morning eager to hear the sound of the sirens, hungry for the excitement of the chase. For such a man, retreat isn't an option. But if anger is depression begging to be released, how that emotional release is accomplished can be life's turning point. Fate had put Dick in just such a place.

He paced in the dark, struggling to collect his thoughts. He felt a primitive kind of anger, one based more on instinct than warped reason. Calling it a descent into the dark side would trivialize the process. The fate of his wife and his son were out of his hands, and unless something changed, he'd lose the house. He felt so helpless! He needed to fight back, to regain some measure of control over his life. He needed to be the one inflicting the pain, not the one being pummeled. As his mind raced, he remembered Jake's strange story about stolen military hardware. The idea was ludicrous, but he was too exhausted to think it through. But, if there was even a slight chance the crazy story could lead to good honest retribution of any sort, against anybody, he'd embrace it. Besides, he felt too weary to look anywhere else for answers, especially within himself. He threw down his cigarette and dialed his cell phone.

"FBI, how can I direct your call?"

"This is Officer Dick Walker, Foothill Division, Burbank California, badge number 11976. I want to report the theft of secret military hardware."

"Officer Walker, stand by please." The voice clicked off, but the line remained active.

Following protocol, the FBI operator keyed in Dick's badge number. For some reason, the computer immediately flashed an alert. It didn't indicate why, but it ordered an immediate cross connect to DIA at Cheyenne Mountain.

"Office Walker, I'm going to patch you through to the proper authorities. Please stand by."

"Go ahead," replied Dick, wearily.

Another click followed, and then a brief delay.

"Officer Walker, this is Lieutenant Latham." He left out the part about his DIA affiliation. "What is the reason for this call?" Latham keyed in the name Walker and pulled up a computer file showing the clearing at Griffith Park. The second panel showed a close-up of Jake Walker's Harley squashed like a pancake, and in a third panel, a close up of the serial numbers visible on a twisted piece of metal. The caller could be a relative of the guy who owned the squashed motorcycle, thought the Lieutenant excitedly…a break in the case, and maybe a promotion!

"Lieutenant, I have information regarding the theft of some top-secret military hardware," said Dick.

A pause on the end of the line followed. "What hardware would that be, Officer?"

"I'm not really sure what it is."

"Did you actually see this hardware?"

"No, Sir, I didn't. But I have an eyewitness who saw it and knows who stole it."

"Okay…can you tell me what this military stuff does?"

"It's some kind of suit that makes the wearer super strong."

"Stand by, please." Latham muted the line and pulled up the

file on Ernie Santos. He played a portion of an audio file. "...Used the thing to toss a whole tree across a creek, like it was a twig...and he crushed a rock in his hand like it was an egg!" So this cop had a scoop on the suit, but not its alien origin or what was going down this morning. Another clue! "Who is that eyewitness, Officer?"

"My son Jake."

Lieutenant Latham pushed back in his chair. They were looking for someone named Walker, and now his father was on the line! A promotion and a medal! "And where did your son, Jake, you said his name is, see the hardware?"

"In an alley near where I am now. Some teenagers have it."

"Some teenagers... Stand by, Officer Walker." Latham placed the call on speakerphone, moved his fingers to his lips signaling silence, and waved over his colleagues. The kook on the phone might be the break they'd been waiting for!

"Officer Walker, this is...the FBI again," said Lieutenant Latham. "Sorry for the delay. We're going to send some boys out there to take a look around," continued Latham speaking into the phone. "So I need to know where I can find the kid who stole our top secret stuff. Did I hear you say he lives in Burbank?"

"Yeah, like I said, he lives across the street from me."

"Got it. And where can I find you, Officer?"

Dick gripped the phone and closed his eyes. "At the same location—the house across the street." He gave Latham the address.

"Maintaining surveillance. Smart idea!"

"Lieutenant, is there a reward for the recovery of your top secret equipment? I got laid off. I could really use the money."

Latham cleared his throat. "Actually, there is a reward, a big one. So stay where you are. See you soon, Officer Walker." He hung up. "This is it!" Latham shouted. "Let's go get this guy!"

"There's a meteor on the way that could take out LA!" exclaimed one of the others. "You can't send any of our guys there now to arrest an insane, out-of-work cop and some punks playing Superman."

"It's the first break we've had to what's going down in that park!"

"That park might not exist in a few hours!"

Latham picked up the phone. "Get me Westlock!" he yelled.

"The general left orders not to be disturbed," said the operator.

"Get him now, it's an emergency!"

The operator shook her head. "Okay, I'll do it…but honey, I wouldn't throw away the want ads." Latham slammed down the phone.

He felt better than he had in some time. He was in command! The phone rang. He picked it up. "General?"

"I said I didn't want to be disturbed!" the general shouted, back in his hotel room.

Latham's stomach clenched, but he held his ground. "I found the father of the guy who owns the squashed motorcycle in L.A.!"

There was silence on the other end of the line. "Is this a secure line?"

"Yes, Sir."

"I want you to fly to Los Angeles, arrest that man, and bring him to Griffith Park by 0800."

"What about the meteor?"

"For your ears only, Latham…there's no meteor—it's a cover story. The saucer's coming back and we're rounding up everyone who's had any contact before we take control of it."

Latham's hand started to shake. This was the biggest assignment of his career, a chance for a promotion, maybe a medal! "I won't let you down, General!"

"I know you won't, son. And remember, this is top secret! If anybody questions your orders, tell them to contact my office."

When the conversation ended, everybody in ops was staring

at him. "The general's ordered me to L.A. to help with…the evacuation."

"What about Walker and the kid with the superman outfit?" someone asked.

"Walker's an idiot, and the kid got his hands on an exoskeleton someone stole from the military." Latham turned off his computer console, straightened his desk, and hurried out of the operation's room.

Finally, someone said, "Cover-up." The others nodded their heads and returned to their work.

Chapter Forty-Two

General Westlock sat in the jump seat behind the pilot of the lead Black Hawk helicopter code-named Alpha One. Westlock grabbed the microphone and started broadcasting to the other helicopters, one orbiting over the house, and four more hovering over downtown Los Angeles waiting for orders.

"Alpha One to all units. Suspect vehicle is attempting to escape! Abort landing. I repeat, abort landing! Alpha One and Two will track vehicle. All other Alpha units are to converge on Griffith Park. Alpha One will notify ground units to set up a roadblock. Alpha units, do you copy?"

"Alpha Two copies."

"Alpha Four copies."

"Alpha Five copies."

"Alpha Six copies."

"Alpha Three copies." Alpha Three was one of choppers orbiting over downtown L.A. "Uh, Alpha One, Sir…I thought we're supposed to be capturing a flying saucer." He snickered, but everyone heard it.

"Maintain radio silence Alpha Three. This is a stealth attack!"

"Roger that Alpha One, but I think we can scrap the idea of this being a stealth attack."

"Say again Alpha Three?"

"I got the Channel Seven News chopper flying formation with me right now. Damn, that blonde news lady is hot!"

A brightly colored helicopter with a large number seven painted on its side flew parallel to the Black Hawk special ops helicopter, call sign Alpha Three. An attractive blonde woman wearing headphones in the passenger seat was smiling and waving, holding a microphone. One of the fifteen heavily armed commandos in the back of the Black Hawk waved back at her.

Melanie Dilman and the Channel Seven news chopper were

covering the impending meteor strike. Since nothing interesting would be happening unless there was a tsunami, or the civic center got squashed, they decided to shadow the Black Hawk helicopters hovering over downtown. Her instincts were rewarded as the helicopters peeled off heading toward Griffith Park, and not out of town like everybody else. The news chopper followed them.

"What do you suppose they're doing?" she asked the pilot, as her cameraman filmed the Black Hawks.

"Don't know, boss. "

Melanie smiled and waved at the soldier in Alpha Three. "My reporter's instinct says we keep following them."

"The tsunami would be in the other direction…you know, toward the ocean? Aren't we supposed to film it?"

"Those four heavily armed military copters know something we don't."

"You got it." The news chopper circled around, following the military birds. As they approached the park, they saw two other Black Hawks following an SUV and veered off to film the pursuit.

A green army ambulance and a jeep drove up the road leading to the clearing in Griffith Park. Half a mile before the turn off, the two vehicles pulled to the side and stopped. The ambulance driver and two soldiers ran to the back of the ambulance, hopped inside, and shut the door. The third soldier stood outside cradling an automatic weapon.

One of the soldiers, who was really a nuclear technician, wore gloves and carefully opened a metal suitcase strapped to the ambulance's floor. Inside was a twenty-kiloton nuclear device, big enough to vaporize everything in the clearing but leave most of the city intact. He adjusted a few dials, synchronized a detonator shaped like a cell phone, and put it in his pocket. Then he carefully closed and locked the metal case.

"Okay, this baby's armed," he said. "If I call the right number, *boom*!"

"What about us?" one of the soldiers nervously asked.

"If we don't want to glow in the dark, we need to be five miles upwind when the sucker blows."

"Then let's get out of Dodge!" said the ambulance driver.

They locked the ambulance door, disabled the engine, placed red traffic cones around it, then hopped in the jeep and sped away.

Since all traffic was moving in the opposite direction, the teens were making good time on the mostly deserted surface streets heading over the Hollywood Hills. Both sides of the I-5 Freeway had cars heading north. They turned off Riverside Drive onto Zoo Drive leading into Griffith Park, which had even less room for a helicopter landing. The two military helicopters pursued Mickey's SUV like killer bees, while the Channel Seven helicopter filmed the whole pursuit.

Vickie looked out the back window. "They're still behind us!"

"We've got to reach the clearing!" Mickey said.

"How? The choppers are right on top of us!" said David.

"They can't land at the clearing—too many trees. They'll have to land in the Observatory's parking lot, and that's a ways back." Mickey kept glancing in the rearview mirror.

The combined downdraft of the helicopters buffeted the SUV with an earsplitting sound.

The girls covered their ears. "Why are they chasing us?" shouted Vickie. "We didn't do anything!"

"They've got to be onto us!" yelled David. "I bet my brother blabbed before he got shot."

"What if the saucer doesn't come?" Vickie shouted back.

"It's coming. Look at your palm," said Pam in her weirdly serene voice. Even in daylight, the car's interior pulsed with white flashing light.

A lone stealth helicopter landed on the street between David and Mickey's houses. Latham hopped out wearing body armor. He hadn't been on an actual mission in a few years and the armor looked a little snug. The other member of their special ops team dismounted. Latham consulted a GPS and pointed at David's house. "Walker lives there," he said.

The street was deserted. "Place looks like a ghost town," said Corporal Hicks. Hicks was the only special ops guy who'd volunteer for the mission. He looked up at the sky. "I hope you're right and there's no meteor coming."

Latham went to David's front door and rang the bell. A moment later, Walker opened the door.

"The general sent us," said Latham.

Walker looked like he hadn't slept in days, because he hadn't. "I thought you were FBI?"

"It's our phone cover."

"Did you bring the money?"

"It's in the helicopter," Latham replied. "We want the kid with the suit, and we know where he is. Help us nab him, and the money's yours."

Walked forced a smile. "Time for some payback."

Latham pointed at the chopper's open door. They hurried over and climbed inside. The copter lifted off and headed for Griffith Park only three miles away.

The car careened up the winding road to the clearing. The two Black Hawk helicopters and the Channel Seven News helicopter were trying to follow, but the terrain was making it difficult. They now met up with the other four helicopters hovering over the clearing.

"Alpha One, this is Alpha Three. Over."

"Go ahead, Alpha Three."

"Boss…ah, I mean Alpha One, Sir…if we're going to continue pursuit, we have to land somewhere."

There was silence on the airwaves for a few seconds. General Westlock leaned forward toward his pilot.

"Biggs, can you see any place for us to land?"

Lieutenant Biggs consulted his digital maps and radar.

"There's a parking lot at the Observatory."

"Alpha units, this is Alpha One. Stand by."

Lieutenant Biggs continued consulting his computer displays. "But there's room for only one chopper."

"Where's the nearest flat area that will hold all six of us?" asked the General.

"Hollywood and Vine, Sir."

The general frowned. "How about something a little less obvious, soldier?"

"There's a parking lot at the Los Angeles Zoo with enough room for five choppers, but it's two and a half miles back from the clearing where the saucer last landed," replied Lieutenant Biggs.

"Alpha One to Alpha group. Alpha Two through Six will land at the zoo and hike to our rendezvous point. Alpha One will land at the Observatory and secure the area until your arrival. Do you copy?"

"Alpha Two copies."

"Three copies… But, Sir, in full body armor and lugging all our equipment?"

"Suck it up, soldier! All Alpha units maintain radio silence until arrival at our rendezvous point! Do you understand Alpha Units?"

"Alpha Two copies."

"Alpha Three copies… But, Sir?"

"Now what?"

"When our five big black choppers full of commandos land at the Los Angeles Zoo followed by the Channel Seven News helicopter, do you still think we can keep this operation a secret?"

"Just follow orders, Alpha Three! Anybody with a brain is already on the road out of town! Alpha One out!"

The pilot of Alpha Three covered his microphone. "He said it, not me."

Mickey slowed the car as they arrived at the dirt road leading to the clearing. He carefully eased down to a slower speed avoiding another altercation with a tree. When they reached level ground, he pulled to the side and parked. The teens piled out.

"Mickey, call the saucer!" David yelled. Pam leaned against the side of the SUV looking up into the sky while Vickie grabbed her braces. They heard a helicopter approaching, but after a minute, it flew away.

Mickey opened the trunk and removed the suit. "One of the helicopters must've landed, probably at the Observatory!"

"What's the plan?" said Vickie sounding perfectly calm. She'd definitely changed since the trip to Europa.

Mickey put on the suit and closed the visor. All the buttons were dark. He stabbed at them several times, but nothing happened. He took off the helmet again. "I guess that's it for this getup."

"What does that mean?" asked Vickie, moving closer to him.

"It means the Test is over and I can't stop bullets."

Chapter Forty-Three

They heard rustling coming from the shrubbery, and an amplified voice blared at them. "Drop your weapons and put your hands up! This is the United States Military!"

"Great!" Mickey groaned, shaking his head.

"What weapons?" asked Pam, leaning on Vickie.

David looked up into the sky. "No sign of it."

The teenagers pulled together into a tight group. They saw fifteen soldiers from Alpha One in full combat gear advancing down the dirt road. One of the soldiers, the platoon leader, turned and signaled to the others to halt.

"Jesus, it's just a bunch of kids!" he shouted. "Safety your weapons!"

Another soldier stepped forward with a chest full of medals. "Which one of you is David Walker?" General Westlock demanded.

David stepped forward. "I am."

"The other boy there, is your name Mickey…something?"

Mickey stepped forward too. "That's me."

"Where's that UFO?" demanded the general. The soldiers anxiously glanced around the clearing.

None of the teens responded.

"I want this clearing surrounded, now!"

"With fifteen guys?" asked the platoon leader.

"Where the hell are the rest of the men?" shouted the general.

"Hoofing it down from the Zoo. Should be here any minute."

A ruckus of voices echoed from the road. The loudest was Jerry's. Mickey's parents had followed them in the car. "Mickey!" Jerry screamed. She and Max came running down the road followed by more commandos from the other five helicopters, all with their weapons drawn.

Jerry ran right through the cordon of soldiers and grabbed

her son in a bear hug. Then she gathered up David and yelled to the two girls. “Get behind me!” She faced the gathering of some ninety black-clad soldiers with the fierce look of a mother bear protecting her cubs. “Don't you dare come near these kids!” she yelled at the top of her lungs. “I'm a US citizen and I know my rights!”

A blonde woman speaking into a microphone, and a man carrying a portable television camera on his shoulder came slipping and sliding down the dirt road. A former Huey pilot in 'Nam, the news helicopter pilot had found a place to land his smaller helicopter. Several soldiers whistled at Melanie. She smiled and took a bow. After that brief exchange, she shoved her way to the front of the soldiers and stuck the microphone close to General Westlock's face, hitting him in the chin.

“Sorry about that, General,” she said. She turned to her cameraman. “Bill, is the camera on?” The cameraman signaled yes. “Erase the part where I hit the General, okay?”

“That's General Westlock, young woman,” snarled the general.

She smiled at him, and then looked straight into the camera. “This is action reporter Melanie Dilman, live in Griffith Park at the scene of a clandestine military operation.” She turned back to General Westlock. “General, would you care to tell our viewers what's happening here?” She batted her eyelashes at him. “Are there terrorists in Griffith Park?”

“Shut that thing off!” he shouted, pointing at the television camera. “This is a top secret military operation, and this is a restricted area!” He signaled with his hand, and one of the soldiers confiscated the television camera, ripping out the power plug and removing a DVD. Melanie calmly dropped the dead microphone and pulled a hand recorder from her pocket. She smiled and thrust it back in General Westlock's face. This time, she didn't hit him.

“Have you ever heard of freedom of the press, General?”

He turned to his men. "Get her out of here!"

Seconds later, Latham came down the road followed by Walker and Corporal Hicks. The clearing was becoming crowded.

Frankel's face blanched when he saw Latham. Latham glared at him.

"Who's he?" asked Frankel, pointing at Walker.

Latham pushed out his chest. "The father of the guy whose motorcycle was squashed by the flying saucer!"

Frankel threw up his hands in frustration. "Great!"

General Westlock glared at Frankel. "And the father of one of the flying saucer kids!" The general turned to Latham. "Good work, soldier."

At that very moment, they all heard the sound.

A haze blanketed the sky overhead. Directly above the clearing, a patch of it began to boil. Thick clouds billowed into existence, and then sullied like the sudden appearance of a storm. A whining sound accompanied the atmospheric disturbance. The newly formed clouds then blazed with light, as if backlit by the sun. Everyone in the clearing stood transfixed, gawking at the climatic display. Behind the glowing clouds, flashing lights became visible. With each passing second, the unnatural whining increased. Roiling clouds and brilliant lights started descending over the clearing.

Some of the soldiers instinctively backed away.

Pam gazed up with an angelic smile. "It's coming."

"Yep," was all David could say.

Mickey dropped the helmet on the ground and reached for Vickie's hand.

A hundred meters above, the clouds churned and the bottom of the saucer became visible. A ring of colored lights pulsed under its surface. The kaleidoscope of colors was ever changing.

Mickey looked at General Westlock. "You and your men may want to move back, General. The last time this saucer landed, somebody's motorcycle ended as a big silver dollar."

General Westlock stared at the saucer. "Pull back!" he shouted. The order wasn't really necessary, as his soldiers had already run back up the dirt road and dispersed into the surrounding foliage.

Max ran to the teenagers still huddled behind Jerry. He looked at his son. "You know about that thing, don't you?"

"Gotta trust me on this, Dad," Mickey replied. The five of them followed Mickey and moved next to the tree that the SUV had hit the first time.

The saucer settled to the ground and the whining sound faded. Within moments, the door formed on its side and the ramp flowed to the ground. A bright light streamed from the doorway. Within the light, a lone humanoid figure appeared.

General Westlock crouched in the bushes with some of his men. "Prepare to fire on my command!"

Melanie Dilman from Channel Seven was one bush away. "Bill, you've got to get this! This is a fucking Pulitzer and an Emmy, maybe the Nobel Prize!" Her cameraman took out his camcorder and started filming. Half the soldiers were recording as well with their cell phones.

"Jesus, look at that!" a soldier shouted. He dropped his rifle and bolted away.

Wearing a silvery coverall, Ernie Santos stepped out of the light in the saucer's doorway and stood at the top of the ramp. He smiled and waved. Everybody gaped at him.

Ernie motioned the teens up. "You kids gotta come up here," he called down. "We have to talk." He never stopped smiling.

"Who's that guy?" Pam asked.

"Holy shit—is that Ernie?" David exclaimed.

"Who's Ernie? How'd he get in the saucer?" Vickie asked Mickey.

"I have no idea! This is freakin' unbelievable!" said Mickey. "He runs the marina where David and I go every summer. Takes us fishing. He's totally cool!"

Vickie looked at Pam and shrugged. "Just when you think you've got it figured out." Mickey turned to his mom. "We have to go."

"You're not getting into that thing!"

"I've already been in it, twice. We've traveled all over the solar system in it."

Jerry paled. "What?"

"Me too," said David.

Pam and Vickie nodded too.

Mickey faced his dad. "Please trust me on this!" Max put his hand on his son's shoulder, looked in his eyes, then nodded at Jerry. She hugged and released her son, and the teenagers walked toward the saucer.

The general pushed his way forward. He had Dick Walker by the arm.

Dick pointed at Mickey. "That's the kid."

"You kids aren't going anywhere!" barked General Westlock. "As the officer in charge here"—he glared at Major Frankel—"in the name of the President of the United States, I order you not to set foot inside that thing! That flying saucer is now the property of the US government!" He turned toward his men. "Take these kids into custody and lock down that UFO!"

The teens started up the ramp with David and Vickie assisting Pam.

"Stop, or we'll fire!" yelled the general when they were halfway up.

Ernie touched his sleeve. A bright blue veil descended over the kids. They continued upward.

"Fire!" ordered the general.

"No!" screamed Frankel and Mickey's parents. But it was too late.

Several high-powered rifles and a machine gun started firing with a deafening sound. The smell of cordite filled the air.

Simultaneously, a series of bright flashes erupted where the bullets impacted the protective blue force field. Everyone heard several *pffzt* sounds as the hail of projectiles was vaporized. Bewildered, the soldiers stopped shooting. The teens reached the top of the ramp and turned around.

"Don't let them get away, you idiots!" shouted the general. He rushed forward, drew his pearl-handled Colt 45, just like General Patton's, and started shooting. Unfortunately it had been awhile since he'd fired the gun, or cleaned it, and bullets sprayed everywhere. One stray bullet hit Max in the shoulder. His knees buckled, and he fell to the ground. Jerry started shrieking.

"Dad!" screamed Mickey from the top of the ramp. He took a step downward, but Ernie held him back.

"He'll be okay." Ernie showed him a silver disc in the center of his own palm. "Let's go inside. We've got some serious business to conclude, and not a lot of time. I'll fix your dad when we're done." He smiled. "I promise!"

The teens followed Ernie into the saucer, and then the door disappeared.

Chapter Forty-Four

Inside the saucer, they gathered around Ernie.

"What are you doing here?" asked David.

Mickey appeared nervous. He kept glancing at the wall where the door had been.

Ernie sensed Mickey's discomfort. "Don't worry," he reassured him. "I'm going to fix your dad. You know ol' Ern never breaks his promise, right?"

Mickey still didn't seem convinced. "How?"

Ernie removed an object from the pocket of his silver coveralls and held it up. It looked like a ball the size of a grapefruit comprised of the same silver substance as the saucer. It pulsed with white light, just like their palm discs.

"What does that thing do?" asked Vickie, peering at it.

"Tons of cool stuff," replied Ernie.

"How does it work?" asked David.

"Not a clue, except I know it does amazing things. Saw the whole thing on TV while I was sleeping."

The teens looked at each other, wondering if they heard correctly. Ernie smiled. "You've been to Europa and know the silver guys have things we can't understand…yet!"

"Not good enough," said David. "There's too much at stake here!"

"I'll tell you kids everything, or at least what little I know or understand, but first there's something real important to decide, and everyone knows what it is." Ernie studied the face of each of the teens.

Pam hobbled over to one of the silver pillars and leaned against it. As soon as she came in contact with it, an appendage sprouted and flowed around her waist. After several seconds, she started flexing her legs.

"That's better!" she said with a big grin. The appendage

withdrew and Pam stood up straight, undid her braces, and tossed them to the floor. She began bounding about the saucer like a gazelle, but then stopped and looked embarrassed. "Sorry!" she apologized, and rejoined the group. David gazed at her with tears in his eyes.

Ernie smiled. "One of those silver seats did the same thing to me! When I first got into this saucer, one of them lassoed me. Told me I had diabetes, heart disease, and a tumor on one kidney. Of course I wasn't too happy to hear all that stuff, but I started to feel funny all over, and after that real good—I mean *really* good. Then it released me and a strange voice told me I'd been repaired. The other weird thing is that I haven't had anything to eat or drink for hours, but I'm not hungry or thirsty. Good thing too, cause I haven't located anything that looks like a refrigerator." He laughed.

"You still haven't told us what you're doing here," said Mickey.

"How did you get in the flying saucer?" David added.

"Well, I got this feeling that I needed to drive to L.A. Not sure why. Headed out about five-thirty this morning, got as far as Indian Wells, and then I'm driving along and my truck starts to glow. Before I know it, I'm onboard this saucer."

"What happened to your truck?" David asked.

"Mexico's first satellite."

They all laughed. Finally Mickey interrupted. "Really, do you know what's happening?"

"Yeah, I do. Part of my TV download. You and David and the girls, the Test, and the Choice." Mentioning the Choice made everybody turn serious. "So, what are you guys going to do?"

"I need to decide if I'm going," said Mickey.

Vickie gave Mickey a pensive look. "And if you go, who goes with you," she said in a silky voice. His heart skipped a beat.

"You guys got part of it right," said Ernie.

"What do you mean?" asked Vickie, still staring at Mickey.

"Two of you must decide if you're going back with the saucer to Europa. But which two has already been decided."

"I was the one who passed the Test," stated Mickey.

"And I was thinking of going with him," added Vickie, looking down. Mickey grinned.

"Yes, but you two guys don't really want to go." Mickey and Vickie looked at each other and nodded in agreement. Ernie gave them a comforting smile. "Kids, take a look at your palms."

Each of them held up their hands. The silver discs on the palms of David and Pam were still strobing brightly. Mickey and Vickie's discs were dark.

Mickey stared at his palm. "What does that mean?"

"It means that Pam and David are the ones. It's *their* Choice." Ernie beamed at them. "It's the biggest decision of your lives, kids. Actually the biggest leap any human has made since…well, since discovering fire."

"Do I hear a drum roll?" said Mickey, trying to lighten the mood. David playfully punched him in the arm. Inside, David was so nervous he could barely stand.

"It's going to take a while to restart the civilization on Europa," continued Ernie, "and it's got to be done right, not just with technology, but with maturity and the proper code of ethics. This time Adam and Eve are staying in the garden and making it their home."

David moved closer to Pam and took her hand. When he did, the same aura they'd seen earlier reappeared and enfolded them with a golden light. David pulled Pam closer and kissed her, and the aura sparkled like a galaxy of twinkling stars. Mickey put his hand around Vickie's waist and she rested her head on his shoulder. For a moment, nobody moved.

"But I was the one who passed the Test," said Mickey, breaking the silence.

"Yes, you did," replied Ernie. "You passed the Test for the whole human race, not just for yourself. You're the one who made it possible for the beings who built this flying saucer to finally find the right flesh-and-blood species to rebuild their world. You're a real hero! But David and Pam are the two best candidates to move to Europa." He turned to face David and Pam. "Why don't you two talk it over. But I gotta tell you, we don't have much time." Ernie stepped over to the window with his back to the teens.

Pam smiled at David, her glistening eyes filled with excitement. "Davie, I'm going," she said. "And not just to walk again. I can't tell you why…because I don't know…but I feel like my entire life has been heading for this moment!"

"'Be all you can be,'" David added with a smile. Pam nodded her head.

Ernie, the Army ranger, turned back to them. "Gives a whole new meaning to the old army slogan, guys." He chuckled.

Pam smiled at Mickey and Vickie. "But I'll miss my friends!" Vickie ran over and hugged her. Pam looked into her best friend's eyes. "Vic, I've got to do this, for me…for us, for everyone. Does that make any sense?" She was crying. "And I want to be with Davie!" They hugged again. "Tell my mom I love her," said Pam. With tears rolling down her cheeks, Vickie pulled away.

Mickey stared at his best friend. "Are you really going?"

"Yeah." Davie wiped his eyes with his shirtsleeve. "I love Pam, but it's more than that. Lately, before all this happened, I was starting to wonder what I was going to do with my life. I want to do something that matters, so there's a reason I was born. My dad never had any use for me, but my mom always told me I was special, that someday I was going to do something important." Tears were flowing down his cheeks. "She loves me, and believes in me…but now she's sick." He looked down, as if he struggled to continue. "I'm scared to leave her, but…" Pam touched his cheek. It was a simple caress that communicated volumes. He took her hand in his, reigniting the aura, and they faced Mickey and Vickie. "But this is my chance to prove she was right about me, that I was right about me, and my dad was wrong." He gazed into Pam's eyes. "Is that being selfish?"

Ernie placed one hand on David's shoulder and one on Pam's. "Your mom's going to be okay," he said. "Good as new, just like Mickey's dad."

David wiped his eyes. "How do you know?"

Ernie pointed towards the saucer's window. "Look."

David ran to the window. Captain Stevens was helping David's mother down the road to the clearing. Her hair was disheveled, and she was obviously weak, but when she looked at the saucer her eyes were clear, more so than David could ever remember.

"What's wrong with her?" David asked.

"You might say she has the same problem we all do, Davie, even the Europans. We all need to figure out who we really are and get on the right path. Your mom needed to stop and take a deep breath, look in the mirror. But she'll be fine now. We all will."

Mickey moved next to them. "What about my dad?" He could see Max lying on the ground tended by a medic.

Ernie took out the sphere again. "I'll fix him with this thing. He tossed it from hand to hand, as if he were juggling.

"How's that thing going to cure Mickey's dad?" Vickie asked skeptically.

"Beats me… It generates the same energy that powers up the City on Europa, and this flying saucer too." He pointed at Pam's legs. "You already know what this stuff can do. And you know what the suit does too." David and Mickey nodded their heads. "It's also a kind of…a holographic computer containing every technological advance of the Europan race."

David smiled at him. "Hey, Ern, when did you get so smart?"

Ernie looked at his watch. "About ten minutes ago."

"Can I try that thing?" asked Mickey.

"Me too," Vickie added. "I've got calculus next semester."

"Sorry, it's programmed so only I can use it. Anybody else touches it and they get zapped. Won't kill 'em, unless they use lethal force."

"You haven't told us what you're doing in the saucer, except you saw something on TV," Mickey said.

"Now that David and Pam have decided to go, I'm staying here with you and Vic, to help out, to give humanity the gifts. The silver guys told me it didn't work out too well when they showed up the first time, so they made some modifications."

"The first time?"

"They showed me..."

"On your TV set," Mickey interrupted. "We got that part. Showed you what?"

"They handed out one of these technology gizmos down here once before."

"Roswell!" shouted David.

Ernie shook his head. "That was somebody else. The Europans were here twelve thousand years ago. It's how the Great Pyramid was built...levitating the stones and all that. It was originally a power plant for the whole planet, converted the earth's own energy into..." The sphere now turned an angry red in his hand. "Guess I'm not supposed to share that yet."

"Early man didn't pass the Test," said David.

"But we had potential," Ernie continued, "so they kept an eye on us. Tried again six thousand years ago without the gizmo. Check out the history books—not much better. This time around, the Test was tailored to one individual using the suit. You, Mickey."

"What are you supposed to do with that sphere thing after you cure my dad and David's mom?" asked Mickey.

Ernie had a faraway look in his eyes. "That's up to the people of the world."

"You know that crazy-ass general out there will try to confiscate it."

"Then he's in for an…expanded experience, him and his men, and anybody else who tries to use force against us and the sphere."

Ernie seemed to shake himself loose from his "altered self" and became the old fly-fishing Ernie once again. "Okay, gang. Let's get this show on the road!" He turned to Mickey and Vickie. "You kids say your goodbyes, 'cause David and Pam need to make tracks back to Europa. I've only seen it on TV, but it sure looks like a great place. You know how much I like being around water!"

Behind them, the doorway started reforming. Mickey hugged David hard. Vickie did the same with Pam.

David held up his hand. "Wait!"

Everybody looked surprised.

"What's the catch?" asked David.

"What do you mean?" Mickey asked his friend.

David stared at Ernie. "The last time humanity took a bite out of the apple, things didn't go so well."

"Not going to disagree with you, Davie," said Ernie. "But this time we've come of age…hopefully."

David nodded and took Pam's hand again.

"We're never going to see each other again!" Mickey said somberly.

Ernie held up his hand. "Actually, some day you will!"

"When?"

Ernie continued smiling, but shook his head. "I'm not allowed to say." He winked. "But trust me on that one, you will."

"Wait!" yelled Vickie. She stared at Pam with more tears in her eyes. "They told us on Europa that we could make phone calls, and text…and do Facebook."

Ernie nodded. "We all can, as often as we want. Just have to make sure it's not during one of my favorite TV shows."

With feigned seriousness, David turned to Mickey. "I wonder if Jerry's Famous Oatmeal Cookies delivers to Europa."

Mickey's face burst into a smile. "I'll ask Mom, but I'll bet Domino's does!"

Ernie pointed to the doorway. "We need to go."

Chapter Forty-Five

Mickey and Vickie slowly walked down the ramp holding hands, followed by Ernie. General Westlock, Dick, and the cordon of soldiers waited at the bottom. Melanie Dilman was filming and narrating the entire event. A medic tended to Max while Jerry stayed by his side, holding his hand. She was relieved to see her son. Frankel kept looking anxiously up the road.

When Mickey, Vickie, and Ernie reached the ground, the general gave a signal and a commando unit tried to run up the ramp. Halfway there, the ramp dissolved into its liquid form and the men tumbled to the clearing. Before the door disappeared, another soldier fired a shoulder-launched missile, but the force field wrapped itself around the projectile and contained the blast. The only sound anybody heard was a *pop*, like a champagne cork.

When the saucer's door disappeared, the ground began to tremble. Then the whining sound started up again. Leaves on the ground flew around the disc like a cyclone. Everybody stepped back. The saucer lifted off, gaining altitude and moving straight up. The sound coming from it was deafening, and the downdraft of air underneath was so strong everyone in the clearing had to shield their eyes from the flying dirt and debris.

They were watching satellite imagery of the clearing in the conference room six thousand miles away. Everybody's eyes were fixed on Ernie and the glowing sphere.

"Sir, do we detonate?" asked the soldier at the site, his voice on the speakerphone.

The man with the orange signet ring looked around at the others. "The mechanic is the intermediary, and the sphere is the repository of the alien technology. If I don't give the order to detonate the weapon we'll lose the saucer, but we can still gain possession of the sphere." The others nodded their heads.

"Secure the weapon. Do not detonate."

"Yes, Sir," said a voice on the phone. The soldiers hopped into the jeep and sped back up the Griffith Park road.

A hundred meters above the ground the lights on the bottom of the disc began to flash blue and gold, faster and faster. It hovered, tilted slightly on its side, and a scintillating ray of golden light shot from it towards the road. A few seconds later, there was only a dark stain on the pavement where the ambulance with the nuclear device had been.

When the soldiers arrived, their ambulance was gone.

"Damn!" exclaimed the driver.

"You set the emergency brake, didn't you?" asked one of the soldiers.

The nuclear technician took out his Geiger counter and waved it around. "Nothing," he said.

"Did you see that ray, or whatever it was come out of the saucer?"

A few seconds later, Frankel heard a voice in his ear coming through a miniature transmitter embedded in his ear canal. "As you're still alive, you can surmise that the nuclear detonation has been aborted. You will allow the general to secure the alien device and we'll relieve him of it later."

When the beam winked out, the saucer shot straight up into the sky, and with a loud sonic boom, it disappeared.

Mickey ran to his father. Max was lying on a stretcher on the ground. He looked pale. There was a blood-soaked dressing on his shoulder.

"Ernie, do something!" shouted Mickey. "You promised!"

Ernie took the sphere out of his pocket and bent down. "Excuse me," he said to the medic.

"Why?" said the medic, eyeing Ernie's silver jumpsuit. In the sunlight, Ernie resembled Elvis Presley.

Ernie ran the sphere over and around Max's shoulder, and then down the front of his torso. Nobody could detect any light or other emanations coming from it. Ernie stood again. "That should do it," he said. "You can take off the bandage now."

"That should do what?" asked the medic, apparently confused.

"Take a look."

The medic removed the bandage. Underneath, there was no sign of a wound. Max's skin was pink and unblemished.

"But the bullet's still in there. It'll turn septic."

Ernie shook his head. "Take some X-rays—totally dissolved, no fragments."

Beaming, Jerry helped her husband up. Max swung his arm around in a circle with no impediment.

Ernie put his hands behind his back, turned, and faced General Westlock and his soldiers. "Gentlemen," declared Ernie, "time to put down those guns and go home."

"I give the orders around here!" shouted the general. "And I say"—he pointed at Ernie—"arrest that man! And those kids!"

Ernie didn't flinch. "Never disobeyed an order before, Sir, but this time I will."

"Give up your sphere weapon and stand aside soldier!" bellowed the general.

"Can't do that, Sir!"

"Men, take them into custody and confiscate that sphere or whatever the hell it is," barked the general.

As the soldiers stepped forward, a force field formed around Ernie, the teens, and Max and Jerry. One of the soldiers pushed it with the muzzle of his rifle. The weapon sailed back over his head into the bushes. The rest of the soldiers backed away.

The general shook his head in frustration. He spotted Melanie Dilman and her cameraman filming the event, but before he could shout any orders to stop them, Ernie shook his finger.

"I wouldn't do that, General," said Ernie. "The world needs to know what went down here today. No more cover-ups."

The general was fuming. Major Frankel handed him a cell

phone. "Sir, somebody wants to talk with you."

The general grabbed the phone. "Who is this!" he barked, heard a response, and then walked off. He seemed to be standing at attention. "Sorry, Sir." He paused, and then nodded his head. "Live feed. I get it, Sir." He looked toward Melanie and forced a smile.

Frankel appeared relieved. He turned to Ernie. "Okay, soldier, it's your show. What do we do now?"

Ernie relaxed. "Well, Sir, there's two parts to this mission."

Everyone in the clearing leaned closer. Frankel put his hand in his pocket activating a hidden microphone hooked to his secure phone. The signal bounced off a satellite and came through the speakerphone on the conference room table six thousand miles away.

Ernie started, "First, David and Pam have gone on a trip to Europa. They agreed to go, and they're safe."

"Why?" asked Frankel.

"Can't tell you that."

"Are they coming back for you?"

"No, I'm staying home to help us improve things around here. That's the deal the Europans made if Pam and David chose to go."

"He's the intermediary!" shouted the voice in Frankel's ear, making him wince and grab his ear.

"Improve things? What does that mean?" Frankel asked when he recovered.

"You okay, Major? Want me to fix that ear?" Ernie held up the sphere.

"I'm fine. Old war wound. Acts up once in a while, but I'm used to it." He pointed at the sphere. "What else can that thing do?"

Ernie held up the sphere. "Got stuff in here that can improve everybody's life."

Frankel edged closer. "Like advanced technology?"

"You betcha, Major." Ernie smiled and looked into the camera. "It's really cool stuff. Like unlimited clean energy, for free."

"That works," Frankel said.

"Yep. Everything we'll need to turn things around, stop global warming, the cure for lots of diseases, and an end to famine. Shouldn't be any reason to have wars anymore."

"What's in that little sphere gizmo that can do all that?" Frankel asked.

"Information," replied Ernie. "We'd have figured it for ourselves, eventually. Think of it as a serious jumpstart."

"What's the catch?" asked Mickey.

"We'll have to learn to cooperate with each other, to share our resources and know-how with the entire planet, as the Europans are sharing with us."

Frankel braced for another painful burst of sound in his ear.

"This is American soil, soldier," sneered the general. "Everything in that sphere is propriety information. The White House decides which stuff to share…or not."

"Actually, Washington doesn't decide—we do!" boomed the voice in Frankel's ear.

"No longer your call, General," said Ernie. "I can upload the contents onto the Internet right now, if you like."

"No!" shouted the voice. Frankel winced again, but he thought quickly. "Sounds like we need to involve the United Nations, get everybody together…maybe hold some kind of symposium."

Ernie smiled. "I like the way you think, Major."

"What is he doing?" asked one of the men gathered in the conference room. An international symposium? Preposterous!"

"He's providing us with a venue more conducive to stealing the alien device," replied the man wearing the signet ring.

Jerry hugged Mickey and Vickie and wouldn't release them. "Can we go home now?" she asked Ernie.

Dick pushed forward and pointed at Mickey who was still wearing the garment. "It's not over! Get that suit, General! That's how the kid controls the saucer!"

Before the general could bark out any more orders, Ernie turned to Mickey. "Give him the helmet." Mickey handed the helmet over to Frankel. The general and Dick huddled around Frankel who carefully examined the helmet from several angles. Then Frankel raised the visor and examined the helmet from the inside. He smiled at General Westlock. "This costume looks like something left over from Halloween. There's no technology in here!" He dropped the helmet on the ground and put his foot on top of it. As if made of cardboard, the helmet caved in. Frankel shook his head. "I think we're done."

Dick started shouting. "You saw the kid get out of that flying saucer! I told you—he controls it with the suit!" He pointed at Mickey with a visibly shaking hand.

Mickey unzipped the suit and stepped out of it. He tossed it to Dick.

Dick held it up. "The technology is in here somewhere…I know it!" He ran his hands over the suits several times searching for embedded technology, but all he could see was rumpled black cloth.

The general looked at the dented helmet, then at the rumpled suit. He shook his head and walked off, disgusted. Still filming, Melanie Dilman thrust her microphone at him as he passed by.

"General, what are your final comments for our viewers?"

"God Bless America."

Melanie turned to her cameraman. "I think He just did."

Alone now, Mickey, Vickie, Ernie, and Mickey's parents remained in the clearing with Dick. Melanie and her cameraman had rushed back up the road. She left mumbling about what she would wear when she accepted her Pulitzer.

Mickey looked at Dick. "I feel sorry for you. You lost

something important today—besides almost losing Jake and your wife. You lost your son David."

Dick stared at him with trembling lips.

"He really loves you," Mickey continued. "Most of the time if he was depressed, it was because he wanted to make you proud of him. Somehow, he just never could.

Dick turned away. His shoulders started to heave.

"Maybe it's not too late." Mickey took Vickie's hand and turned to his parents. "Davie and Pam are returning someday." Jerry's face brightened. "We don't know exactly when." Ernie nodded. Mickey turned to face Dick again. "But we can talk to them whenever we want." Ernie nodded again, this time more vigorously. "In the meantime, maybe you and Jake, when he gets out of jail, can take time to reflect and start talking to Davie, become a real family."

"Why don't you start right there?" Ernie pointed towards the dirt road where Linda stood. She began walking toward Dick.

Mickey led his parents, Ernie, and Vickie back up the dirt road leaving Dick and Linda alone in the clearing. Some time later, when they too had left, the suit turned to quicksilver and vanished into the ground.

The astronomer at the Keck Observatory looked away from the telescope's eyepiece. He turned to his associate who was staring at columns of numbers cascading down a computer screen.

"Is it gone?"

"Yeah."

"Same trajectory as last time?"

"Straight back to Europa."

"When is the Europa Lander scheduled to touch down?"

"2016, if the NASA funding holds up."

"Been watching TV? Something tells me that's not a problem."

Epilogue

Mickey and Vickie walked side by side to their last class of the day, science.

Vickie looked around at their classmates, who were giving them a wide birth, and pulled closer to Mickey. "Everybody's eyes are glued on us," she said, feeling uncomfortable. "Gives me the creeps."

Mickey shrugged. "Might as well get used to it." He nodded toward two men in suits wearing earpieces scanning the crowded corridor ahead of them. "That's what I can't stand," Mickey smirked. "Like we even need them."

Vickie glanced at her palm. Ernie had given each of them another silver disc…a replacement for the one the Europans gave them. Best they could tell, this new disc was some kind of link with Ernie and the sphere gizmo. In many ways, it was like wearing the suit again, except without the fancy getup or most of its super powers—just enough to stay out of trouble. "It's kind of cool," Vickie said, flexing her palm.

Mickey laughed. "You liked it when that stalker bounced off your force field and ended up in the bleachers."

"Yeah, maybe." She grinned sheepishly. "Life's good! I even get calculus now—me who can't count change without a calculator."

Coach Dunivant tapped Mickey on the shoulder.

"Hey, Coach," said Mickey, stopping and greeting him.

"Mickey, how about trying out for the baseball team? I saw what you did on TV. Bet you could throw a hundred-mile-an-hour fast ball!"

"That wasn't me, Coach—it was that alien suit. Don't have it anymore." Mickey shrugged. "I'm just plain ol' Mickey again."

"What about the alien sphere?" the coach asked. He dropped his voice. "Aren't you…sort of connected to it?"

"Yeah, but…" Mickey glanced at Vickie. "We can't use it for any personal gain. That's part of the deal."

The coach's disappointment was obvious. His team had come in last the prior three years, an embarrassment to the high school. "Well, if you change your mind, let me know." He tossed Mickey a baseball and walked away.

That afternoon, Mickey and Vickie passed the baseball field on the way home. Mickey still had the baseball. He stopped and stared at the backstop behind home plate. Their Secret Service escort remained ten paces behind.

"What's up?" asked Vickie.

Mickey threw the baseball as hard as he could at the backstop. It punched a hole in the wood like a cannon ball.

Vickie poked him in the arm. "Why'd you do that?"

Mickey shrugged. "Just curious."

One of the agents started dialing his cell phone.

A week later, Ernie walked up the steps to the UN Building in New York surrounded by a cordon of Secret Service agents. He didn't really need them for protection. The display of agents was more to hold off the world's press. Of course Melanie Dilman waited right up front. A celebrity now, she had her own entourage and a television contract that made Barbara Walters' seem like minimum wage.

Inside the UN Building, Ernie strode to the podium and placed the Sphere on the lectern in front of him. He smiled at Mickey and Vickie sitting in the front row. A hush fell over the crowd that included not only prominent world leaders, but also the leading members of the world's scientific and medical communities. Every spy agency in the world had a representative present too. It was amazing how well built all the janitors and food workers appeared, and how most of them spoke with foreign accents. General Westlock leaned forward in his chair and stared at the Sphere like a man in the Sahara Desert who sees a McDonald's sign. Major Frankel had a seat in the back of the auditorium.

Ernie cleared his throat, and the world waited.

"Hi there, everybody!" he said waving. "Beautiful day, isn't it? Sure wish I had my fishing pole with me."

There was complete silence.

Ernie cleared his throat again, and then picked up the Sphere. Some of the delegates in the first row cringed, as if Ernie might zap them. "Never been much good at public speaking," he said. "Why don't you folks just ask me some questions?"

Instant pandemonium followed. Half the attendees stood and started shouting. The Secretary General pounded her gavel. The room quieted down. "As we agreed"—she glared at the crowd—"the members of the Security Council will go first." She nodded at the delegate from the United Kingdom, who stood.

"Mr. Santos," said the delegate. He paused. "Am I addressing you correctly, Sir? Do you perhaps have a different title now, such as Lord Santos, or His Alien Highness?" the delegate asked sarcastically.

Ernie smiled. "Just Ernie will do."

"Very well...Ernie, Sir. Could you expound further, please, on what that sphere device of yours can do?"

"Sure! It's chock full of information on all kinds of things."

"Like a computer?"

"Sort of."

The delegate from the United Kingdom cleared his throat. The air in the UN Building must have been awfully dry. Seemed like everyone was doing it. "And how, Sir, is the information retrieved?"

"I ask it a question."

"Can anybody else ask it a question?" The entire auditorium silently waited for his answer, including all the janitors and food workers.

"Just me."

"Pity," drawled the delegate. He started to sit down.

"Hang on there. Asking the right questions is the key," Ernie hastened to add. "And that depends on you." He gestured toward the audience.

The delegate from France stood up next. "Bonjour, Monsieur Santos." Thankfully, he didn't clear his throat. "Permit me to ask what categories of information the device contains."

"I've thought about that one for a while," said Ernie scratching his chin. "I think the best answer would be that it's a manual for better living. You know, like how to grow organic food without pesticides, clean the air, cure disease…that sort of thing."

"And the file format, monsieur?"

"Excuse me?"

"Is it analogue, digital, or something else perhaps?"

"Not sure," Ernie confessed, and then he smiled. "It has an AE port."

"Is that similar to a USB?"

"Stands for *Ask Ernie*!" The French delegate grimaced and sat down.

"Did you get that?" General Westlock whispered into his lapel microphone. "We have to trick him, ask something that sounds humanitarian, but has military value!"

The delegate from China stood and bowed. "Your honor," he began. Ernie looked embarrassed. "Wouldn't it be more efficient, safer perhaps, to have a spare device, or two? My people are most adept at making copies…"

"Thanks, but I've been told that any tampering would cause…you don't want to know. Believe me, one of these things is enough."

The Russian delegate stood, a bear of a man with a scowl etched on his face. He surveyed the auditorium. "How do we know this isn't an American trick, like pretending to land on the Moon?"

"Ask a question," replied Ernie completely unperturbed.

The Russian delegate put on his glasses and consulted a page of notes. "What is the formula for lithium-based nuclear fusion…for peaceful purposes!" he hastened to add.

"Hold on there," said Ernie. He pulled a projector from a shelf under the lectern and placed it next to the Sphere. The projector was aimed at a large screen behind the podium. Ernie spoke into the Sphere and it shot a beam of light at the back of the projector. Immediately, a series of complex equations filled the screen. Physicists in the audience furiously copied it all down.

"Stop!" shouted General Westlock. He ran to the stage. "That stuff's top secret!"

Armed with their notes, several scientists got up from their seats and began running for the exits. A food worker with a muscular physique followed each of them. The race for the Nobel Prize in Physics had begun.

Pretending to look at his watch, Frankel spoke into his cufflink. "Now," he said, and the lights went out in the auditorium. There were scuffling sounds and cries from the stage before the lights came back on. Several faux delegates planted by the cabal limped off leaving Ernie surrounded by the blue haze of a force field, and General Westlock waiting for the feeling to return to his hands.

Ernie smiled at the general. "The Sphere and I are protected at all times."

The general glared at Ernie, grabbed the projector, and tucked it under his arm. "You can't give our enemies the recipes for bigger bombs!"

"The Sphere only provides information that's good for peaceful purposes." Ernie held a cell phone in front of the Sphere. A light beam linked the two devices for five seconds, and then it winked out. "Besides, it's all on the Internet now. So long as everyone has it, it's no big deal."

The general stormed back to his seat to a chorus of boos from the audience. Before sitting down, he nodded and a janitor approached and took the projector from him. When the general was sitting, he spoke into his lapel microphone. "Wake up all those teenage hackers you have on the payroll. Find some way to keep that stuff off the Internet! And while you're at it, find some way to hack into that sphere!"

"That was embarrassing. Desist for now," Frankel heard in his earpiece.

The audience became restive again. "I heard you say that thing can help cure cancer," shouted the American Security Council delegate. Hushed silence again filled the auditorium.

Ernie beamed. "It can. Send up somebody to have a look."

Three of the world's top cancer scientists, who'd been previously selected for just this question, rushed forward and crowded around Ernie and the Sphere. Ernie asked the question and the Sphere sent pages of material to each of their iPads and to the rest of the medical researchers in the audience. The three scientists at the podium quickly read through the material.

"Oh my God!" exclaimed one of them. "Why didn't we think of that?"

Trembling with anticipation, another scientist pointed at the Sphere. "May I ask it a question?"

"Tell me, and I'll do the talking," replied Ernie, smiling.

The scientist stated his follow-up question. Ernie listened, squinted, then leaned forward and spoke to the Sphere. This was quickly followed by another download. The three scientists almost danced off the stage.

Shaking his head in frustration, General Westlock started walking to the exit talking into his lapel microphone. One of the really beefy janitors in the lobby stopped sweeping to listen. "We need another plan to get control of the Sphere, in case the geeks can't get it done," the general said.

"Yes, Sir. We're on it."

Vickie stood on the porch of Pam's house and tried to control her emotions. Her best friend was four hundred million miles away, and her departure left a gaping hole in Vickie's heart. She rang the doorbell and Phyllis answered. A soon as she saw Vickie, Phyllis grabbed her in an embrace and led her into the living room. They sat on the couch next to each other. Phyllis offered her a Kleenex and they daubed their eyes.

Vickie started to say something, but Phyllis beat her to it. "I miss her too," she said, smiling sadly.

"She said to tell you she loves you," Vickie said. As Phyllis dissolved into tears, Vickie hurriedly added, "We'll be able to talk to them, even see them on a special TV." This made Phyllis smile again.

They sat in silence, holding hands. When the emotional moment passed, Phyllis handed Vickie a framed picture of Pam and Vickie together. "Her sixteenth birthday. Take the picture," Phyllis offered.

"I remember. It was a special birthday." Vickie stared at it, then pursed her lips and tried not to cry again. "I have a sister a few miles from here, but my real sister is halfway across the solar system."

"So's my only daughter," murmured Phyllis.

Cradling Pam's picture to her chest, Vickie slumped against the cushion. "You couldn't have any of your own?"

Phyllis appeared uncomfortable.

Vickie put her hand to her mouth. "How insensitive of me!"

"It's all right. I was injured in the same accident that cost Pam the use of her legs."

Vickie looked confused. "But you're her adoptive mother."

"Yes I am."

"So you were in the car with her real parents, when they were killed?"

Phyllis fidgeted. "No, of course not."

"What happened?"

"I'd rather not talk about it. I'm sure you understand."

"Of course."

Alone that night, Vickie performed a Google search on Pam's adoptive parents and found a newspaper article about the accident—Malibu California, December 31th, 1997. Two cars had collided on a rain-slick road. Phyllis, referred to by her maiden name, and another man, now her husband, had been driving one of the cars. The other car had gone over the rail into the surf. Odd, no names were provided for the victims in the second car, except to mention a three-year-old female who survived with serious injuries. Obviously somebody had been driving, presumably the child's parent or parents. Why weren't they referred to in the newspaper account? Vickie wondered. She picked up the phone and dialed the Malibu police station.

Europa, one earth year later.

Pam and David walked hand-in-hand through the garden. A silver robot moved fluidly in stride with them, while two more trailed behind.

"David, may I inquire if you require any changes to the habitat's enhancements?" asked the alien. It spoke with only a modicum of flashing lights.

"None that I can think of," replied David. "Looks pretty good to me."

Pam nodded. "Except perhaps two shades lighter on the lemons, and up five decibels on the afternoon wind. Oh, and down two and half centigrade on the spring cycle. It's still too hot."

One of the trailing aliens swiveled its head toward the other. Its face erupted in flashing lights. "A characteristic of the female of this species. Most interesting."

"The Pamela unit's behavior is unpredictable," said the second alien.

"Precisely," said the first alien.

"Your logic is flawed," noted the second alien.

"Errors in logic are impossible. Explain," asked the first alien.

"If it is precise, it is predictable, and since it is not predictable, it cannot be precise," replied the second alien.

The first alien stopped moving forward. Its face went blank. "That does not compute…does it?"

"This has not happened since we assumed these forms," said the second alien. "I must investigate." It increased its pace. Once abreast of Pam, it extended a projection of silver from its torso. "May I link with you?" it requested. "I need a *warm fuzzy*, as you refer to it."

Accustomed to this by now, Pam agreed and held out her hand. Ever since she and David had awakened from their first sleep as residents of Europa, the silver aliens started linking with them. At first, they observed that more aliens were awakening and becoming active again. But as time went on, the aliens' behavior began changing as well, almost as if they were becoming more human.

During this time, Pam and David also began to change, but in a different way. They looked the same on the outside, but both knew that's where it ended. Their change was similar to what occurred on their first visit to Europa with Mickey: that feeling of an expanded awareness of everything and its interconnectedness, except now, the feeling remained with them constantly. With enhanced awareness, and the knowledge of the universe at their fingertips, a different view of life and its possibilities was inevitable. David was right. There had been a catch. They'd lost their innocence, and life would never be the same. They were sixteen going on…a hundred.

But there was also a catch for the Europans, one they hadn't foreseen. While they could store and process information at unfathomable rates, they'd given up the ability to feel, and they lacked intuition. Furthermore, when the Europans abandoned their sense of self, they lost their self-awareness, something earthlings with their relatively puny brains had in abundance. Now these two earthlings had both an expanding intellect and heightened awareness. Where would this change take them? Who would be the real children of this new civilization, Pam and David's offspring, or the Europans?

The alien's projection touched Pam's silver disc, withdrew, and the alien slowed its pace until it joined the other.

Colored lights flashed across the face of the alien that had remained behind. "I have yet to try the link. What did you experience?"

After the link, the second alien altered its stride. It rhythmically swayed from side to side—its answering light display had a rhythm to it as well. "It was cool, Dude," it replied.

Finally alone, Pam and David continued strolling the verdant fields of their habitat. Still holding David's hand, Pam stopped walking, forcing him to stop. She sighed and spun around. "I know it's not real, but it's so beautiful here."

"The beauty here is very real," said David. "It's you."

They kissed, surrounded by an aura that now had twinkling stars in all the colors of the rainbow.

David reached up his hand, as if trying to grab one of them. It was like trying to hold a twinkling soap bubble. "This thing is different now," he said.

Pam smiled at him. "It's not the only change."

Hand-in-hand, they resumed strolling along a now familiar path. It led to a house constructed in a 21st-century-style architecture found on Earth

"Have you noticed how our silver friends are changing?" asked David. "Every once in a while I catch one of them acting all goofy—at least for one of them, when he thinks none of the others are watching."

"There's more," added Pam.

They approached the front door of their house.

"By the way, I like all the things you've done with the house," continued David. "It looks great. You've got a real flare for decorating, and landscaping—all that kind of stuff."

Pam stared into his eyes. "I added another room."

"Why?"

"I'm pregnant."